Atlanta Stories
Reconstruction

G.M. Lupo

Lupo Digital Services, LLC
Atlanta, GA

Second edition (Paperback).

The cover image is downtown Atlanta taken from the North Avenue bridge over Interstates 75/85 (the Connector), facing South, taken 23 March 2018 at 18:16. Copyright © 2018, G. M. Lupo.

Library of Congress Registration Number: TX 8-943-325

ISBN: 978-0-9981595-3-9. Published by Lupo Digital Services, LLC, Atlanta, Georgia (www.lupo.net). Printed in the United States of America.

Acknowledgements

The author wishes to acknowledge the good folks down in Moultrie and Colquitt County, Georgia, in particular, Paula Mc-Cullough, Darren Roberson, Steve Saunders, and Wes Lewis for welcoming me while I was working there in 2020. Also, a shout-out to manager, Ora Coots and the staff at the Holiday Inn Express in Moultrie, which was literally my home away from home for much of the first half of the year. Many thanks to Lee Raines for talking baseball. Also, thanks to Sigrid Economou and Melissa Mullaney for all your support and to Liz Dooley for your insightful comments and suggestions while editing this work.

Other Work by the Author

G. M. Lupo is the author of these works:

- Words Words Words: Essays, Poetry, Stories
- Rebecca, Too
- Atlanta Stories: Fables of the New South
- The Long-Timer Chronicles (Kindle)

For new stories in development visit the author's blog Raised by Wolves at http://gmlupo.com.

G. M. Lupo can be found on the web at http://lupo.com.

To contact the author or to be added to the mailing list for future releases, send an email to author@gmlupo.com.

You cannot qualify war in harsher terms than I will.

—William Tecumseh Sherman to James M. Calhoun, mayor of Atlanta, 12 September 1864

I want to say to General Sherman — who is considered an able man in our hearts, though some think he is a kind of careless man about fire — that from the ashes he left us in 1864 we have raised a brave and beautiful city; that somehow or other we have caught the sunshine in the bricks and mortar of our homes; and have builded therein not one ignoble prejudice or memory.

—Henry W. Grady, "The New South"
Delivered 22 December 1886

House Band

Rebecca Jean Asher takes a seat at the bar in Eddie's Attic in Decatur, Georgia, and picks up a menu. It's her first time here, attending an "all ages" show featuring local Atlanta performers. She's been anxious to visit, as it regularly hosts artists Rebecca follows on the radio — Billy Pilgrim, The Indigo Girls, and others. She doubts any national acts will be in the lineup tonight, but one of her older friends told her that sometimes big-name performers show up to watch the shows, and will go up for a song or two, if asked. Following her friend's advice, she arrived early, just as the house opened, and has been rewarded with a great seat at the end of the bar, with an unobstructed view of the stage.

The blonde woman behind the bar comes over and points at Rebecca. "Can I get you something to drink?"

Rebecca sits up, and in her most adult voice, says, "Bring me a rum and Coke."

"Sure," the bartender replies. "Can I see your ID?"

Rebecca sighs. "Bring me a Coke."

"Coming up," the bartender says with a wink and starts to go.

Rebecca says after her, "No ice" which the bartender acknowledges. She looks over the menu, deciding on fries, and mac and cheese (*Decatur's Best!*) by the time the bartender returns. Her food order handled, Rebecca sips her Coke and turns so she's facing the stage. There are, at least, three guitars, a small drum set, and a set of keyboards onstage, with a couple of tambourines and a harmonica holder hanging from the mic stands. Rebecca looked at the poster describing the artists performing when she bought her ticket, but other than one called Echo, who she's not sure is a person or a group, she can't recall them.

Lately, Rebecca has felt in need of some sort of release. A sophomore at Decatur High School (*Class of 1999!*), she's the oldest sibling in her family, which consists of her, brother Steven, and mother Sharon. For the past six months, her aunt, Rachel Lawson, has been living with them, having come to look after Sharon, after she was diagnosed with advanced ovarian cancer. It was Sharon who suggested Rebecca have a night out, correctly sensing her daughter could use a break.

As upbeat and positive as Rachel tries to be around Rebecca and Steven, she's never sugarcoated the stark facts of Sharon's illness or chances for survival. While living on the West Coast, Rachel always warned Sharon not to ignore the symptoms she complained about; by the time Sharon stopped putting off treatment, it was too late. Rebecca has seen her mother's energy level drain away, as Sharon moved from aggressive chemotherapy and radiation to what Rachel now calls "maintenance of pain". Rebecca and Steven have both been reluctant to leave the house for fear their mother might slip away while they're gone, but tonight, Sharon insisted, giving Rebecca plenty of money to do whatever she wanted, once Steven left to spend the evening with a school mate.

Rebecca's food arrives, and she tastes the mac and cheese, then douses it with a generous helping of Tabasco sauce, then tries another bite.

Best gets better, she thinks.

As the crowd starts filling in, a tall, shapely, dark-haired woman who looks to be in her mid-twenties, wearing a Nirvana T-shirt enters and leans against a stool near Rebecca. Something about her seems familiar to Rebecca, who can't tear her eyes away. The woman sits with her back to the bar and seems to be watching the door for someone.

Leaning toward the woman, Rebecca says, "Excuse me. Are you performing?"

The woman glances over her shoulder, before returning her eyes to the door. She gives a terse, "No."

"I'm Rebecca. Ah, Becky."

"Good for you," the tall woman says without looking.

She rises, and Rebecca looks to see a slender man with dark blond hair, accompanied by a small woman, whose hair is strawberry blonde — like Sharon's was, before the chemo. The small woman doesn't seem much older than Rebecca. The two head toward the tall woman.

"We set?" the man says.

"Yeah, I talked to the sound guy," the tall woman says. "He seems to know what's what."

"What, what, what," the smaller woman says, all the while twisting her head slightly to the left. "Let's get ready."

They move from the bar to the stage and Rebecca keeps her eyes pinned on the tall woman. She suspects it could be love at first sight.

For more than a year, Rebecca has been trying to come to terms with the feelings she has for some of her female classmates. She's fully aware of what it means, having been exposed to the topics in human sexuality class, but had not anticipated how it would affect her on a personal level. Still, she concludes, if it's how she is, there's nothing she can do about it, so as far as she's concerned, she might as well embrace it. She doubts her mother or Steven would care, and considered raising the topic with Rachel, but Rebecca isn't sure how much she trusts her aunt. Rachel isn't quite what Rebecca was expecting from her mother's description of her older sister.

Sharon has always described Rachel as a "classic free spirit" and always seemed in awe of her older sister. Rachel moved to California with her best friend in the 70s, and her life there has been shrouded in mystery. From what little she's been told, Rebecca knows Rachel's friend died, and Rachel became a nurse, but Sharon hasn't spoken much of what Rachel was doing during the 80s. Prior to Rachel's arrival, Rebecca formed an image of her as a wild party girl, hobnobbing with celebrities and cruising LA in a hot sports car.

The woman who appeared at the house this past November was totally different, more "flannel" and "new age" than Rebecca expected, with few stories of her exciting Hollywood lifestyle. Whenever Rebecca prompts Rachel with lines meant to get her to open up about her life in Los Angeles, Rachel usually deflects with vague phrases, such as, "It's not all glitter and glamour" or "The lifestyle takes a heavy toll on someone".

The trio of the tall woman and her two companions are now on stage, the man behind the keyboards, and the smaller woman holding a guitar. The tall woman appears to be helping with setup, communicating by hand signals with the person in the booth as the smaller woman strums the guitar. The lights dim, and the tall woman takes a seat just offstage. A man comes to the stage who identifies himself as Eddie, tells the audience to "hush up" while the singers are performing, and introduces the first act, Echo.

Instead of a flashy "good evening Atlanta, we're Echo" type greeting, the smaller woman simply introduces herself as Charlotte, and acknowledges her brother, Brian, who waves to the crowd. Charlotte then launches into a song that leaves Rebecca blown away. For such a small person, Charlotte has a huge voice. It floods into every corner of the room and puts Rebecca in mind of Alison Moyet or Annie Lenox.

At one point, midway through the thirty-five-minute set, the tall woman goes to the booth and speaks to the man running sound. She spends the remainder of the performance stationed in front of the booth, arms crossed and tapping her right foot, listening intently.

Afterward, Rebecca heads to the lobby between the music room and the patio, where Charlotte is speaking to some audience members, and signing people up for Echo's mailing list. Brian and the tall woman are packing up their instruments.

"I enjoyed your performance," Rebecca says, as she's adding her name to the list.

"Thanks," Charlotte says. "We're putting together songs for our first album right now." Her drawl reminds Rebecca of how her father's relatives from below Macon talk. Charlotte holds up a cassette tape. "We made this demo in our living room if you'd like to hear that."

"Sure," Rebecca says, taking the tape. "Is that other woman your sister?"

"Sister, sister, sis—" Charlotte begins, reinforcing Rebecca's notion of where the group gets its name. "No, that's our friend, Claire. She does our sound and helps set up."

Brian enters and joins Charlotte, who introduces Rebecca.

"Always nice to gain a new fan," he says as he shakes Rebecca's hand.

"Fan, fan, fan. Is Claire downstairs?"

Brian nods.

Charlotte looks back to Rebecca. "It's great meeting you, Becky. Hopefully we'll get some stuff out to the mailing list about our next show."

"I'll look for it," Rebecca says.

Once Charlotte and Brian leave, Rebecca goes back to the music room and settles her tab. She hangs out for a couple more performers, but can't stop worrying about her mother, so she decides to call it a night and heads home. She makes a mental note to try and keep up with Echo, but in the meantime, life intrudes. Less than a month later, Sharon Asher loses her battle with cancer.

As far as endings go, Jack Standridge had one of the easiest. He simply went to sleep and didn't wake up the next morning. His wife, Nancy, always an early riser, discovers when she comes to rouse him for breakfast, that Jack is cold and not breathing, but still wears his customary smile. She remains calm, allowing herself only a few sniffles as she goes into another room to summon the authorities, then begin the process of alerting the family. Grief will come later, when it's official, when all the details have been ironed out. Then she will mourn.

A Marine, who served in Korea, Jack came home to Decatur, Georgia, where he found a job with his father's insurance agency. He took over the business when his father retired. Along the way, he married Nancy Belmonte, a lively woman he met in college, and they had two sons, Rex and Lawrence, and a daughter, Claire, who they lost at age eight to a congenital heart defect. Just before the kids started school, he and Nancy bought a nice home in Avondale Estates, now devoid of all but the two of them. The day before, the house had been filled with family, Rex, his wife, and the two youngest of their four kids, stopping in on their way from Florida to Chattanooga.

Before eleven that morning, Lawrence arrives from Ansley Park, without his partner Elijah Parker, who's in Washington until the end of the week. When Lawrence enters, he finds Claire Belmonte already there. Claire came to their home at age sixteen, after running away from a nightmare situation in Middle Georgia. Claire remained with the Standridges for just under four years, taking Nancy's family name as her own, completing her high school equivalency, and starting junior college as a sound technician. Though she moved into Atlanta just prior to her twentieth birthday, she remains close with the family.

The medical examiner has come and gone, having supported Nancy's belief that Jack passed, quietly, in his sleep the night before; with the examiner went Jack, to the coroner for an official determination. There's already a small crowd, consisting of close neighbors alerted by the police cars and coroner's van that something wasn't right, and universally complimentary of the man now gone. Nancy alerted Rex but insisted he and his family continue their brief vacation, though she's certain they're on their way back now.

Chizuko Collins has arrived from her home across the street to relieve Nancy of hosting duties, so Nancy finds herself seated on the couch, with Barbara Stewart, her next-door neighbor, and with Claire, both of whom have taken over the roles of chief comforters. Barbara assures Nancy that "Jack's in a better place" while Claire frequently asks if Nancy needs anything. From here, Nancy entertains a continuous stream of well-wishers as word of Jack's passing filters throughout the enormous community of those who knew him. She relaxes, and settles into the role of grieving spouse, knowing fully well that she will need to make many tough decisions in the days to come. The most difficult of these decisions arrives a few days following the funeral, in the person of an agent representing Walker Development, inquiring about Nancy's plans for her property, and promising a competitive offer on the home.

Depending upon point of view, Walker Development is either a dynamic force for revitalization around Atlanta, or an unfeeling corporate behemoth, mercilessly dotting the landscape with gaudy, overpriced McMansions that only the super-wealthy can afford. As young people from the suburbs of the Atlanta Metro area have moved back into town, fueling gentrification in formerly minority neighborhoods, Walker has, among others, been there to encourage demolition of the older structures in favor of new, more upscale dwellings. The previous residents, many of whom have lived in the neighborhoods their entire lives, suddenly find the costs of taxes and utilities becoming unbearable, and always — always — the speculators are there, offering low-income residents less than the "book value" of the property.

Along the way, old neighborhood names are resurrected, kept alive by the elderly black residents, who learned them from their parents and grandparents. The Fourth Ward becomes The Old Fourth Ward; the areas south of the tracks from Decatur, Candler Park and Lake Claire become Kirkwood and East Atlanta Village. Once-quiet little neighborhoods find themselves overrun with coffee shops, corner bars, art galleries, and consignment shops, many with living quarters overhead, and choked with increasing traffic, as non-residents flock there, sometimes from as far away as Bartow or Henry County, to sample the local ambience.

The representative from Walker is a first contact: a deferen tial, self-effacing young woman, who makes a point to complement the home and express condolences for Nancy's loss within five minutes of introducing herself. She doesn't stay long and leaves a few brochures for Nancy to look at "when the timing is right". Nancy knows, however, that once she's on their radar, the phone calls, mailings, and visits will become more insistent, not just from Walker, but from any number of developers or real estate agents. She doesn't relish the thought of having her family's memories demolished, but without Jack, maintaining the household no longer seems desirable for her.

Claire maneuvers her Jeep Wrangler into the side driveway at the home of Manny and Deanna Savage in Norcross, and parks by the red Nissan that belongs to Brian Sanger. She's there to help Brian and Charlotte plan out the sound requirements for their upcoming CD release show at Smith's Olde Bar in Atlanta. She's worked with the duo, who still call themselves Echo, for seven years, since their earliest shows, which included open mic events at venues such as Smith's and Eddie's Attic, after Charlotte came to Atlanta. In addition to planning the show, Claire has a huge favor to ask her friends.

Instead of heading straight to the guesthouse Charlotte shares with her son, Izzy, Claire walks around to the front of the main house and rings the doorbell. She's greeted by Gloria, the middle of Manny and Deanna's three children, an early-teen girl with dark blonde hair. Her sweatpants, red and black checkerboard sneakers, and Michelle Malone Beneath the Devil Moon T-shirt remind Claire of how she dressed as a teen living with the Standridges.

"Hey, Glo," Claire says, giving Gloria a hug. "I see the Volvo's missing. I guess that means your folks are gone."

"Mom took Prudie to get a dress for a talent show she's in and Derek went to the game," Gloria says. "Dad's in the kitchen."

Claire points to the shirt. "Good album. I ran into Michelle in the studio the other day. She keeps saying we need to work together, but neither of us can schedule anything, with her on tour all the time."

Claire follows Gloria through the house and into the kitchen, where Manny is carefully measuring and placing lumps of cookie dough onto a greased baking sheet. Manny Savage's dark, unruly hair (which is currently stuffed into a ridiculous looking chef's hat) and powerful upper body with very broad shoulders make him look younger than his forty years. The effect is negated by his salt and pepper beard; he normally has a heavy five-o-clock shadow, but today looks like he hasn't shaved in a couple of days. Looking up as Claire enters, he says, loudly and enthusiastically, "CC!"

"How're you doing Manny?" Claire says. Not wanting to interrupt his baking, she rubs his back, rather than hugging him.

"I hope you'll stick around for some cookies," he says. "We're making twelve dozen."

"I can probably help you out with a few," Claire says.

"So, getting set for the big show at Smith's, are you?" Manny says.

"You know it," Claire says.

Glancing at Gloria, Manny says, "Brian let me hear a track from the album. Looking forward to it."

"I bet you are," Claire says with a knowing smile. "I'll stop back in for some cookies later."

Claire exits into the back yard and stops to play with Lex, a medium-sized mongrel, with brown, shaggy hair, that the Savage family rescued from animal control a few years earlier. As she approaches the door to the guest house, she can hear Charlotte's contralto voice singing a tune Claire recognizes from their upcoming album, accompanied by Brian on piano. Charlotte has recently been immersing herself in Sacred Harp and shape note singing, trying to figure out how to incorporate these styles into her songwriting even though they work better with a group than a duo or solo artist.

As Claire lets herself in, Charlotte and Brian acknowledge her without pausing. For the past several months, Charlotte has been wearing her hair in dreadlocks and has a fake nose ring she puts on when she's onstage. She also wears round, wire-framed, rose-colored sunglasses when performing, further emphasizing her offbeat image.

"Where's Izzy?" Claire says.

"He's visiting the Branches this afternoon," Charlotte says. "Ned's taking the family with Izzy and Derek to see the Braves."

"Sounds like fun," Claire says.

They're familiar with the sound requirements at Smith's from the many times they've played there, so most of their meeting deals with several songs on which Brian and Charlotte will be using some new instruments they've not played in concert before. Deanna Savage has been teaching Charlotte to play the banjo, and Brian will be playing a saxophone and trumpet, which he's used in the studio, but never live. After about an hour, they have a good handle on what's needed, so Claire decides to approach them with the favor she needs.

"A family I'm close to recently lost their father," Claire says. "Brian, you attended the funeral with me, Jack Standridge."

"Right, I remember," he says. "They struck me as good people."

"They are — the best," Claire says. "Jack's death has been really tough on his wife, Nancy. She's all alone in this huge house in Avondale Estates and misses her grandkids, who live in Florida."

"Florida, Florida," Charlotte repeats. "Is there anything we can do for her?"

"Maybe," Claire says. "Nancy has decided to put the house on the market and move down near her oldest son and his family. If your financial situation allows it, I'm hoping you'd consider making an offer on the house."

"House, house, house. Why would we do that, assuming we can?"

Charlotte glances at Brian, who shrugs.

"Bickering pays me well enough. I assume your salary with the Forestry Service is adequate. A mortgage is probably cheaper than the condo I'm renting in town."

Claire says, "Walker Development has been buying up property around the area. They want to tear down the houses and build these hideous monstrosities that will drive up the property values and tax assessments."

"How's the neighborhood reacting to that?" Brian says.

"Split fifty-fifty," Claire says. "Many of the older residents just want to sell out and leave. The other half, mostly families with school-age kids, want to fight it."

"Fight it, fight it. I'm happy where we are, Claire. Izzy's happy. The school system suits us — and I especially like having babysitters right next door."

"DeKalb has a good school system, too," Claire says. "It's a larger house, with a huge back yard, and has a wooded area. Izzy would love that."

"Charlotte would love that," Brian says, to which Charlotte nods.

Claire leans toward them. "Look — this place has a lot of sentimental value for me. The Standridges were there when I really needed them. My whole life started over in that house."

Brian touches Charlotte's hand, and says to her, "It won't hurt to meet with them. Take a look at the place. Decatur's got a great music scene, too, and we'd be right near the thick of it in Avondale."

"Avondale, Avondale. We can take a look. The woods do sound tempting. Just don't get your hopes up, Claire."

Claire nods. "That's all I ask."

There's a knock at the door, followed by Gloria looking in and saying, "Dad said to tell you the latest batch of cookies just came out of the oven. Actually, he told me to look in and yell 'Cookies!'

like Cookie Monster, but I'm not doing that."

Gloria is sitting on the back porch, when Brian comes out with a guitar and joins her.

"Hey, Glo," he says, "want some company?"

"Sure," she says. "You going to play something?"

"I wrote a song for the album," he says, "and I wanted to get your thoughts on it."

"Okay," she says, wondering what he's up to. "Why me?"

"I wrote it for you," he says.

"For me? Really? Why?"

"I think you'll figure it out," he starts strumming the tune. He sings:

"When times are bad, and no one understands
Someone's there with a loving hand
Reach out
When your friend's just a friend, not something more
Remember, there's an open door
Reach out
When it seems like love is meant for all but you
Someone's waiting whose love is true
Reach out
Reach out when people stare
Reach out when life's not fair
Reach out when love alludes you and
You don't know what to do
Reach out — someone's there
Reach out — someone cares"

There are tears in Gloria's eyes when he finishes. "How did you know?"

"Intuition, I guess," Brian says. "Kindred spirits, perhaps."

"This is the track you let Mom and Dad hear, isn't it?" she says, to which Brian nods. "I guess I'm lucky to have the coolest parents on the planet. I was pretty sure they knew but are just waiting for me to say something. It's the kids at school. I don't think they'd understand."

"Some probably would," he says. "The ones who really care, they'll understand."

"Thanks, Brian," she says and gives him a hug. "I just feel so alone, sometimes."

"One day, you're going to meet somebody, and she's going to knock your socks off."

"If I'm lucky."

"She's the one who's going to be lucky," he tells her. "Because she'll know you."

"Charlotte sings it, right?" Gloria says.

"She sure does," Brian says. "She adds a few flourishes of her own, of course."

"I'm sure she sounds awesome. Maybe it will help someone else figure out they're not alone."

"Let's hope so," Brian says. "Charlotte wants to invite you to come up on stage and perform it with us at Smith's if you want. Your folks said it's okay with them."

Gloria hesitates. "I don't know. Some of my friends will be there." She considers it a long moment. "But hey, reach out, right?" She hugs Brian again. "I'll do it."

Rebecca turns off Piedmont Road into the parking lot for Ansley Mall, and parks behind the filling station that's on the corner of Piedmont and Monroe Drive, half a block from Smith's Olde Bar. Tonight, she'll be using information she gained from an associate to introduce herself to someone she finds intriguing. Tonight, she has decided she won't drink much, because she needs her wits about her. Tonight, she's planning to make her move.

The words of a Patti Smith song she remembers from a record her mother used to play run through her head as she maneuvers her copper-colored Mini Cooper into a space and kills the engine. "I'm going to make contact tonight."

The past six years haven't been easy for Rebecca, starting with the death of her mother. Her unmarried and childless aunt, Rachel, became the guardian of Rebecca and her brother and wasted no time in instituting, in Rebecca's terms "her autocratic rule" over the siblings. Rebecca did her best to endure, sometimes directly challenging Rachel's authority, like when she packed her ancient Toyota and drove to Florida for Spring Break her senior year, over Rachel's objections. Before she graduated high school, she was accepted into Columbia University and once she moved to New York for school, she became part of a group of progressive feminists who agitated for equal pay, reproductive freedom, and gender equality, on campus and in the community.

Rebecca's college career ended abruptly her junior year, due to a surprise and very unwelcome visit by her father. Following Sharon's death, Owen suffered an attack of conscience, and felt guilty about losing touch with Rebecca and Steven and began trying to contact them. His attempts were blocked by Rachel, who let him know his presence was not welcome. About a year and a half after she moved to New York, Rebecca began receiving cards and letters from Owen. He had somehow tracked her down there. Rebecca usually shoved them into a shoebox, so she could bring them out and rant about them whenever her friends were around.

One evening, halfway through her junior year, she returned to her dorm, where she was startled by a familiar voice calling her name as she moved through the lobby. She turned to see "Owen the Pilot" as she and her mother derisively called him, approaching her. She angrily confronted him, as he tried to plead his case, then told him to "hop back in your damn plane and fly the hell out of here!"

The encounter sparked a month-long binge of drinking and smoking pot, which led to her failing all her classes and being placed on academic probation. She fled New York, hoping to regain her momentum.

The situation didn't improve once she was back in Atlanta. Using her experience with publications in New York, she was able to find work with Creative Loafing, Atlanta Magazine, and several Neighbor newspapers around town, but her drinking and recreational drug use increased. Her relationship with her aunt, strained before she left for school, was now reaching the breaking point, as she began staying out until all hours, wandering home intoxicated, angrily rebuffing attempts by Rachel to talk or insist she seek help. At last, Rachel changed all the locks on the doors, and Rebecca showed up one afternoon, drunk, to find all her belongings packed up on the porch.

Since then, she's drifted from friend's couch to friend's couch, sometimes sleeping in her car, remaining just coherent enough to hold down her job, reporting on cultural events around town. That is, until several weeks ago, when she recognized the name of a favorite band appearing at Blind Willie's, and attended the show, where she found herself in close proximity to someone with whom she's become obsessed.

Rebecca is a regular presence around the club scene in Atlanta, and it's here she first heard of a red-hot female deejay who bills herself as CC Belmonte. A mystical presence in the clubs, CC, sometimes called "The Phoenix," cuts a massive figure — some say she's over seven feet tall — with long, dark hair and what Rebecca regards as a total badass bitch attitude, all the while spinning some of the tightest House mixes in all of North Georgia. Rebecca has acquired several of her compilations. Given her height, there's a rumor rampant in the clubs that she's actually a drag queen, but Rebecca confirmed through reliable sources this isn't the case, though information on her is fleeting, fueling the mystery.

Then came the show at Blind Willie's, where Rebecca was catching up with the brother and sister duo, Echo. Working the board for them was a tall woman the band called "Claire" who Rebecca remembered from the first time she'd seen them back in high school. Claire had ditched her club attire for jeans, a Steely Dan T-shirt, a backwards baseball cap, and slip-on Vans, which de-emphasized her height; it wasn't until Rebecca purchased a CD, and read the engineering credit, that she realized Claire was none other than the deejay who has come to dominate Rebecca's every waking thought.

She couldn't stick around after the show at Blind Willie's but enlisted the aid of an acquaintance who she's used for background on stories, to run down info on the elusive CC Belmonte. Rebecca considers herself an information junkie, and the more she can learn about a subject, the more of a rush she gets. Her contact found her a wealth of tidbits about CC's past and armed with the results, Rebecca heads into Smith's Olde Bar, ready for Round Two.

She camps out at the bar downstairs, where she can smoke, and watches the entrance to the upstairs music room. The show tonight is the official release event for Echo's new album; aside from the possibility of a second run-in with Claire, Rebecca is excited to review the new CD.

While she's waiting, Rebecca notices an older woman, wearing a polka dot dress, faded denim jacket, and a railroad cap peering into one of the windows. She looks, to Rebecca, like a refugee from Cabbagetown. She seems confused when she first comes in, then moves to the bar and leans against it, near Rebecca.

"Where's that concert supposed to be at?" the woman says.

"Upstairs," the bartender says and points to the entrance. "Doors open in about twenty minutes."

"Listen, I ain't here to see no show," she replies. "I just need to give a message to somebody with that band."

The bartender shrugs. "I think they're doing the sound check now. They might let you up. You can try."

The woman nods and goes to the door. Finding it open, she heads up. Rebecca doesn't see her come back before the light goes on, letting the crowd know doors are open, and people start heading up. Once she gets to the music room, Rebecca sees the woman seated near the far end of the room, nursing a drink in a Styrofoam cup.

Guess she changed her mind about the show.

She takes a seat at the bar, and debates whether to get a drink. By the time the bartender arrives, she's decided against it for now. "Let me start with water," she says. When it arrives, she leaves a dollar tip on the bar. She'll drink something later, especially just before she's ready to approach Claire, but she decides to at least hear the first few songs with a completely clear head. She watches as the crowd filters in.

Among them, Rebecca notices a woman she's seen at open mic nights around town and tries to remember her name. She's with a man who has dark features and unruly black hair, and three children, two early-adolescent girls and a boy, who appears to be in his mid-teens. They situate themselves near the stage. The crowd is a good mix of people in their teens to thirties and forties. Rebecca glances back toward the sound booth and notes when Claire goes into the booth and gives a thumbs up. The lights dim, and in the darkness, Rebecca sees the band getting in place. The announcement for them comes over the loudspeaker, and they start playing as the lights come back up.

While Rebecca had heard them at Blind Willie's a few weeks before, the duo had concentrated on their older work, with just a song or two from the new album. Tonight, the first set is all new, and Rebecca feels it's the strongest work yet by the band. Charlotte's voice sounds even more powerful than she'd been at Blind Willie's, and Brian's repertoire of instruments has grown to include a saxophone and trumpet, while Charlotte plays flute and recorder in addition to her guitar. Rebeca spots a banjo on stage as well and remembers Charlotte referencing it at the previous performance.

The new material builds considerably on their earlier work. Rebecca has noted over the years a change in the lyrical content from the usual teen topics of unrequited love and teen angst, to more socially conscious lyrics, with a particular concern for the environment and human rights. Charlotte's interaction with the crowd has also evolved from simply announcing the numbers and thanking the crowd to telling jokes and stories or interacting with Brian as they segue into each song.

Charlotte introduces what she describes as their newest single and asks someone to join them onstage. The older daughter with the couple goes up. Charlotte introduces her as Gloria Savage.

"Savage," Rebecca says, recalling the name of the older woman, "Deanna Savage — Banjo Girl."

"Gloria is an aspiring musician herself," Charlotte tells the crowd. "We asked her if she'd like to help us out on this new song and she said, 'Oh yeah!' Give her a hand, everyone."

The crowd responds warmly.

Gloria gets a guitar and they launch into a song called "Reach Out". Rebecca is impressed at how unaffected Gloria seems at being onstage, and how well she plays, though, at first, Rebecca can't understand why she's there. As soon as she hears the lyrics, however, the answer dawns on her, especially when Charlotte starts singing Gloria's name at the end.

"Welcome to the club, sweetie," Rebecca says, raising her glass in a toast.

Rebecca predicts it will be a breakout hit for the group and starts making a mental list of her contacts in radio who might be open to getting it airplay. When the song finishes, Charlotte and Brian each give Gloria a hug, and she returns to her family as the pair go into their final song of the first set.

The band takes their break. Rebecca stands and looks to see Claire come down from the booth, and walks over, pointing at Claire, and saying, "You remind me of someone."

Claire gives Rebecca a long look. "I get that a lot."

Rebecca sips her drink. "No. Really. Someone I used to know." She focuses on Claire's face as she says, "Her name's Christine Messner."

Claire's expression changes and she takes a quick glance in the direction of the older woman Rebecca noted earlier, with a mix of what Rebecca senses is fear, panic, and outright rage. Whatever it is, Claire keeps it under wraps and speaks calmly. "You've mistaken me for someone else. Excuse me."

She goes to the stage and starts tinkering with the equipment. Looking after her, Rebecca says, "Got your attention, at least."

Rebecca heads to the exit, then drops her empty cup into the trash. She walks around to the hallway behind the stage and, finding the line manageable, waits for the women's restroom. Once she's done, she heads back out, but as she's approaching the door that leads backstage, Claire steps out and confronts her.

"Where did you get that name?" Claire says.

Rebecca is startled but recovers with a laugh. She leans toward Claire and says in a confidential tone, "Name changes are public information. They're on file at the courthouse. Anyone can look them up."

"Who are you, and why are you poking around in my business?" Claire says.

"I'm Rebecca Asher," she says. "Becky, if you prefer. We met once before, but it was a long time ago. As to why, let's just say I find you very fascinating."

"Fascinating," Claire says, with a knowing smirk. "Well, I believe what you're doing is called stalking. I don't like it. Back off."

"I'm not stalking you," Rebecca says. "Am I? I'm a big fan of your work in the clubs. I'd just like to get to know you a bit better."

"Ah. You know me from the clubs. Just out of curiosity, have you ever come up and introduced yourself?"

Rebecca starts to say something, then shakes her head.

"Yeah, didn't think I remembered you. Here's a newsflash: I work in the clubs, but I don't patronize them. I don't swing that way."

"Bummer," Rebecca says. "Let me buy you a drink. A peace offering, if you will, since it seems like we got off on the wrong foot."

"I don't think so."

"Come on. I'm a fun person in many situations. It doesn't have to mean anything."

Claire shakes her head. "I don't drink when I'm working."

With that, she disappears backstage.

"That wasn't a total disaster," Rebecca says with a chuckle.

Back in the music room, she once again notices the older woman seated to the side, who's been watching the show with little apparent interest. Occasionally, the woman looks toward the sound booth. Rebecca takes more of an interest this time and walks over. As she's approaching, the woman looks in Rebecca's direction. "What you looking at?"

"You stand out like a sore thumb, you know," Rebecca says.

"Not really here for the music, so I'm guessing you must be related to someone in the band."

"Don't see how that's any of your business," the woman says.

"Just making idle chat," Rebecca says. "I'm Becky, by the way."

"Yeah, well you can just keep on moving, 'cause I ain't one of them kind of women."

"Didn't think you were," Rebecca says, noting the similarity in how Claire responded. "Apologies if I gave you that impression. I just like meeting new folks. I'm a people person."

"All right, then. I just want to make sure we're clear," the woman says. "My name's Selma Messner."

"Messner," Rebecca says. "Let me buy you a drink, Selma, just to show there're no hard feelings."

Selma lifts her cup and shakes it. "I could go for another Coke Cola, I suppose."

"Coke it is," Rebecca says. "I'll be right back."

Rebecca chats with Selma for the duration of the break, learning where she's from and that she's in Atlanta to deliver some news to someone. Whenever Rebecca presses her for more information on her background, or her interest in the band, however, Selma becomes defensive. Rebecca notes that when Claire returns to the booth, she stops, looks over at Selma, and shakes her head, but does not approach them.

Rebecca returns to her seat at the bar for the second set. It's mostly old favorites, to the delight of the crowd who respond with cheers, dancing, and waving their hands in time with the music.

Once the set is over, Rebecca visits the ladies' room again, and when she returns, she sees Claire is seated at the table with Selma, having what appears to be a heated exchange with her. Brian and Charlotte are hanging out, talking with the Savages, and other fans. Rebecca purchases several copies of the CD, then waits until Brian and Claire head to the stage to begin the load out before she approaches Charlotte.

"Great show, as usual," Rebecca says.

Charlotte gives Rebecca a quick hug. "Thanks for being here — ah, sorry — help me out."

"Rebecca. Becky," she says.

"Becky, Becky, Becky. Didn't I see you at Blind Willie's?"

"You probably did. I was there," Rebecca says. "I couldn't hang around then. I definitely hear a lot of evolution in your sound."

"You've been following us?" Charlotte says.

"I'm with Creative Loafing," Rebecca says. "It's a job and in this case, my pleasure. I bought copies of your CD to send out to some friends across the country who own indie stations. They might be able to get you some airplay."

"Wow, that sounds great, Becky," Charlotte says. "Listen, Brian, Claire and I like to hit the Majestic after a show. You're welcome to join us."

"Sounds like fun," Rebecca says. "I'd love to join you. Maybe find out more about the album."

"Great," Charlotte says. "We'll be headed over as soon as we're packed up."

Rebecca heads back downstairs where she sees Selma sitting at a table. Rebecca approaches her. "You going to the Majestic as well?"

"What's the Majestic?" Selma says.

"All night diner," Rebecca replies. "The band and Claire are going."

"No. I'm headed back to Perry," Selma says.

"Quite a drive this late at night," Rebecca says.

"I can always stop at some cheap hotel along the way, if need be," Selma says. "I ain't much for sleeping, though."

Rebecca rummages in her bag. "Let me give you my card." She removes one and hands it to Selma, who looks over it.

"Asher. You got kin down around Cordele?"

"Yeah. My grandparents. They own a crop dusting business. You know them?"

"I've heard the name," Selma says, pocketing the card.

Rebecca heads over to the Majestic, where she finds Charlotte and Brian seated in a booth. Charlotte introduces Brian.

"Claire change her mind?" Rebecca says.

"She'll be along," Brian says. "She needed to have a few words with someone."

They talk about the show and Charlotte tells Brian about Rebecca's offer to send CDs out to her contacts in radio. About twenty minutes after Rebecca arrives, Claire shows up.

"Selma all squared away?" Brian says as Claire approaches.

"She says she's staying in town," Claire says. "We're getting together tomorrow."

No, you're not, Rebecca thinks.

Seeing Rebecca, Claire puts her hand on one hip and says, "What's she doing here?"

"She's a reporter," Charlotte says. "She's doing a writeup on the show and also offered to send some CDs to her contacts in radio."

"A reporter?" Claire says. "Did you mention your sideline as a stalker?"

"Stalker, stalker, stalk— What are you talking about?"

"Let's just say she's really into research," Claire says.

Rebecca points to a news bin at the front of the restaurant. "Creative Loafing, page 53. My write up on Music Midtown. I'm also a huge fan of Echo. Have been for quite a few years."

"You're a fan, are you?" Claire says. "Then tell me, what's your favorite song from the first album?"

"Album, album, album. Why so suspicious?"

"Really? Claire?" Brian says.

"No, that's okay." Rebecca thinks about it. "Do you mean the first studio album or the EP they distributed on cassette at Wax N Facts? I know a lot of the songs ended up on the album, but there's a gritty, raw quality to the tape."

"I thought only ten people bought that cassette," Brian says.

"Me and nine others, I guess," Rebecca says.

"Come on, Claire," Charlotte says. "I think she passed your test."

"Oh, all right," Claire says and sits beside Rebecca, who's glad to note that once Claire relaxes and they have a chance to talk, the two hit it off.

A week after the show, Claire takes Brian and Charlotte to meet Nancy Standridge. Claire greets her with a long hug before the introductions. They talk for about an hour, and Charlotte especially enjoys hearing Nancy's stories about Jack and living together in the house. Lawrence is there and gives them a tour. Brian likes the basement space, which he and Claire agree would make a nice recording studio, and Charlotte likes the finished attic which served as Jack's office and would make the perfect room for Izzy — complete with wall space for his guitars. She especially loves — as Claire suspected — the back yard with a wooded area.

"How far back do the woods go?" she asks.

"All the way to the edge of the property," Lawrence says. "Maybe three quarters of an acre. There's a little creek that runs through about halfway. We had a lot of good times out here as kids."

"Kids, kids, kids. I bet growing up here was wonderful."

"Given how they've handled other properties, Walker Development would most likely clear cut the whole lot and put in a pipe to bury the creek," Lawrence says. "Build five hundred thousand-dollar McMansions or condos.

"Condos, condos, c-condos," Charlotte says. She turns to Brian. "We can afford this, right?"

"With what we have in savings, easily. Either of our credit unions would let us take out a mortgage also," he says. "My credit's good and I assume yours is, too. If we put a studio downstairs, we can write that off as a business expense and save money on recording — maybe even make money offering studio time."

"Then what are we waiting for?" Charlotte says.

The sale of the house goes through quickly, and two and a half months later, once Nancy is happily ensconced in a senior community in Florida, Brian, Charlotte, and Izzy start moving in. The neighbors from across the street, Alfred and Chizuko Collins, with their sons, Aaron and Genzo and daughter, Midori, who's Izzy's age, come over with platters of food and household items to welcome them.

"There's so much that gets overlooked when moving," Chizuko says.

Alfred tells them he's an Air Force veteran, who works at Hartsfield as an air traffic controller, and Chizuko, a native of Japan, is an interpreter with the Georgia Division of Family and Children's Services. Izzy hits it off with the kids, especially Midori, and the family is happy to learn Chizuko and Midori play violin and flute and sing. They invite them to come by to jam.

Alfred takes Brian and Charlotte around and introduces them to others in the neighborhood. Charlotte asks about the possibility of having musical gatherings at the house. Most are amenable, provided they don't run very late and parking doesn't become a problem.

A few weeks after settling in, Charlotte is in the back yard, when an older, black man, with close-cropped hair and beard, and wearing an Army jacket comes to the back gate. "Morning, ma'am. I'm looking for the Standridges."

"Morning to you, sir" Charlotte says and waves him in.

"My name's Theodore Gaston," he says. "You can call me Ted. I used to do some work for Jack and Nancy when I lived in the neighborhood some years ago. I take it they moved."

"Moved, moved," Charlotte says, then stops herself. She introduces herself and explains about Jack's death and Nancy selling them the house.

Brian steps out onto the back porch with a cup of coffee and some sheet music under one arm then sees Ted. "Hello there."

Ted greets Brian and Charlotte introduces him.

Brian comes down off the porch and shakes Ted's hand. "I guess Charlotte filled you in on who we are and why we're here."

"She did," Ted says. "Jack was a good man. Sorry to hear of his passing, but I'm glad to hear Nancy's doing well. I've been out on the West Coast living with my son's family, and just moved back a few days ago. I was just stopping in to pay my respects."

Claire comes through the back gate and when she sees Ted, she throws up her arms and calls out, "Chicken Man!"

He looks at her. "Hey, Miss Claire. Good to see you again."

She hurries over and gives him a hug.

"Chicken, Chicken, Chicken Man?"

"Yes ma'am," Ted says. "That's what they called me in the Army. My family owns a poultry business near Statesboro."

"We're from down that way," Brian says. He thinks for a moment then snaps his fingers. "Gaston Poultry."

"That's right," Ted says. "My family's been selling chickens down there longer than any of us can remember."

To Charlotte, Brian says, "Mom used to buy eggs from there."

"Eggs, eggs, eggs. I remember chasing the birds around there when I was a kid. Can we have chickens in DeKalb County?"

"Yes ma'am," Ted says. "With some restrictions, of course."

Charlotte looks at Brian and says with excitement, "Brian, we can have chickens!"

"Sounds like it," Brian says. "Why don't you come on in, Ted? We've got some coffee brewed, and some doughnuts and pastries, if you'd like. It would give us a chance to get better acquainted."

"You can meet my son, Izzy, when he decides to make an appearance," Charlotte says.

Several weeks later, with Ted's help, Charlotte, Brian, and Izzy build a chicken coop, and stock it with some hens and a rooster. The Sangers hire him as a general contractor to oversee some needed electrical and plumbing upgrades among other repairs and to provide his expertise in raising and caring for the birds.

In the days following the show at Smith's Rebecca goes into overdrive promoting Echo's album. She predicts that "Reach Out" will be their breakout hit and sends copies of the CD to several friends across the country with indie radio stations, including Buffalo, Denver, San Diego, Minneapolis, and Seattle. She also writes a glowing review of both the show and the album in Creative Loafing and mentions the album and individual tracks on her blog.

Over the next year, songs from the album start getting into rotation across the country. Demand for shows throughout the Southeast increases substantially and Echo starts playing larger venues and opening for known acts. As Rebecca predicts, "Reach Out" becomes a favorite among gay teens.

Rebecca's relationship with Claire remains in the "friend zone" despite Rebecca feeling a distinct connection to Claire she can't explain. The feelers Rebecca sends out to test whether Claire's interested in expanding their relationship are shot down promptly.

"Becky, stop trying to get me into bed," Claire finally tells her. "Otherwise, I'm cutting you off completely."

This cools down their relationship a lot, though Rebecca remains hopeful Claire will have a change of heart.

Brian and Charlotte spend much of 2004 touring around Georgia, the Carolinas, Tennessee, Alabama and Florida. Owing to their jobs and the demands of motherhood on Charlotte, they've never taken gigs that require them to be away longer than a night or two or are outside reasonable driving distance from Atlanta. With the success of the album, however, demand for the group increases substantially, and the Sangers have difficulty keeping up with requests for performances. Claire introduces them to a friend of hers, Amy Yarborough, who Brian and Charlotte know as a performer, but also as the manager to an enigmatic performer named Shayna Banks, who've they've opened for in smaller venues.

Amy dives right in handling their schedule and negotiating with venues, freeing up Brian and Charlotte to begin work on a follow up album late in 2004. Since Izzy's older, and there's a contingent of people who can look after him, they begin working with Amy on plans for a cross-country solo tour. They decide to divide the country into segments and hit each one throughout the following year, finally hitting the West Coast by late 2005 or early 2006.

Claire hasn't been touring with them, instead focusing on building her client list and appearances as a deejay at clubs. She becomes part of the entourage who'll be watching over Izzy. He'll stay at the house or with the Collins family throughout the week, spending weekends with the Savages or Branches. Claire and Ted have volunteered to coordinate being there a few nights a week to look after him and be available as needed. Charlotte provides photos of each to the school, with written instructions that they are to be contacted, whenever Chizuko or Alfred are unavailable.

As they're preparing for the West Coast tour in December 2005, Claire delivers the sad news that Rebecca has been killed in a car accident. Charlotte insists that Echo dedicate the remainder of their tour to Rebecca, since she played a large part in making it happen. She's also inspired to write a song about Rebecca and asks Claire to see if Steven would mind. He gives his okay and the result, "Becky Jean", is finished in time to make it onto a rough-cut EP they'll distribute to fans along the way. Claire arranges a private listening for Steven and Rachel at Charlotte and Brian's home, and Steven is very moved by the song.

Their West Coast itinerary includes San Francisco, Los Angeles, Portland, and finally Seattle. At their last show in Seattle in February 2006, a dark-haired teen girl, who introduces herself as Abigail hands Charlotte the EP she's just purchased. While Charlotte is signing the CD, Abigail leans in and in a voice just above a whisper, divulges that, "I really love 'Reach Out'. I learned to play it on guitar and sing it all the time."

Charlotte wraps her arms around Abigail and says, "You hang in there, Abigail. You're not alone."

"Thanks so much," Abigail says.

Brian joins them, and Abigail introduces herself as, "Abigail Worthy".

"Worthy, Worthy, Worthy," Charlotte says. She bows to Abigail and says, "You are Worthy!"

The words — "you are worthy" — get stuck in Charlotte's head. Several weeks later, with no recollection of why she's thinking them, she'll use them as the basis for a new song.

Morning Star

Chénxīng can no longer distinguish between that which she knows to be true about her past and that which she wishes to be so. The only reliable memories she has start with her time in the orphanage. Those are true whether she wants them to be or not.

Chénxīng knows very little about her mother and most of what she knows was told by the woman who explicitly said she wasn't her mother. Chénxīng doesn't know how much she can believe. She cannot recall a time from before she went to the orphanage when this woman wasn't around. At the time this woman left Chénxīng there she provided some details about Chénxīng's history that did not match with the few memories Chénxīng did recall from when she was smaller.

The story given was that Chénxīng's mother worked in a factory and left Chénxīng with the other woman. Her actual mother died in an accident at work, so the woman who was not her mother brought her to the orphanage. Chénxīng knows this isn't true, but she cannot remember enough to recall how she knows this and is not certain what the truth is.

The only story she heard that she does believe is how she got her name. The woman who said she wasn't Chénxīng's mother told the man at the orphanage that when Chénxīng was born the morning star was shining through the window of the room in which she was born. Her mother named her after it. Chénxīng wants this to be true, so it is.

Chénxīng does not know for certain how old she is. The earliest memories she has are bits and pieces of life in the house with the woman who said she wasn't her mother and they are not connected enough to form a coherent picture. The woman was always very angry. She constantly yelled at Chénxīng to stay quiet and not cause trouble; sometimes, if this "didn't work," she struck Chénxīng. Chénxīng learned to steel herself and shed no tears.

Chénxīng can remember cleaning around the house, washing dishes, and clearing the table after meals. The woman who said she was not her mother yelled at her to work quicker and to stop singing "that noise" — the songs she heard people from outside the windows singing. It was usually just the two of them, but sometimes, the woman who said she was not her mother would make Chénxīng go into a smaller room and be very quiet — quiet enough that Chénxīng could clearly hear other voices outside, though never clearly enough to identify who they were.

Her most vivid memory is of being taken to the orphanage, hearing the woman who said she wasn't Chénxīng's mother tell the official how Chénxīng was born and ended up with her. Since Chénxīng was small and had no birth records, her date of birth was listed as the date she was brought to the orphanage. The woman who said she was not her mother claimed she was four, though Chénxīng knows she was older. She cannot remember how she knows this, though.

After she entered the orphanage, Chénxīng avoided the other children and sometimes fought with them. She never displayed fear and became very good at defending herself. The others learned to stay away from her.

One morning, some months after she arrived, Chénxīng heard a small voice crying out in the dialect Chénxīng spoke. She followed the sound to the sleeping quarters and discovered a tiny girl crouched against the wall, crying and calling out for her mother. Other children were on their beds, ignoring her.

"Why does no one help her?" Chénxīng asked.

"All she does is cry," another child said. "We tell her to stop and she does not. She will not last long if she will not be quiet."

Chénxīng went to the girl and crouched beside her. She touched the girl's cheek and said, "What is your name, little one?"

"Hû Bâihé," the girl answered.

"Tiger Lily," Chénxīng repeated. "Are you afraid, little Tiger?" The girl nodded.

Chénxīng offered her hand. "We appear to be from the same province. We could be sisters. Would you like to be sisters little Tiger?"

Hû Bâihé nodded and took Chénxīng's hand.

From then on, Chénxīng protected the girl and they called themselves sisters. Chénxīng taught her songs she could remember from when she was younger. Looking out for Hû Bâihé gave Chénxīng a sense of responsibility. They were inseparable.

Then one day, the Americans came.

For months, Chénxīng and Hû Bâihé supported one another and looked out for each other. As time went on, Chénxīng came to think of her little Tiger as truly her sister. The other children left them alone and even the workers at the orphanage did not try to separate them, though their being together might hinder one or both of them from being adopted.

As Chénxīng got older, she would hear talk from the workers at the orphanage about finding someplace for her to work, since she would be harder to place. She worried that a day would come when she and Hû Bâihé would be unable to remain together. She concentrated on teaching her sister not to show her emotions around the other children, and how to sneak into the kitchen for a nighttime snack and helping her to memorize the schedule by which the custodians checked on them.

The day came when there was much excitement around the orphanage. A rich American couple had been visiting and now, they were there to adopt a child. Chénxīng could recall seeing them, walking around with the workers in the orphanage and talking to children. They had shown a particular interest in Hû Bâihé during one of their visits, and Chénxīng had encouraged her to talk and be friendly to them. A few days later Hû Bâihé was taken to the office and did not return.

Chénxīng missed her sister and thought of her constantly. Sometimes, after the lights had been turned out, she buried her face in her pillow and sobbed as quietly as she could. She took solace in knowing that Hû Bâihé would have a better life now.

Once her sister was gone, talk increased of sending Chénxīng to a job. One of the workers in the orphanage told her she might get the option to choose something, but otherwise, she'd be sent wherever she could be placed. Chénxīng prepared herself to be sent away.

At last, Chénxīng was brought to the office, expecting to receive an assignment for work. Instead she found the American man was waiting with the director. He explained that Hû Bâihé had not adjusted well to the separation.

"She keeps crying and calling out your name," he said. "Are you really her sister?"

Chénxīng regarded him with a long, emotionless stare. "Yes. We are sisters."

The director shook his head.

"The orphanage says you are not," the American said.

The orphanage is run by fools, Chénxīng thought.

To the American she said, "They would not know. Our papers were lost when we were separated. Can you not tell we speak the same dialect?"

"Yes. You do." The American stared at her for several long moments. Finally, he nodded to the director. Chénxīng was led out into the reception area and told to wait. The American emerged from the office and went to her.

"Is there anything you need to take with you?" he asked.

"Nothing," she replied.

"Come with me, then," he said. "I will take you to your sister."

Chénxīng learned the Americans were Peter and Helen Joiner and that they had been in China working with a religious group. When she and Peter arrived at the hotel, Hû Bâihé rushed to her and they embraced. Of the two, Peter seemed better at communicating with them in their home dialect specifically.

"There she is," Helen said. She was tall and seemed well-fed with a nervous sense about her. She went to Chénxīng, crouched beside her, and rubbed her shoulder. "Welcome to our family, Chénxīng."

"Family?" Chénxīng said, looking between Helen and Peter.

"That is right," Peter said to her. "We talked about it and have decided to adopt you as well."

"When Hû Bâihé got so upset without you, we prayed about it, and the Lord reminded us we have enough love in our hearts for two children," Helen said. "Tomorrow, I will take you out to get new clothes and we can begin our lessons."

What caught Chénxīng's eye were several porcelain dolls on a dresser that Helen purchased while in China. Helen explained that she collected them. Chénxīng couldn't help thinking that she and her sister had also been added to Helen's collection, but she didn't think it would be productive to say anything to anyone.

The following day, Helen took her shopping and they purchased more clothing than Chénxīng had ever owned. Looking at herself in the mirror at the hotel, she could not recognize the rich, Americanized girl in such fine, new outfits. They spent the rest of the day with their lessons.

Helen explained she was a teacher back in America and Peter was an executive with a technology company. Helen spent the afternoon tutoring the girls in English. Chénxīng picked up the words quickly but sometimes had trouble putting them together. Despite Helen's suggestion that she and Hû Bâihé try to communicate in their new language, whenever Chénxīng wanted to talk to her sister, she did so in their dialect, which Helen found difficult to follow.

Chénxīng recalls there being a long wait before they could leave China but had not yet picked up enough English to understand why. She recalls hearing Helen speaking to Peter in the other room and Helen sometimes seemed upset but whenever they were with the girls, Helen was cheerful and positive. Finally, they went to an office where they received papers and a few days afterward, they were on a plane bound for the United States.

When they landed in America, the sisters were given new names. Hû Bâihé was called Lily Francesca. Chénxīng became Amanda Lucille Joiner.

As long as they were in China, Chénxīng was very polite and not too talkative around the Joiners. She was afraid if she angered them, they'd send her back to the orphanage, despite the fact that they never threatened to do this. Once they arrived in America, she slowly began rebelling against them, and in particular, her new mother.

There was no reason for any animosity on her part toward Helen, who was always upbeat and very patient with Chénxīng. When she reacted awkwardly to Helen's spontaneous hugs and other displays of affection, Helen became more cautious in how she touched Chénxīng, unlike Hû Bâihé, who opened up to Helen almost from the beginning. When Chénxīng pretended not to understand an English word or phrase, Helen would explain it multiple times without displaying any frustration.

Chénxīng picked up English rather quickly, especially reading, graduating from the children's stories with which they started to more advanced texts within a matter of months. Around Helen, however, she always acted like she didn't understand her and continued to speak to Hû Bâihé in their native dialect. Peter would often scold Chénxīng about this, but Helen would reply that she could handle the situation.

Chénxīng's main point of contention was her name. Hû Bâihé quickly adapted to using the name Lily, and eventually stopped answering to her Chinese name. Chénxīng refused to answer to "Amanda" or "Mandy" as she was sometimes called. Chénxīng usually sat in silence whenever Helen spoke to her using the name. She could tell she was having an effect if Helen left the room to avoid getting emotional around her. While she could never explain why when Lily would ask, Chénxīng convinced herself she should not trust Helen.

The focus of Chénxīng's animosity became the dolls Helen collected. She had several shelves full of them and would sometimes take one down to show Chénxīng and Lily, explaining how she gave the doll its name. Lily listened with fascination to Helen's stories and asked lots of questions, but even though Chénxīng was sometimes interested, she pretended not to be, so Helen wouldn't notice. Chénxīng continued to see herself as one of Helen's collection and resented them more because of it.

One evening, Helen took a blonde doll with blue eyes from the shelf. "This one is Amanda. I named her that because she reminds me of my sister." To Chénxīng she said, "You're named after my sister, too, and your middle name is equivalent to your Chinese name, just like Lily's."

Something in Chénxīng snapped and she said in Chinese with much anger in her voice, "This is all we are to you. Your little China dolls."

"No. Why would you say that, Amanda?" Helen said.

"That is not my name," Chénxīng said, her anger growing. "You brought me here. You call me by another name, just like you do with your dolls."

"Oh. No. Amanda," Helen said. "We love you. We wanted you here with us so we could be a family."

"You showed no interest in me at the orphanage before you chose Hû Bâihé," Chénxīng said. "I am only here because Hû Bâihé was upset without me. You think you can put me on the shelf and name me like one of your dolls. I am not your China doll. My name is Chénxīng."

To drive home her point, Chénxīng overturned the shelf with dolls on it.

"Chénxīng no!" Lily screamed, in Chinese.

Helen broke down and buried her face in her hands.

Peter hurried in and stepped in front of Helen. "Amanda, go to your room." Chénxīng did not immediately comply and Peter said with much more firmness, "Go to your room now."

Chénxīng retreated to her room, slamming the door behind her. After she had been there alone for a long time, Lily visited her and climbed onto the bed. She laid her head on Chénxīng's shoulder.

"What is on your mind, little Tiger?"

"You're wrong, you know," Lily said in English. "These people love you. You should let them."

Chénxīng hugged Lily.

Sometime later, Helen came in and spoke to Chénxīng in English.

"I'm speaking to you this way because I know you can understand me despite always pretending otherwise. I am aware that you and Lily aren't actually sisters. She told me that when we got her back to the hotel in China, but she said that when she went to the orphanage, all the other children were mean to her and mistreated her. You were the only one who showed her kindness and looked out for her."

Helen moved to the end of the bed.

"Peter only wanted one child. But I convinced him that someone capable of that level of selflessness deserves a chance at a much better life. We also know that you're a lot older than the orphanage told us you are, but I don't think they were lying to us about your age. I think they didn't know — or didn't care. No matter. Peter and I decided that we had enough love in our hearts for two children and we meant that. You are definitely testing me, but I'm not going to give up on you. It would be nice, however, if you could try to meet me halfway."

Chénxīng remained silent and would not face Helen.

"Well," Helen said. "Whenever you're ready."

She turned to leave.

"I do not know my mother's name," Chénxīng said in English, causing Helen to stop and turn back. "I cannot see her face. All I have left of her is the name she gave me. Chénxīng."

"The brightest star in the morning sky," Helen said. She sat beside Chénxīng. "My mother was a very careless woman. She claimed she didn't realize that she was feeding my sister something Amanda was allergic to, and she was dismissive and slow to react when I told her Amanda was having a seizure and couldn't breathe. That's how I lost my sister."

Chénxīng sat up and faced Helen.

Helen went on. "The county took me away from my mother twice, but for some reason, the court sent me back both times. The third time they removed me, I swore I'd kill myself if they sent me back, but I was finally placed with a family who cared about my welfare. Just like you, I was very angry and rebelled against them at first."

Chénxīng said in English, "I hope I did not break any of your dolls."

Helen put her arm around Chénxīng and said, "They're a bit roughed up, but with a little care, they'll be good as new."

"I am glad you told me of your sister," Chénxīng said. "I will try better to honor her name."

"Your mother left you at an early age and is probably who sent you to the orphanage," Helen said. "I don't know if what you went through before that was better or worse, but it brought you to us and we love you and care about you. You may not remember her, but you do know your mother's name and what she looks like. I have chosen to be your mother and I swear to you I will never abandon you."

She hugged Chénxīng tightly and for the first time since being separated from Lily at the orphanage, Chénxīng allowed herself to cry.

Accepting Helen as her mother did not solve all their problems but it lessened the tension between them and Chénxīng began to confide in Helen. She sometimes still speaks to Lily in Chinese, but Lily always responds in English, and over time forgets how to respond otherwise. Chénxīng tells Helen she does not want to forget how to speak her native language, so Helen starts taking her to local businesses owned and staffed by Chinese immigrants, where Chénxīng can converse with them. Chénxīng starts exclusively speaking English in all other situations. Her nickname for Lily continues to be Tiger.

When they move to their new home in a place called Lawrenceville, Chénxīng learns there's a problem enrolling her in school, due to uncertainty about her age. Peter and Helen insist that the only information they have are her records from the orphanage, which indicates she's eight, which is equivalent to her educational level. After much discussion, the situation is resolved and Chénxīng is enrolled in third grade.

Chénxīng notes that most of her classmates are white, though there are some blacks, people from South America, East Indians, other Chinese, and Korean students. Chénxīng keeps to herself, not approaching anyone. She is left alone by the others.

One day, on the playground, she notices a blonde girl approaching her with a black girl following. Not sure of their intentions, Chénxīng puts up her guard, but the blonde girl smiles as she gets near and folds her hands in front of her to address Chénxīng.

"We noticed you're alone a lot and thought we'd introduce ourselves. My name's Alyssa, but my friends call me Aly. This is Sandy."

The black girl nods to her. She seems more guarded than her companion.

Chénxīng starts to respond, "My name is Chénxīng," but pauses, considers it, then says, "I am Amanda. My family calls me Mandy."

"Would you like to sit with us at lunch, Mandy?" Alyssa says. "We talked about it and would like you to join us. Right, Sandy?"

Sandy shrugs. "Yeah. Sure."

"I would like that," Chénxīng says.

Chénxīng finds Alyssa to be very friendly and interested in getting to know her, but Sandy remains quiet and on guard whenever they're together. She rarely speaks directly to Chénxīng, but filters everything through Alyssa. Chénxīng suspects that approaching her was Alyssa's idea.

The Joiners attend the same church as Sandy's family and one Sunday, when she sees Sandy sitting alone, Chénxīng has an idea and sits beside her.

"In China, my name was Chénxīng," she says.

Sandy repeats, "Chénxīng."

"It means morning star."

"That's a nice name."

"This is something I've told just you and not your friend."

"You're not going to tell Aly?" Sandy says.

"Only when you say that I can."

Sandy nods. After that, she begins to open up to Chénxīng. One afternoon, several weeks later, while Alyssa is with them at Sandy's home, Sandy asks Chénxīng, "What did they call you in China?"

From that point on, they become what Alyssa calls, "The Three Musketeers".

Events of 1985

Leah **Walker** sits at the console of the Amiga 1000 computer in the basement of her family's home in Buckhead, a box of Lucky Charms on the desk nearby. Two years earlier, she was enthralled by the film *War Games*, which inspired her interest in computing, and she planted the notion with her father that if they had a computer, he'd be able to get more work done without having to waste time driving to the office. Her subtle hints were rewarded when Paxton, acting on an idea that "just came to me" brought home a Commodore 64, which Leah completely mastered in a matter of days. A few months ago, she saw a report on a network news magazine show about teen hackers in California who compromise the phone companies and invade computer networks, which coincided with her learning about a BBS run by a local computing nerd, and she began connecting with other enthusiasts.

Then came the crown jewel, the Amiga 1000; the most advanced computer Leah has ever seen with its brand-new Windows operating system. Not even Pace Academy has one of these yet. Leah has been learning Windows on her own through trial and much error, though she's considered taking a course at the Learning Annex to supplement what she already knows. The local BBS is visited by people from across the country, and it was here she learned about boards in California which attracted some of the folks she heard about in the news report. Since then, she's been trying to tap into these groups who could teach her how to pull off lots of interesting, and not-remotely-legal tricks.

"Doctor, doctor, can't you see I'm burning, burning," Leah sings along with the radio, tuned to WRAS 88.5, Georgia State University's radio station.

Her four-year-old sister, Alyssa, is seated at the Commodore across the room, playing her favorite game — one with cartoon bears in it; Leah can't remember what it's called. Alyssa's wearing headphones, but sometimes sings along to the songs in the game. She was the "surprise" child, born when Leah was twelve, and both Leah and Paxton refer to her as "Princess," a name Leah's mother, Melinda, has not adopted.

Leah opens the cereal and takes out a handful, which she crams into her mouth and crunches on as she clicks on the modem software and selects a number from the list. The modem makes its wavering and staticky noises as it connects her to a box just outside Los Angeles. She logs in with her handle, Jo-eMamba, then begins exploring what's new since her last visit. So far, she's lurked more than posted, not wanting anyone to suspect she's a high school kid from Georgia. She's set up her profile as Lee Johannes, a male college student from Gary, Indiana. As she explores the message board, she keeps notes on a yellow pad by the computer.

Melinda calls from the top of the stairs, "Leah, Gita's here."

Leah rolls to the door and yells back, "Tell her I went to the North Pole."

"She's standing right here," Melinda yells back.

"Oh. Don't tell her that, then," Leah says. "Are her legs working?"

Melinda calls back, "They appear to be."

"Well use them, Gita," Leah yells then rolls back to the computer.

A minute or so later, her classmate and best friend, Gitanjali Ramachandra, or "Gita" as she prefers to be called, enters.

Gita's wearing sandals, cut-off jeans, and a bulky "Frankie Say Relax" T-shirt that engulfs her entire midsection. Her father is the chief financial officer at Bickering Plummet. She and Leah met at school in second grade after her family moved into the palatial colonial revival house across the street from the Walkers in Buckhead.

Gita regards Leah with frustration, and says, "Why are you playing around on the computer? We're supposed to be going to the park."

"I heard it's supposed to rain," Leah says.

Gita stops and says with a disappointed tone, "Really?"

"No. Of course not."

"Very funny." Gita jostles Alyssa's hair, which prompts Alyssa to look up and say, "Gitanjali Ramachandra!" with all the confidence of a four-year-old proving she can. Gita reacts with amusement.

"Want some cereal?" Leah says, offering the box to Gita.

"Lucky Charms?" Gita says, with a sour look.

"Hey! They're magically delicious," Leah says, snapping the box away from her friend. "Never mind, then." She takes out another handful and crams it into her mouth.

"Have you ever heard of the Arpanet?" Leah asks between bites.

Gita shakes her head. "What is it?"

"It's this gigantic network of networks that connects the military with colleges and government agencies."

"Why would they need to be connected like that?" Gita says.

"I guess schools that do research need to connect with the places that fund them. I read someplace the Arpanet was built to withstand a nuclear war."

"That's helpful to know," Gita replies with more than a hint of sarcasm. She falls back into the chair and sighs.

Twenty minutes later, she has shifted in the chair, from leaning on her elbows — watching Leah become increasingly consumed by whatever she's doing on the computer — to sitting sideways with her feet, sans footwear, dangling over the side — humming along with the tune Alyssa keeps singing from her program — and finally with her feet over the back, and her head hanging backwards over the seat.

Finally giving in to frustration, she pleads with Leah, "How long are you going to screw around on that damn computer?"

"Sorry," Leah says. "It does get addictive." She disconnects from what she's doing and shuts down the Amiga, then rises. "Anyone meeting us?"

"I said something about it to Stewart," Gita says.

"Stewart, the ass wipe who calls you Rama-lama-ding-dong? Honestly, Gita, what do you see in that idiot?"

"He's cute," Gita says. "Besides, he said he'd stop calling me that."

"When's he going to start? Monday?" Leah says. Gita rolls her eyes. "Why are you even talking to Stewart, anyway? Aren't you supposed to be getting married?"

"Not before I'm twenty," Gita says.

"I cannot believe there's a guy sitting over in Bombay waiting for you to come over and marry him," Leah says.

"No. Raja's in Canton. His family moved here five years ago."

"Well, good luck with that. I'm never getting married."

Leah takes the cereal and goes over to Alyssa, who's engrossed in her game, and pulls one of the headphones away from Alyssa's ear. She sets the cereal beside the console.

"You're on your own, Princess," Leah says, then kisses Alyssa on the forehead.

They go upstairs into the kitchen, where Melinda is sitting at the counter reading the Atlanta Constitution. She's Leah's height and build, with dark auburn hair and hazel eyes. A Virginia Slims is burning in an ashtray nearby.

"Is Dad using the Mercedes today?" Leah says. She goes to the counter and takes a draw from the cigarette. Melinda takes it from her, swats Leah's hand and gives her an aggravated look, then puts the cigarette back in the ashtray.

"What's wrong with Margaret's car?" Melinda says.

"The Karmann Ghia doesn't have a phone," Leah says.

Leah learned how to drive in her aunt Margaret's Karmann Ghia, and Margaret's been letting her drive it since then. One of the stipulations Margaret had for letting Leah use it is that she learn how to change the oil and perform other basic maintenance. Margaret doesn't trust mechanics in the area since her favorite repair shop closed. Leah has become adept at most repairs and service on the vehicle and won't let anyone else touch the car.

"I think he's golfing at noon," Melinda says, "but I'm not sure if he's driving today or riding."

"Let's just take the convertible," Gita says. "It's a nice day out. We can put the top down."

"Oh, all right," Leah says. "But if we get stuck someplace and can't call for help, don't blame me."

"What's Alyssa doing?" Melinda asks.

"Playing that bear game for the five thousandth time," Leah says. "Honestly, she probably dreams about singing bears."

"I'll check on her in a minute," Melinda says, massaging her temple. "Where are you girls off to today?"

"Piedmont Park," Leah says.

"I heard it might rain," Melinda says.

Leah shakes her head. "Not today." She kisses Melinda on the cheek. "Love you, Mom."

"Have fun," Melinda says.

Contrary to Gita's speculation, none of their schoolmates are at the park, which suits Leah, so they spend an hour or so roaming around, people watching, before retiring to the lawn to hang out and toss around the frisbee. At one point, Gita's throw is just outside Leah's reach. She follows it with her eyes and watches as it grazes the head of a guy walking near them with a camera, who stops, picks it up and turns to see where it originated. Leah and Gita laugh, and Leah goes to retrieve the frisbee and apologize.

Avis Collins sets a stack of paper plates at the end of the food table her mother and others from the church have set up and reaches into the bag for a box of plastic utensils. Her brother and sister, Alfred and Annabelle, disappeared into the park, leaving all the work to her, as usual. Her father encouraged her to go out and enjoy the nice summer day as well, but Avis isn't one to idle while things need to be accomplished. She put her little brother, Avery, in charge of ice and drinks, but now he's wandered off somewhere and, since all the others keep stopping to converse with friends and family, Avis is mostly working alone. But she has a job to do and she's going to get it done, despite all the distractions; hopefully, her parents will see that she, at least, is dedicated to giving her brother a fitting send off, even if he's not there to appreciate it.

Celebrating Alfred's graduation from Georgia State University, and enlistment into the Air Force as an Airman First Class, warrants a church-wide picnic at Piedmont Park. Since Georgia State doesn't have an Air Force ROTC program, he's been attending the one at Georgia Tech, and his commander, a reserve officer and local pilot, Captain Asher, has been encouraging Alfred to enroll in flight training, with an eye toward qualifying for the space program, an idea Alfred has whole-heartedly embraced. An avid model builder, he has a replica of the Challenger on the dresser in his bedroom, and he's always wanted to emulate Guion Bluford.

The turnout is more than likely a reflection on Avis's father. Aaron Abel Collins is pastor at the Edgewood African Methodist Episcopal Congregation of Atlanta; his congregation of around three-hundred and fifty members considers him a "mighty man of God," no doubt in part to the significant neighborhood outreach, that gives the congregation — and the pastor —an influential voice in the community.

As his oldest daughter, Avis has always been very conscious of her role in the family and community, and she holds herself to a higher standard of decorum than that of her friends and acquaintances — and, at this moment, her siblings.

Certain that she's neither of her parents' favorite child — Avery gets most of her mother Maxine's attention, while Annabelle is clearly the apple of Aaron's eye, and Alfred, as first-born, holds an exalted position — she nevertheless endeavors to be worthy of their praise and attention. In her second year at Spelman, Avis doesn't have any special accomplishments to her name beyond being a good student with perfect attendance at the schools she attended whilst her father was assigned to various churches around the region. Aaron calls her "the serious one" and her maternal grandmother has always claimed Avis has "an old soul". Eternally hyperconscious of other people's opinions, Avis tries to keep everyone around her within the prescribed boundaries, prompting Alfred to nickname her "Mother Avis".

"Where did they get off to?" Avis hears Maxine say.

"Oh, they'll be along sooner or later," Aaron says. "Probably just having a good time in the park."

"I'll go find them," Avis says, without any prompting from either of her parents.

Before Aaron or Maxine can stop her, she sets down her box of plastic flatware and heads away from the pavilion, in the exact same direction she saw Alfred and Annabelle go nearly an hour earlier, knowing fully well they're most likely on their way back as she starts. She wants some time to herself to stroll around and enjoy the park.

On some level, she knows her parents won't mind her taking the time, but never feels quite right spending time on herself when there are other responsibilities. She likes to stay busy — she isn't good at simply "hanging out" and gets self-conscious when she's around others and doesn't have anything to occupy her. She likes getting away from everyone where she doesn't feel the need to conform to how others think she should act. On her own, she allows herself to relax and take in the sights in the park.

Though Avis is closer in age to Alfred, he's always had more of a kinship with Annabelle. As children and teenagers, Avis felt her older brother was allowed far more leeway than she was. He would often take off from the house for hours on his bike without either parent apparently worried where he was or when he was coming back, whereas her mother would mercilessly grill Avis on her plans, even when she was just headed over to a friend's house to work on school assignments. Once, Alfred consumed an entire box of Lucky Charms on his own over the course of several days, carefully resealing it and placing it back on the top shelf in the kitchen so it looked undisturbed, and when Avis finally convinced her mother to open it, they found it empty.

In college, Alfred pledged Omega Psi Phi fraternity, and bears, on his right arm, a brand of the Omega symbol, which had been a point of friction between Aaron and Alfred for several weeks before and after he got it.

"Our people didn't march for their freedom just for you to be branded like livestock," Avis recalls Aaron stating during one of their many arguments at the dinner table.

"You're just upset because I didn't pledge Alpha Phi Alpha like you did," Alfred countered. "The Q-Dogs were good enough for Langston Hughes and Jesse Jackson."

Avis finds she also doesn't have much in common with her younger sister, separated by four years. There's nothing particularly wrong between them, it's just that their personalities don't mesh. Annabelle is a track star at her high school and is already being evaluated by colleges. In church, Annabelle seems mostly going through the motions of her faith rather than truly believing and during the few times they've discussed it, Annabelle seems to have more questions "why" than assurances that the answers found in the Bible or the pulpit are correct. She confides more in Alfred, who encourages her by quoting Eastern philosophy he's learned in his martial arts classes.

The youngest, Avery, has yet to demonstrate what he's most passionate about and spends his time listening to rap artists who have been screened by Aaron and Maxine, and cracking jokes he makes up about his experiences in school and church. His teachers mostly have positive things to say about him, though they do note a tendency on his part to be the class clown. He is very popular among his fellow students, and his grades are sufficient for him to be on the basketball team at school, where his height usually leads to his being the center. While he displays a talent for it, his coach has stated he doesn't feel Avery's interested in pursuing it long term.

The only thing Avis has ever truly been passionate about was her friendship with Myesha Kittredge, a young woman she met when her father was assigned as pastor at Edgewood AMC when Avis was a junior in high school, and she let that friendship go rather than face an uncomfortable truth about herself. Myesha was loud and funny, the complete antipathy of Avis, who likes to keep to herself and not draw attention. When they were together, Avis felt she could drop her guard and share more of her personality, without her friend judging her.

Avis came to realize her feelings for Myesha ran much deeper than friendship and she found Myesha occupying her thoughts during times they were away from one another. These feelings disturbed her and put her at odds with her upbringing. She wasn't aware of anything explicitly in the Bible against women being with other women, but the opinions of those in her congregation seemed to discourage relationships other than a traditional husband and wife pairing. She was certain that her family and those who knew her would be very disappointed if she followed her heart as it were.

Everything would be fine, though, as long as she never acknowledged it. Myesha was her friend, a good friend and nothing more. As long as that's what Avis told herself, nothing could go wrong. It turned out that Myesha felt the same and Myesha wasn't Avis. She didn't care what the congregation, kids at school or even her parents thought. She always followed her own path, and this was no different.

On prom night, Avis went with Wiley Johns, a classmate at Carver High, who also attended her church. Her family got along well with Wiley's and encouraged Avis to show him more consideration than she usually did. Avis liked Wiley, but she never felt much of a connection with him, even though he was always polite and courteous toward her. Myesha was at the prom, alone, and sat with them and several others. Avis spent the majority of her time talking with her friend, except for the few occasions when Wiley convinced her to dance. Toward the end of the evening, Myesha disappeared and Wiley suggested he and Avis could go to one of the after parties.

Avis said she was tired and asked to be taken home. She said good night at the door and gave Wiley a quick peck on the cheek before disappearing into the house. Maxine wanted to grill her about the prom and how she and Wiley got along, but Avis claimed exhaustion and excused herself to go to her room.

Twenty or thirty minutes later, after Avis had changed into shorts and a T-shirt, there was a tap on her window and she looked out to see Myesha there, armed with a bottle of champagne. Avis slipped out the window and she and Myesha hurried through the yard, suppressing their giggles until they exited onto the street behind, where Myesha's car was waiting. Once inside, they burst into raucous laughter.

"Where are we going?" Avis asked.

"My aunt's apartment," Myesha said. "She's out of town and asked me to take care of her cats."

Once there, they opened the champagne while they joked about people at the prom. Wiley came up and Myesha teased Avis, calling Wiley "the man you'll marry, if your family has anything to say about it."

Avis sighed. "Wiley's okay. I just wish my folks would stop trying to push us together. If something was going to happen, it would have happened by now."

"They just want you married, girl," Myesha said, taking Avis's hand. "Or working toward it, at least."

"I don't see that happening anytime soon. Not with Wiley anyway."

They fell silent for several long moments. Myesha touched Avis's cheek then leaned forward and kissed her. Avis returned the kiss. A jolt went through her, a feeling she'd never experienced before, and the feeling grew as the kiss intensified. Myesha laid back with Avis over her, who started to move her hands over Myesha and under her shirt.

She could no longer remember what specifically had gone through her mind, whether it was the image of her parents, or the thought of their congregation learning of what they were doing. All Avis could recall was that suddenly, she felt the full weight of what was happening between them drop on her at once and she sat up and moved away from Myesha.

"We need to stop," she said.

"What's up?" Myesha said, out of breath.

"We shouldn't be doing this. It's not right."

"Feels right to me. Seems like it felt pretty right to you, too."

"Well, it's not. Two women aren't supposed to be together like this."

"Says who?"

"You know who. The Bible says men and women are supposed to come together as husbands and wives."

"That was thousands of years ago." Myesha slid toward her and touched her shoulder. "Avis, I love you. I thought you felt the same."

"Of course. We're friends."

"That's not what I meant, and you know it."

"Can't we just forget this?" Avis said. "Go back to the way things were."

"No. I don't think we can."

"What would people think? Are you going to tell your parents? I'm not."

"Why does that matter?" Myesha said. "Why would we even need to tell anyone? It's not their business."

"I would know. I couldn't hide it."

"We'll make it work," Myesha said. "If we really care about

each other, that's all that matters, isn't it?"

"No. No it's not."

It wasn't that Avis didn't want to agree with Myesha. It's that she decided she couldn't and, having decided that, she would not waver. She asked Myesha to drive her home, which she did without further discussion.

That Sunday, they didn't sit together at church and though Myesha looked in her direction frequently, Avis kept her eyes focused toward the front and never once glanced at Myesha. She also avoided her as much as she could at school. Once, Myesha cornered her in the halls.

"Don't you at least want to talk about it?"

"No," Avis told her and walked away. They made no other attempts to discuss it throughout the remainder of the year. After that, Avis decided that she would never again let anyone get that close to her.

She spends around fifteen minutes wandering through the park, absorbed with her thoughts before pausing a moment near the nature trail to admire some violets growing there. Her thoughts are interrupted by the click of a camera nearby and she turns to see a guy just lowering his, facing her direction.

"Oh, no you didn't," Avis says to herself and goes to confront him. "Did you just take my picture?"

He seems somewhat embarrassed.

"Were you standing over there?" He points toward approximately the spot she was standing.

"Yes."

"I pointed my camera in that direction and took a picture. You might be in it. I won't know until I get it developed."

"That's very rude. Photographing people without their permission."

"Sorry."

"Oh, you're going to be sorry." She encircles her face using her index finger. "Take a look. Take a good look. This lady is off limits. You got that?"

"Okay."

"I know all about you" — with air quotes — "photographers, walking around, saying 'Hey baby, why don't you give me a smile?' Well here's a newsflash. Avis Arielle Collins is not your private dancer."

The man gives her a curious look. "Collins? Do you know Alfred? I work with him at GSU."

The invocation of Alfred's name catches Avis off guard, and it takes her a moment to regroup.

"Don't you worry about who I know." She pokes her finger at him. "You see me again you just better not be pointing that camera at me."

With that, she storms off.

When she gets back to the pavilion, Alfred and Annabelle have returned and Avery is hovering by their table.

"There she is," Maxine says. "Avis where have you been?"

Avis starts to answer but Aaron speaks up.

"It's okay, Maxey. She's here now."

Avis sits with her family as Aaron addresses the crowd.

"We are blessed by everyone's presence here today. Alfred is concluding an important part of his life, and preparing to embark on another, and I know he appreciates everyone's thoughts and prayers as he moves into this new phase of his life. I just want him to know how proud we all are of his accomplishments and we know the Lord has big things ahead for him."

Everyone applauds and Aaron leads the congregants in the blessing before settling down to lunch.

"You know who I ran into at Kroger the other day?" Maxine says. "Nell Kittredge. She asked about you, Avis."

"Did she?" Avis says without much interest.

"How are they liking their new congregation?" Aaron says.

"They like it just fine," Maxine says. "Said she hasn't heard a word out of that daughter of hers, since Myesha moved to the West Coast."

"Whatever happened between the two of you, anyway?" Annabelle says.

Avis gives her an angry stare. "What makes you think something happened?"

"She stopped coming around right after you went to the prom with Wiley Johns," Annabelle says.

"Way Wiley told it, she went to the prom with Myesha," Alfred says. "He just drove her there."

"Wiley is an idiot," Avis says.

"That idiot, as you call him, is working on a law degree from Howard University," Maxine says. "You could have done a lot worse than Wiley Johns, young lady, as sweet as that young man was on you."

"We just didn't click, I suppose," Avis says.

"Personally, I wasn't sorry to see Myesha stop hanging around so much," Aaron says. "That girl was a bad influence on you, Avis. Good family, but she had a wild streak in her."

"You two were thick as thieves for a while there," Maxine says. "I was surprised she disappeared like she did."

"I guess she just found other things to do," Avis says. "I thought this day was supposed to be about Alfred, not me."

"I loved it when Myesha was around," Annabelle says. "She always made me laugh."

"Why didn't you stay in touch with her, then?" Avis says. She looks at Alfred, hoping to change the subject. "What time do you have to report Monday?"

"O-Eight-Hundred, sharp," Alfred says.

"When do you get to be an astronaut?" Avery says.

"Not right away," he replies. "I've got to go through basic, then make it into flight school. That could take months, or maybe a year or more. Lots of people want to fly."

"You haven't even flown in a plane," Avis says. "What makes you think you can pilot one?"

"They'll need to train me," he says. "That's why there's flight school."

After lunch, Avis starts to help out with cleaning up, but Alfred touches her arm and says, "Why don't we take a walk?"

"Annabelle is over there."

"I don't want to talk to her," he says. "I want to talk to you."

She walks with him away from the pavilion.

"So? Talk."

"Look, I know we haven't been all that close," he says. "That's on me as much as it is you. But I'm going to miss you, Avis."

"Don't you mean Mother Avis?" she says with a slight smile.

"Okay. I guess I deserve that," he says. "Hey, you'll be the oldest finally. At least until I get back."

"That's something, I guess," she says and gives him a hug. "I'll miss you too, as aggravating as you are."

"That means a lot," he replies. "Let's try to stay in touch, okay?"

"That'd be nice," she says. "Be careful flying those planes. I wouldn't want to permanently become the oldest."

"Not a chance," he says.

David Cairo — pronounced "kay-ro" — enters the kitchen of his family's modest, ranch-style house in East Point, Georgia, and pours himself a bowl of Lucky Charms, then drowns the cereal in milk. It's eight a.m. and so far, he's heard no evidence that the rest of his family is up. His father, Joseph, reads meters for the East Point Water Department, and is usually out of the house by the time David starts his preparations to head to school, but Joseph doesn't work on Saturdays, and usually sleeps late as does David's mother, Miriam.

He doesn't hear his brothers, Rand or Terry talking, as they often do when they wake up but aren't ready to get out of bed, so he takes that as a sign they're not awake yet either. He debates whether or not to turn on the television, then decides against it, since that would certainly get the rest of the family going, and he prefers the quiet. The Cairos are a close-knit group, but usually communicate at an amplified volume and David's not in the mood for it just now. Unlike his brothers, he has a room to himself where he can retreat if the family gets too much on his nerves, but he prefers eating at the dining room table instead of lying on his bed.

David is twenty-two, a native of Atlanta, and in his third year at Georgia State University, where he's majoring in English. An uninspired student in high school, he's done much better in college, hardly Dean's list, but he maintains a much higher GPA. Tuition at a state university isn't high and David is the oldest of three sons in a single-income family a few notches above poverty level, so he's been able to finance his entire college career with Pell Grants, holding down jobs as a student assistant to provide himself with a little spending money. Despite their lower middle-class status, the family is living comfortably, with a decent home, more than one car whenever Joseph finds a deal, and plenty to eat, though lacking in a few luxuries, such as a color television. Joseph has never stressed the need for another wage earner contributing to the family's resources, so David has never really felt it necessary. Anything he earns he usually spends on himself.

His plans for the day include heading over to Piedmont Park to give his Minolta X-370, its first real workout. A coworker at school, Alfred Collins, sometimes brings his camera and often shows off photos he's taken around town, usually with lots of women in them, and brags about how introducing himself as a "photographer" has gained him numerous phone numbers. This inspired David to subscribe to *Modern Photography*, where he researched the ads in the back for the latest camera models. An electronics shop in New York City listed several at prices David considered reasonable, so he sent them a check. The camera, extra lenses, and filters cost him just under three hundred dollars, and represents the cutting edge in existing technology.

Photography is turning into an expensive, and somewhat time-consuming hobby for him, having found a Wolf Cameras at a nearby mall that can process photos in an hour. He's constantly running over there to get his pictures developed. So far, his main subjects have been items on the dining room table, or pictures on the walls of his home, or the family's cats. It took him several tries and a few rolls of 24-exposure film before he figured out how to turn off the automatic shutter and exposure controls which were causing his indoor, low-light photos to blur, but now he has a reasonable handle on the settings and is ready to start taking his hobby seriously. A few days ago, he went downtown and snapped several rolls of black and white film around Lucky Street and the Omni.

Finished with the cereal, he rinses out the bowl and leaves it in the sink and goes to his room, where he switches on his radio, set — as always — to WRAS. His room fills with the sounds of the Thompson Twins. He changes into jeans and a T-shirt and puts on a pair of black Reeboks, then places his camera bag on the bed and goes through it to be sure he has all his desired filters and lenses, and plenty of film. He's started using larger, 36-exposure rolls, which allows him to take many more shots, and increases his processing costs, but he usually doesn't obsess over how much money he's spending. Usually he just plops down his credit card and makes his usual monthly payment.

Satisfied he has all his equipment, he gets his wallet, keys, and pocketknife. When he heads back into the living room, he finds his father sitting at the dining room table, smoking, with his mother in the kitchen starting coffee.

"Where you headed today?" Joseph says.

"Piedmont Park," he says.

"Got that expensive camera, I see," his father says.

"It wasn't that expensive. Besides, I paid for it myself, so what difference does it make?"

Miriam steps into the doorway to the kitchen. "You're not taking the car, are you? I need to do some shopping."

"No. I'm taking MARTA."

"Do you want something to eat?" she says

"I had some cereal."

"Will you be back before lunch?" she says.

"Probably not."

"Well, be careful out there," she says then goes back into the kitchen.

Joseph shakes his head and looks away. David waits a moment to be sure his father isn't planning to say anything else, then exits and heads out to the bus stop.

Depending on how the trains are running, the trip to the park usually takes a little under an hour, including the time it takes to walk there from Midtown station. David grew up on public transportation in Atlanta, and MARTA has been his primary means of travel in college. Use of the family car is prioritized for his father to get to and from work.

In high school, college had been the last thing on his mind. One of his teachers concluded that David was the type of student who only put forth a meaningful effort when he felt challenged and otherwise didn't worry about his grades. David found this to be an accurate description of him. He usually understood most subjects, and before high school had been a good student who always tested well above his grade level in reading and math; but found the grind of classwork too repetitive and he was easily distracted.

When he graduated, he decided he was done with education forever and found a job working as a courier at a local business. It took about six months in the work force for him to grow tired of the limited opportunities afforded by his low-wage position and he finally decided college was his best option. Most of his friends were already going to school, and, after finally being laid off when the company relocated, he applied and was accepted at Georgia State. Mid-way through his second year, he started taking classes in the late-afternoon and evening and found them more to his liking with fewer students than the crowded morning classes.

He often finds himself second-guessing every decision he makes. He swore he'd never go to college right up to the point he enrolled. He constantly tells himself he needs to quit his nowhere, student assistant position, and find something more lucrative, but lacks the motivation to make good on his threat. A close friend of his is fond of saying David might be dangerous if he ever acquires the means to make something of himself.

David exits MARTA at 10th Street and walks the few blocks to Piedmont Park. He's hardly been there for ten minutes before he runs into Alfred Collins, with a young woman who looks to be in her teens.

"Hey Cairo. Got your new camera with you, I see," Alfred says.

"Yeah," David says, holding up to show it. "Thought I'd give it a workout."

"Nice." Alfred indicates the young woman. "This is my little sister, Annie."

She swats his arm. "I'm not your little anything, Alfie." To David. "Nice to meet you."

"Are you in college?" he asks.

"No, Carver High," she says.

"Annie's a track star," Alfred says. "She can outrun just about anyone."

"Not difficult in my case," David says.

"Lots of sunbathers on the lawn," Alfred says in confidence to David with a wink, as he and his sister head off.

"Good to know," David says to him.

Running into Alfred reminds David why he got the camera, but his experiences haven't been as fruitful as Alfred claimed his were. He wonders if it's because Alfred is more outgoing and has no trouble talking to anyone. David rarely meets any of the people he photographs, especially not women, and can't imagine even approaching them when he's not taking photos. In everyday social situations, he usually works his way into conversations by hovering around a group of people who are talking and listening for an opening, where he can comment. Consequently, he spends a lot of time on the periphery, watching everyone else have a good time.

He spends some time along the lake, taking photos of the ducks and a squirrel, or interesting plants. He snaps a couple of the tree line and gazebo reflected in the water, then circles around the playground area and snaps a photo of a mounted policeman on a horse. His favorite subjects are buildings and plants, which usually don't require permission to photograph.

Passing near the nature trails, he spots a young woman standing near the entrance, deep in thought, and he snaps a photo then looks around to see where he'd like to go next. She focuses on him with her hands on her hips, then walks over.

"Excuse me, did you just take my picture?"

"I don't know," David says, somewhat self-conscious. "Were you standing over there?" He points in the direction he was looking.

"Yes, I was."

"I pointed my camera in that direction and snapped a picture," he says. "If you were standing there, you might be in it. I won't know until I get the photos developed."

"That is very rude, taking someone's photo without permission."

"Sorry. I didn't mean anything by it."

"Oh, you're going to be sorry," she says. She waves her hand around her face. "Take a good look, mister. This lady is off limits. You got it?"

"Okay."

"You men don't fool me with your cameras. Walking around, saying, 'Hey baby, why don't you give me a smile?' Well for your information, Avis Arielle Collins is not going to be your private dancer."

The name registers with David. "Did you say your name is Collins? Do you know Alfred? I work with him at GSU."

This seems to catch her off guard and it takes her a moment. "Don't go worrying about who I know. You just watch where you're pointing that camera. You run into me again, I better not see it pointed at me."

"Okay, okay. I apologize if I inadvertently took your picture. I swear if you're in any of my photos, I'll burn them and the negatives."

She waves her hand around her face again then shakes her finger at him and storms off. David waits until she's far enough away and snaps one more photo.

He spends another hour wandering around, taking pictures of flowers, artwork, and women who catch his eye. As he's heading across the lawn, something grazes the back of his head. He sees a purple frisbee hit the ground near him and stoops to pick it up, then turns and focuses on the auburn-haired, teenaged girl moving toward him, dressed in shorts, an over-sized rugby shirt, and white sneakers.

"Sorry," she says, her hands folded in front of her.

"I think I'll survive." David hands her the frisbee.

She takes it, gives him a quick smile, then points. "Nice camera. Minolta?"

"Yes, it is." He holds it up. "May I?"

She poses, holding the frisbee like a hat beside her head, as he snaps a shot of her.

Another girl, wearing an enormous "Frankie Say Relax" T-shirt, calls out, "Leah, let's go."

Leah motions to her. "Come here." Her friend joins her, and she says to David, "You mind?"

"Not at all," he says and snaps a photo of them posing together. He lowers the camera. "How can I get in touch with you to send you copies when I have them developed?"

Leah shrugs. "Maybe we'll run into one another again someday." She and her friend turn to go.

"Have a nice day, Leah," he calls after her. She waves as they walk away.

David checks to see he only has a few more exposures left on the film he has loaded and finishes the roll as he heads toward the exit. If he has use of the car, he plans to have them developed as soon as he gets home.

Ashes

Each year, close to her birthday on May 11, Claire Belmonte takes a trip to a little church yard in Houston County, Georgia, just outside Perry to visit the grave of Christine Messner, whose life dates are 11 May 1973 to 4 September 1989. Christine "died" on the same day she was declared an emancipated minor in juvenile court in Houston County, and the headstone was placed there by Zachariah and Selma Messner early the following year. No death certificate has ever been filed on her, owing to the fact that she is, still, very much alive in Atlanta.

Claire learned of the headstone from her friend, Jodie Newcombe, about a year after it had been placed there. Jodie found it while visiting the graves of her grandparents and noticed a new stone several yards away. There had not been any funeral services at her church since Deacon James Frederick had been quietly laid to rest at a sparsely attended service just after Christine left Perry in 1989, and his grave is on the opposite side of the cemetery. When she went to investigate, the name on the stone caused Jodie's knees to nearly buckle, and she hurried home and called Claire in Atlanta to be sure her friend was all right.

A few days later, Claire, accompanied by Lawrence Standridge, came to see Jodie, and she, Lawrence, Jodie and her father visited the cemetery. Claire has come down every year since for the past twelve to pay her respects. This year, she's working a show on the Sunday of her birthday, so she goes the following Monday.

She arrives around ten-twenty in the morning, places two white roses, crossed, on the grave of James Frederick, then goes to Christine's grave, where she places a bouquet of red carnations in the vase on the headstone. Claire bows her head and mouths a silent prayer. Finished, she crouches down and runs her finger over the letters of Christine's name.

"It's just you and me, Christine, as always."

She hears a car pull in and rises, then looks to see a familiar black Chrysler LeBaron parking.

She shakes her head. "You have got to be kidding me."

Zachariah Messner exits the car and approaches Claire. He is much thinner than the last time she saw him and leaning heavily on a cane. He doesn't look to be in good health.

"Well now, look who we have here. It's been a while, Miss Belmonte."

"What are you doing here?" Claire says. "Can't imagine it's to tend the grave."

"It has been noted that around this time each May, someone places flowers here," he says.

"Noted, yeah," Claire says. "How is Selma these days, by the way?"

"She is as she always has been," Zachariah says. "More or less."

"I knew she was lying about what you'd do to her," Claire says. "You've always been more smoke than fire. She carried out all your violence."

"Selma can be a troublesome individual. But she's there."

"Since I'm certain you didn't make this once in a lifetime return visit to the grave just to chat, I have to assume something's on your mind. Perhaps we should just skip to that, or should I be on my way?"

"We are only allotted so much time on this Earth," he says. "Sometimes a man takes stock of the time he has, and wonders if, perhaps, his efforts could have been better utilized."

"Oh, give me a break," she says. "Soul searching doesn't suit you."

"There comes a time when that's all one has left. Since turning my business over to an associate, I've had much opportunity for reflection. In my line of work, it's best to not leave debts unpaid."

"Don't come out here pretending you've ever cared for anyone other than yourself," she says. "Least of all me. If you're trying to apologize, save it. It's meaningless."

"I have no feelings for you one way or another, Miss Belmonte. You served your purpose."

"My purpose was not to help facilitate your leading Deacon Frederick astray."

"As if one such as him could be led astray."

"I will never forgive or forget what he did, but when I was a child, he was always good to me. You took that from me as well."

Messner chuckles. "There are some former members of the congregation who might disagree with your earliest memories of the not-so-good deacon."

"What's that supposed to mean?"

Messner looks toward the sky, contemplating something. At

last, he says, "I believe you were in school with Davis Robinson's boy, Ernest, were you not?"

"He was a year or two ahead of me, but I remember him."

"He's a rather tall young man. Doesn't look much like either of his folks."

Claire considers this. "Are you saying what I think you're saying?"

"One hears rumors. There were always whispers about those who had received the Deacon's private counseling."

"How many were there?" Claire says.

"Hard to say," Messner says. "More than a few, if memory serves."

Claire shakes her head. "James Frederick should have been held accountable under the law for what he did. His victims had the right to confront him. You took that away from us — away from me."

"It was not my will that was served."

"You don't really believe that, and you know it," Claire says. "It was a vendetta, plain and simple."

"Water under the bridge."

"You still haven't answered my question. Why are you here?"

"There is no answer. I'm here because I chose to be here. That's all." He puts his weight onto the cane and begins to slowly move toward his car. "You take care of yourself, Miss Belmonte."

She turns and watches him walk away, sensing that it will be the last time she'll ever see him. This thought neither fills her with relief nor regret. In fact, she finds that she feels nothing at all for him. Claire watches as he shambles back to his car, gets in, and drives away, then she resumes erasing all trace of him from her memory.

Following her encounter with Messner, Claire decides she needs to see a friendly face, so she drives to the junior high school where Jodie Newcombe, under her full, married name, Josephine Carter, works as a counselor. Claire checks in at the front desk, and a few moments later, Jodie appears. Seeing Claire, Jodie hurries to her and gives her friend a warm hug.

"Christine!" She pulls away, looks Claire over, and corrects herself. "Sorry. I mean, Claire."

"Call me whatever you want, Jodie," Claire says. "You earned that a thousand times over."

Jodie leads Claire back to her office. "Good timing. Lunch is in ten minutes."

"How're Giles and the kids?" Claire asks as they enter Jodie's office.

"They're all doing well," Jodie says. She leans toward Claire. "Just found out, there's another one on the way."

"Congratulations!" Claire hugs her. "That'll be four, right?"

Jodie lowers her head. "Five with Patrick."

"I'm sorry, Jodie. I didn't mean to leave him out."

Jodie takes Claire's hand. "He was our first. It was a long time ago."

"I could do a better job of staying in touch," Claire says. "I get down here once a year. I should stop by more when I'm in town."

"You're here now. Let's catch up over lunch."

They head down to the cafeteria and sit in the faculty area. Claire fills Jodie in on what's been happening in Atlanta, while Jodie brags about her kids. Something Messner said comes back to Claire.

"You wouldn't happen to know what Ernie Robinson's doing now, would you?" Claire asks. "Is he even around?"

"Married, couple of kids. I believe he's the produce manager at Walker Groceries. At least he was last time I was in there," Jodie says. "Why do you ask?"

"I ran into Messner at the church," Claire says. "He was filled with his usual innuendo and double talk. Ernie's name came up in a discussion of Frederick."

"Frederick's still a tender subject down this way," Jodie says. "Not many folks who knew him talk openly about him."

"With good reason," Claire says. "You may recall, though, that in school Ernie and I were often mistaken for kin."

"Think there's a connection?" Jodie says.

"That's what Messner was implying," Claire replies.

After lunch, Claire walks Jodie back to her office.

"We're heading up to Gatlinburg next month," Jodie says. "I'll see if we can stop in on our way through Atlanta."

"Great," Claire says. "I can give you and the kids a tour of a sound studio."

Walker Groceries manages a chain of stores throughout Georgia and the Carolinas and competes with Piggly Wiggly in most markets in Georgia, except Atlanta. Claire heads to the produce section, but stops when she sees a tall, dark-haired man stocking a display shelf.

When they were in elementary school, Ernie's family attended Claire's church, but switched to a Baptist denomination when Claire was in second grade. Now, looking at him, she finds it hard to deny there's a connection between them. He glances at her, and a look of recognition crosses his face.

"Can I help you, ma'am?" he says, stopping his work.

"Ernie, right?" Claire says.

"Yes ma'am," he says. "Do I know you?"

"My name's Claire Belmonte," she says. "We went to school together as kids." He shakes his head and starts to respond, but Claire stops him and finishes, "You'd know me as Christine Messner."

The right side of his mouth curls into a smile. "Christine." Ernie looks to his left and calls to a stock clerk. "Hey Frank, I need to take a break. Could you finish up this display?"

"Sure thing," the clerk says.

Ernie removes the apron he's wearing and says, "Let me buy you a cup of coffee."

At a nearby diner, Claire fills Ernie in on how she came to be known as Claire Belmonte. Ernie hands Claire a photo of him with his wife and kids. He points to the smallest girl. "That's our youngest — Clara, actually, but we call her Clare."

"Really?" Claire says. "You have a beautiful family."

She hands him the photo, but he waves it off.

"You hang onto it," he says. "I've always wondered if I'd ever see you again. After all that went on with James Frederick, I figured you were long gone."

"I've been back from time to time. Usually for short stays."

"Guess I don't have to tell you, there are still a lot of folks from that church who like to believe Christine Messner is really buried in that grave."

"Oh, you know about that." She lowers her head. "Jodie Newcombe — well, Carter, now — told me about all the backlash from what happened with me and Frederick."

"Prominent citizen like the Deacon hangs himself, that sets a lot of tongues to wagging," he says. "Whole lot of truth came out after that."

"When did you find out?" Claire asks.

"I didn't get the full story until about a year afterward." He sips his coffee. "Though I kind of suspected beforehand. I got to hand it to my Dad: he found out when I was still just a kid, but he's never treated me any worse because of it."

"Is that when you left the church?" Claire asks.

He nods. "That's my understanding. Course, they never explained any of that to me at the time. Just said they preferred the preaching in the Baptist Church."

"I remember in school, everybody always saying we looked like we could be related."

"I guess they were right," he says.

They reminisce for nearly half an hour, before Ernie says he needs to get back to the store.

"I suppose you'll be heading back to Atlanta soon," he says.

"I just came down for the day," she says. Noting the look this elicits, she finishes, "But, I don't really have anything going on up there that can't wait a day. I could stay a little longer."

He brightens up. "Would you like to have dinner with my family? I'll need to clear it with my wife, of course, but she usually likes meeting people. If it gets too late, we can probably find a bed for you."

She nods. "I'd like that."

That evening, Claire heads back to Atlanta with a slightly more extended family, and the promise to stay in touch.

Selma Messner enters the upstairs performance area at Smith's Olde Bar in Atlanta and walks to the bar. She's wearing a polka-dotted dress with work boots and white socks, with a faded denim jacket over her dress, and a railroad cap. Her hair is gray, and her face is wrinkled. She asks for Claire and the bartender points to the sound board in the back.

Claire sees her, comes down from the booth, and approaches Selma.

"He's dead, isn't he?"

"I put him in the ground," Selma says. "It wouldn't really bother me much if he's not, truth be told."

"Whatever you're doing here, I'm not putting up with anymore of your crap."

"Yeah. I think you made that real clear when I was up here before."

"You could have just called."

"I ain't got your number. Besides, been a while since I could go anywhere north of Macon, so I figured I'd tell you in person."

Claire leans in and says in a lowered voice, "Last time I was down there, Messner told me about Ernie Robinson."

Selma laughs. "He's just the tip of the iceberg."

"How many do you know about?" Claire says.

"Most of 'em," Selma says. "A whole lot of people knew what was going on and just looked the other way."

Claire points away from Selma. "Find a seat over there. We're going to talk when I have some time."

As Selma takes a seat, Claire goes to the man at the door. "Hey, Tom, see that woman over there? Selma Messner. She's my comp."

He makes a note on his sheet and gives Claire thumbs up.

When the show gets under way, Claire's too busy working the boards and monitoring the situation on stage to worry about Selma, though a few times she glances over to be sure she's still in her seat. When the band takes its break, Claire leaves the booth, wanting to talk to Selma, but instead, she's approached by a short, dark-haired woman who seems vaguely familiar to her.

"You remind me of someone I used to know," the woman says.

"Yeah, I get that a lot," Claire says, anxious to be rid of this person who most likely wants to hit on her.

"No, seriously, her name is Christine Messner," the woman says.

At the mention of her former name, a jolt runs through Claire, but she tries to control her reaction. She shoots a glance in Selma's direction, then says, "You've mistaken me for someone else."

She heads toward the stage but watches out of the corner of her eye as the woman leaves the music room, then circles around and heads straight for Selma.

"What the hell are you up to?" Claire says to her. "Who's that woman?"

"What woman?" Selma says.

"Short, dark curly hair," Claire says. "She called me Christine Messner."

"She didn't get it from me," Selma says. "I drove straight here from Perry and only talked to a couple of bartenders after I got here."

"You had better not be pulling anything," Claire says. She heads toward the backstage area and looks out into the back hall where the restrooms are, catching sight of the dark-haired woman in line for the ladies' room.

She waits until the woman exits, then steps out and confronts her. "Where did you get that name?"

The woman is startled by Claire's sudden appearance but recovers and chuckles. "Name changes are public information."

She introduces herself as Rebecca, "Becky, if you prefer," and offers to buy Claire a drink, which she refuses.

Claire confronts Rebecca about stalking her, but just then, Charlotte calls to Claire from backstage and she excuses herself. She hooks up a pedal Charlotte requests for her guitar and heads back to the booth to check the sound on it, stopping briefly to greet the Savages. On her way, she notices Rebecca talking to Selma and shakes her head. "I knew it."

The second set goes well, and Claire notes halfway through that Rebecca has retreated to the bar, leaving Selma alone. Claire rehearses in her head how she plans to confront Selma to learn what she's trying to accomplish sending someone to antagonize her. As soon as the final encore is finished, she immediately goes and sits with Selma, interrogating her about Rebecca, but Selma continues to deny any knowledge of who she is or how she knows about Claire's name change beyond what Rebecca said while they were talking.

The music room is slowly emptying of everyone not interacting with Brian or Charlotte, so Claire instructs Selma to wait downstairs for her and heads to the stage to begin load out. Onstage, while unplugging the instruments and rolling up the cords, she notices Rebecca talking to Charlotte.

"Do you know that lady Charlotte's talking to?"

Brian takes a look. "Never seen her in my life. Wait." He considers this. "Okay, I think she was in the audience at Blind Willie's, but I didn't speak to her before or after the show. Who is she?"

"I'm not sure," Claire says. "She was hanging out with Selma."

"Doesn't look like her type."

Once the van is loaded, Claire confirms with Charlotte and Brian that they're going to their usual post-show haunt The Majestic, then heads downstairs to find Selma seated in a booth.

"We need to talk about Frederick," Claire tells her.

"I don't want to get into this now," Selma says. "Why don't we talk tomorrow?"

"Will you be here? I find that a little hard to believe."

"I'm staying outside town. Over near the airport."

"Okay. What hotel?"

"It ain't a hotel; it's a motel. Economy Lodge or something

like that."

"They just let you stay there without a credit card?" Claire says.

"I guess they did. I gave them some money."

Claire takes out a pen and writes her number on a napkin. "Okay. Here's my cell number. Call me when you get in and leave me a message on how to find you. We can meet for breakfast."

Once she's finished with Selma, Claire heads over to The Majestic and is annoyed to find Rebecca sitting with Brian and Charlotte. After serious vetting, Claire decides Rebecca is really a fan and may be there for other reasons than to simply rattle her, so she relaxes and gets to know her a bit better. Rebecca's decidedly skewed view of life, and her almost encyclopedic knowledge of movies and music, impresses and amuses Claire, and the two hit it off.

The following morning, after receiving no call, Claire realizes Selma lied about staying in town and once again vows to have no further contact with her.

A few months after meeting Rebecca, Claire realizes that she is familiar with Rebecca's aunt, Rachel, who's active in the Unitarian Universalist church Claire attends, and who Rebecca constantly complains about. She didn't make the connection right away, because Rebecca's description of her aunt is so negative, Claire initially imagined a much older and less attractive person than the vibrant and energetic woman Rachel turns out to be.

Claire does not know her well, but they do have mutual acquaintances, who always speak well of Rachel. She's not in church every week, owing to her work as a nurse and counselor, and her many outside activities, but when she's there, she's always engaged with individuals and small groups. The few times they have interacted, usually when Claire has found herself in close proximity to Rachel, she's gracious, greeting Claire with a warm smile, sometimes a pat on the shoulder. Rachel looks everyone square in the eyes, giving the feeling she's there solely for the benefit of that single person. Their encounters are rarely more than a few seconds, though, and Claire is certain they mean more to her than to Rachel.

In addition to having a tough time reconciling the woman Rebecca describes with the actual person, Claire can't understand why Rebecca has such a problem with her aunt in the first place.

Claire isn't certain of Rachel's sexuality, but does know that she, like Claire, practices celibacy. Other aspects of Rachel's life, however, sound like they'd inspire admiration in her niece, rather than the raw animosity Rebecca displays. Claire has noted, on rare occasions, that Rachel shows up at church with bruises, and once, a couple of sore ribs and a noticeable limp. Claire learns these are from her activities with an organization called Journey from Night, which helps young women and girls escape sex trafficking, and sometimes this involves Rachel openly confronting pimps and johns on the street, who don't appreciate the exposure and react violently to get away from her.

From what Rebecca has told Claire, the tension stems from the time Rebecca's mother died, and Rachel took responsibility for Rebecca and her brother, Steven. Why that rankled Rebecca has never been clarified. Claire notes that most of Rebecca's anger is confined to the time she returned from college, particularly after Rachel locked Rebecca out of the house, fueling her desire to replace her aunt as her brother Steven's guardian. Rebecca won't reveal to Claire why she left New York without finishing school, telling Claire she needs to get to know her better first.

As much as she finds Rebecca's constant flirtations and innuendos tiresome, Claire worries about Rebecca, who seems very much out of control, and headed for a collapse — drinking heavily, smoking lots of dope, often passing out at the home of whichever of her friends she happens to be visiting. On several occasions, when they've been out, Claire has let Rebecca sleep in her guest room, rather than allowing her to drive. In addition, Rebecca has chosen to surround herself with a cadre of "friends" who she mainly knew in high school, who do little more than encourage her bad behavior and with whom Claire has a very hostile relationship.

Early in their acquaintance, Claire sat Rebecca down and let her know in very clear terms she had no interest in a physical relationship. She's never been fully convinced Rebecca accepted this, however. Claire has dealt with such overtures from both sexes the entire time she's been in Atlanta. As a young teen, before her parents pulled her out of school, Claire had, what she assumed, was a regular interest in boys, and often wonders, had her life taken a different course, if she'd have ended up married with a family. This was, in fact, the course she expected to take, before her parents interfered. The situation with James Frederick left her wary and cautious in interactions with men, and working as a waitress after coming to Atlanta, the constant stream of innuendos and solicitations she received from guys, led her to adopt an icy aloofness when dealing with them.

She was surprised, however, to find women hitting on her almost as aggressively as men did. Some misread her restraint toward guys as a declaration of her sexuality, just as Rebecca appears to have done. While adopting her tough CC Belmonte persona intimidated a lot of the men into leaving her alone, it only encouraged the women, who put their own spin on Claire's intentions in presenting the front. While she certainly never means to come across as sexless, she views her deejay persona as more of a statement of her independence and self-expression, not as an advertisement for a date.

Other than her closest friends, the only people to fully embrace her identity as The Phoenix and see it for the humorous façade it's intended to be, are gay men, who've always been at the core of Claire's support system. This dates back to when Lawrence Standridge and his partner Eli Parker helped her overcome the legal problems left behind in Houston County when she came to Atlanta. Her refusal to engage either sex is met with a similar level of distain from both. The two most prevalent rumors Claire hears about herself in the clubs are that CC Belmonte is a lesbian, often initiated by hetero men, or that she's a drag queen, which she suspects may have originated with some of Rebecca's friends.

Once Rebecca sets out to become her brother's guardian, the intense focus she gives to the endeavor causes her to curb some of her bad habits. While she doesn't stop drinking, she does curtail it considerably, and she stops spending so much time with her friends, which only increases their rancor toward Claire. Rebecca claims to have some sort of dirt on Rachel, which, she says will turn the tide in her case, but then, the whole thing fizzles out when Rachel steps aside and lets Rebecca be Steven's guardian without contesting it. She leaves the family's home, which allows Rebecca to move back in, and, consequently, Claire notes the level of vitriol Rebecca spews against Rachel subsides.

Perhaps the only thing that truly keeps Claire close to Rebecca is Rebecca's writing. Always an avid reader, Claire finds Rebecca's work for Creative Loafing and especially her blog The Frantic Feminist, fresh and compelling, with a take-no-prisoners style that's open and brutally honest. Rebecca has stated she found her voice in New York, while working with a women's group, and has since honed her craft. While her personal life slid into disarray, her writing became fiery and expressive. Claire often finds herself hanging on every word, and frequently encourages Rebecca to compile and publish her blog and other work.

Two incidents occur that end Claire's relationship with Rebecca, both occurring in November 2005. The first is initiated by Rebecca, who invites Claire to her house under the pretense of "hanging out" when, in actuality, Rebecca has ulterior motives. At the house, she plies Claire with wine, then makes an aggressive pass at her which Claire rebuffs. Claire's annoyance at the attempt turns to anger when she learns that Rebecca has made a recording of the encounter on her computer and is slow to erase it when Claire insists. This prompts Claire to distance herself from Rebecca.

Late one morning early in December 2005, Claire answers a knock at her door to be greeted by someone she never expected to see at her home, Rachel Lawson, who seems just as surprised to find that the friend her nephew sent her to meet is a familiar face from her church. Claire invites her in and once they're seated on the couch, Rachel tells her, "Steven asked me to speak to you."

"Steven?" Claire says. "Has something happened to Becky?"

"I'm afraid so," Rachel says. "Rebecca was killed in a car accident on her way back from a film festival in South Carolina."

Despite their problems, Claire is still upset by the loss. Rachel consoles her and spends several hours with Claire, listening to her stories about Rebecca and comforting Claire. She offers to meet with Claire to help her work through her grief, and Claire readily agrees, visiting Rachel at her home, and talking to her more often at church. Over time, they become close friends.

As they get to know one another, Rachel notes that Claire is full of stories about her friendships, previous jobs, and activities she enjoys in and around Atlanta; but that her history always starts with her stay at the home of Jack and Nancy Standridge when she was a teen. When Rachel initially enquires about her life before the early 90s, Claire speaks of an individual she calls "Christine" — which Rachel knows is Claire's middle name — but doesn't elaborate on who this person is or was to her. On occasions, though, when speaking to Rachel, Claire's accent will slip from the general, almost newscaster sounding accent she normally uses, to a less polished cadence reminiscent of South

Georgia.

"My way of talking was much rougher when I moved in with the Standridges," Claire tells her one evening.

"You definitely sound like you're from Atlanta now. At least in my limited experience with how people here talk."

"I had to modify the way I pronounced words. That took more than a year to become a habit. After that, I just started sounding like I'm being sarcastic all the time. People assume I'm a native."

Over time, Rachel persuades Claire to reveal more about her past: her life with the Messners; her relationship to James Frederick; how he betrayed her; how she escaped and came to Atlanta. Claire shows Rachel a flyer containing the school photo of a young teen girl with short, dark hair, and full, rosy cheeks, wearing a smile that seems somewhat forced. The flyer has the header "Missing" and describes Christine Messner, said to have run away from home at age sixteen. Claire tells Rachel about Christine's grave and her visits to it every year. Through it all, Claire continues to refer to the individual as "Christine" as though describing someone other than herself. This concerns Rachel.

"In my experience, it's not healthy to disassociate yourself from your past like that," she tells Claire.

"Is that what I'm doing?" Claire says. "I acknowledge it all. I'm not denying what happened or to whom. I was there, remember?"

"I'm just concerned that you've closed off an important part of your life. In whatever way you regard Christine, she's still who you see when you look in the mirror."

Claire shakes her head. "No." She waves her hand around her face. "This is who I see in the mirror. Claire Christine Belmonte. I chose her, created her. I became her." She holds up the flyer. "When I remember Christine, I see the pudgy, 13-year-old, with big feet, and hand-me-down clothes, who was hated by the man she thought was her father; who was beaten by her mother; who was constantly shamed by the other kids in her school because of how she dressed; who tried to love her parents, even though she feared them; who felt special when James Frederick gave her candy and how she wished he could be her father and how she came to regret ever wishing for that. I see the sad little girl who'd been a victim all her life."

Claire breaks off and stares at the floor. "Maybe you're right. Maybe I am disassociating. Whenever I go to visit Christine's grave, I sincerely apologize to her that I had to leave her behind when I came here." She looks up and meets Rachel's eyes. "That's why I go back — why I'll always go to see her. Just to let her know I haven't forgotten her."

"She's you, Claire," Rachel says. "All your strength, your persistence — the amazing woman you are grew from that little girl."

"She perished in flames," Claire says, her Atlanta accent slipping away. "She died in the spare bedroom of James Frederick's house. But I arose from her ashes, and finally understood the lesson Zachariah Messner had been teaching Christine all her life. I learned to hate. I stopped hoping; stopped praying; stopped blaming myself. I started thinking, what do I need to say; what do I need to do to make Frederick drop his guard? The frying pan was my second choice. There was a butcher knife in one of the drawers, and I knew exactly where it was — and I'd have used it, too, but I figured I'd do less damage hitting him. I didn't care. I was leaving, and he wasn't going to stop me again."

She leans forward and rests her elbows on her knees. "Ever since then, there's only been one question I keep asking myself. How could I have been so wrong about someone? Growing up, I thought James Frederick was the most wonderful person in my life. He always took the time to talk to me; always asked how I was. He seemed like he really cared. Was I that naïve?"

"There's nothing naïve about caring for someone," Rachel says. "Even those who don't deserve it. Right now, there's only one person left who may be able to give you any answers."

"Selma." Claire leans back and looks away from Rachel. "The person who devoted her life to punishing Christine. I'm not asking her for anything ever again."

"It's a natural reaction to assign the most blame to the person who abused you," Rachel says. "But many abusers learned it first hand, not from a spouse but from a parent."

"I couldn't tell you anything about her parents. The only time I heard them mentioned was at my uncle's house and he mostly talked about how sweet his mother had been. He never spoke well of his father."

"That's a red flag, then," Rachel says. "Selma's the only person who could clear all this up for you, Claire."

"Then I suppose it's just my cross to bear."

"But you don't have to. Let me help."

"You can't fix this, Rachel," Claire says, meeting Rachel's eyes. "Some things just can't be fixed."

Rachel takes Clare's hand. "I'd like to try. If you'll let me."

After much more coaxing, Claire reluctantly agrees to let Rachel mediate between her and Selma.

Mylene Messner stood on the porch of the home she shared with her husband, Zachariah, watching as he drove away in his light blue Chevy Rambler. They'd said their goodbyes inside at the kitchen table once they'd finished breakfast, but she suddenly had to see him again and rushed to the porch where she threw her arms around his neck and pressed her face to his cheek, taking in the scent of his aftershave, holding him tightly.

"What's this for?" he said with a chuckle.

"Just thought I'd give you a little extra send-off."

"No complaints from me," he said then kissed her on the cheek. "I could ask Mr. Carter to let me go early if you'd like."

She shook her head. "I might not be here. I have some errands this afternoon."

"See you the usual time then," he said.

She lingered a long while, watching until he was out of sight, knowing it was the last time she'd ever see him.

Mylene went inside and began clearing away the breakfast dishes and washing them. She busied herself straightening up the house and returning a small stack of written correspondence. She kept her responses cheery and brief, trying not to think about what she had in mind for that day. After putting the letters into the mailbox, she phoned the Porter's house to see if Selma was there, but no one answered, which wasn't out of the ordinary.

Mylene worried about Selma, because of the situation in the family's home. As a teen, Mylene had known enough about Alec Porter, Selma's father, to avoid being at his house for very long if he'd been drinking — which was most of the time when he wasn't at work on their small farm or doing odd jobs around town.

Selma was often more relaxed and talkative when she spent the night with Mylene when they were younger than when she was at home. She was especially tense when her father was "out of control" as she described it without much elaboration. It was Alec most people blamed for his wife's death — he had, after all, drunkenly caused the car wreck that killed her. A friendly judge kept him out of jail, but his wife's family held him accountable and cut off all ties with him.

Since Selma's mother died no one was ever home during the day. Selma sometimes volunteered at their church when she wasn't working but Mylene did not call there. Hearing Selma's voice might prompt Mylene to reveal what she was planning, and she didn't want to burden Selma with that knowledge. She thought about writing a note but decided against it. She couldn't explain it well enough to herself to be able to articulate it for someone else.

It had been just over nine years since Mylene married Zachariah, leaving her family wondering what she had seen in a man so much older than she was. Zachariah started attending her family's church when Mylene was in high school. While still a girl, she found him to be a curiosity; and she, with Selma, would sometimes snicker at this odd man who, to their eyes, always appeared wearing the same dark suit; always clean-shaven; who'd sit in the same pew in the same place each Sunday, seemingly fully devoted to his faith. His was among the loudest voices when hymns were sung, and he frequently answered the altar call when the pastor invited everyone who felt in need of prayer or forgiveness to come forward.

Her family always believed she'd marry Jimmy Frederick, who graduated a few years before Mylene, but who'd shown an interest in her throughout the brief time their paths crossed at school. After she graduated, they dated a while, but she could never garner much interest for the popular Frederick, who, for his part, had his pick of eligible women. His entourage of admirers prompted Mylene's family to encourage her to make up her mind before it was made up for her. She had to admit, he seemed to be a very good prospect: the top salesman at the largest furniture outlet in Perry, with a nice home on the outskirts of town and a new car every two to four years.

Mylene had been a bright and cheerful young woman in school, who worked on the yearbook staff her senior year and wrote poems and stories for her high school newspaper. She imagined all sorts of wonderful adventures she'd like to pursue, maybe one day moving to Macon, Atlanta, or even New York to pursue a writing career. After school, she contributed poems and short, inspirational paragraphs to the newsletter her church sent out, eventually earning herself the title of editor. She went to work as a cashier at Walker Groceries and it was here where she'd often see Messner, stocking up on food or other necessities.

"Afternoon, Mr. Messner," she'd always say when she saw

him. She noted that when she was on duty, he'd often choose her lane, even if there were other lines open or people ahead of him at hers.

"Miss Tucker," he'd reply, usually with a smile and a nod.

There was always an awkwardness in how he behaved in her presence, unlike the rigid assurance with which he conducted his actions in their church. He knew the Scriptures like no one else Mylene had ever met — including Frederick, who always put an interpretive spin on the verses — and he was quick to volunteer his time for church sponsored projects. His devotion both frightened and fascinated Mylene, especially since it was all he presented to the world. She had never heard him speak of family and, while he had gained the respect of others within the church, he had no apparent friends and did not socialize after services like many other members of the congregation.

Despite their difference in age, Mylene found herself drawn to this quiet and faithful man. She began making every effort to speak to him after services or lengthen the conversation when she'd see him at the store. She found him receptive and before long, rumors were circulating about how this odd duck had somehow captured the heart of the beautiful Mylene Tucker.

They were married in a small ceremony attended mostly by her family and other congregants. No one claimed to be there on the groom's behalf. Frederick had been notable by his absence, having expressed his belief to Mylene that she was only spending time with Messner to make him jealous. In fact, Mylene had come to love Zachariah, his every quirk a hidden joy for her. She looked forward to raising a family with him. It took more than a year before she became pregnant, however, and the joy she felt was undone by her sorrow when she miscarried several weeks later. After that, she waited patiently for the doctor to tell her she was expecting another child, but time passed without the news.

Zachariah, who never dwelt on the situation, was always a source of comfort for Mylene. "It's the Lord's will," he'd say. "He'll reward us when the time is right."

The timing was never right and to make matters worse, always lurking just outside their marriage was Frederick, who had never given up his hope that Mylene would "come to her senses" and see him for the suitable mate she deserved.

Around eleven, she had a call from her oldest sister, Patsy Jean, inviting her to come to Cordele for a visit. Mylene agreed, knowing it would never happen. Patsy Jean married and moved to Cordele just before the start of the Second World War, when Mylene was still just a toddler, so she didn't get to know her big sister until she was nearly in high school and she still didn't know her well. Between Patsy Jean's birth and hers had come five sisters and two brothers, all of whom Mylene had at least a little more chance to know. Still, Mylene enjoyed her visits there, as her brother-in-law, Dud, or her niece Clydie would take her flying in one of their planes which they used for the family business of crop dusting. Of all her siblings, Patsy Jean was the one Mylene regretted leaving the most.

Just after noon, Mylene had a light lunch and took stock of all she had accomplished that morning. The house was cleaner than she'd ever gotten it, the dishes were all washed and put away, and all her correspondence was handled. She felt there wasn't much left she needed to do. She phoned Janice Wolfe, who was taking over the duties of editor of the church newsletter from her. Mylene had gone to see the pastor and asked to be relieved of the job so she could focus more on "family concerns" and the pastor had nodded with a knowing expression.

Mylene had already shown Janice the ins and outs of producing the newsletter, as well as how to work the mimeograph machine, and the schedule of deadlines for placing items in each edition. She'd even gone so far as to give Janice her cherished red fountain pen for editing. She really had nothing new to share with her but felt the need to hear another person's voice one last time, so she called and repeated some instructions she'd already given at least once before, just for the sake of hearing Janice acknowledge them.

"Okay, mother hen," Janice said. "I got it all down. You just wait 'til you see my first issue. I'll make you proud."

"I'm sure you will," Mylene said and concluded the call.

Zachariah, for his part, knew how much Mylene wanted a child, and never gave up praying and hoping the Lord would bless them. His thoughts had turned toward another alternative which he never came out and said, but which Mylene understood very well.

"I love you, Zachariah," she said when the idea was first intimated. "I could never betray you like that."

"It would only be a betrayal if your heart was in it," he replied. "The Scriptures have shown us that God's will overrides that of man."

"The Commandments say otherwise."

"It is through faith and not deeds that we are redeemed. The Lord would forgive."

"I couldn't forgive myself," she replied. "If it's the Lord's will that I never be a mother, so be it."

Zachariah had dropped the argument, but Mylene could still tell that it occupied his thoughts. She had taken to avoiding Frederick in church, because even his words of comfort after her miscarriage had sounded self-serving and meant to steer her in his direction. He had always been very popular with the women as far back as high school, and now, as the manager of the furniture store, he dealt with many as clients — married and otherwise. Mylene had heard many rumors of women receiving "private sessions" from the Deacon.

Once Zachariah put the idea into her head, she wondered if she'd even be able to go through with such a thing. On the pretense of shopping for a new sofa, she stopped in at the store, and found Frederick talking to a young couple about a bedroom set.

"Of course, we have easy finance terms, with no money down," he was saying as Mylene caught his eye. "You two take a moment, maybe lie down to see how it feels, and I'll be right back with you."

Frederick walked over. "Afternoon Mrs. Messner."

"Mr. Frederick," Mylene said. "I'm here to take a look at your living room sets."

"Of course," he said. "You know where everything is. I'll get these two squared away and we'll see what suits your needs."

As she browsed the floor merchandise, she thought about how she'd approach the matter. When Frederick joined her, he showed her several models, all of which met with some objection on her part, too large, too firm, not the right color for their living room. He seemed to sense her mind wasn't on shopping.

"Is there something else you wanted to talk to me about, Mylene?"

"I've just been feeling a little down lately," she replied. "You know our situation. I don't like being in that empty house while Zachariah's at work."

"I understand," he said with a slight smirk. "Is there anything I can do to help lift your spirits?"

She looked around. "I wouldn't want to discuss it out in the open like this."

"My door is always open to you, Mylene. You know that."

"I do. Would you be available to talk tomorrow afternoon?"

"I certainly would," he said. "Come on by whenever you want."

"We'll see."

Mylene wrestled with the decision throughout dinner with Zachariah and had a fitful night of sleep. As the following day wore on, she became increasingly anxious. Just after noon, she drove to Walker Groceries and parked, then walked the two blocks to Frederick's house. She was careful to be sure none of the neighbors were out when she made her way to the door and knocked.

Frederick opened the door and smiled. "Why Mylene. Come on in."

Inside, she sat on the couch while he got them soft drinks. Being in the house had not allayed the nervousness she felt and when he returned and sat beside her, closer than she felt comfortable, her anxiety increased. She couldn't recall what they'd chatted about before an uncomfortable silence fell between them and, all at once, Frederick put his arm up on the back of the couch and leaned toward her, and that's when she knew. She slid backwards, then got to her feet.

"This was a mistake."

"Mylene, relax," he said. "It doesn't have to be unpleasant."

"I can't do this — do you hear me? I need to go."

"You came to me, Mylene."

He rose, took a step toward her and reached for her.

"Don't you touch me," Mylene said, backing away.

Frederick threw up his hands. "I'm not going to do anything you don't want me to, Mylene."

Without turning her back to him, she made it to the door and opened it. On the porch, she caught sight of Frederick's next-door neighbor, a parishioner at their church, getting into his vehicle, and pausing a moment to watch as she moved down the steps and away. Frederick came to the door and with a wave called out, "You stop back in anytime, Mylene" before greeting his neighbor.

All the way back to her car, and on the ride home, the encounter played over in her mind. She hadn't done anything, she knew that, but she also knew no one would believe that. There was nothing she could say, though, even if someone bothered to ask her about it — and nobody ever would. There were never any direct questions, just a lot of knowing looks and whispers behind someone's back.

As she and Zachariah had dinner that evening, all she could think was whether or not he had heard. Since he'd started his job collecting debts for Mr. Carter, he went everywhere and saw everyone. If he didn't already know, he would.

"I went to see Frederick," she told him.

"You did?"

"Nothing happened," she emphasized.

"All right," he said.

"No, I mean it. Nothing happened."

"It wouldn't matter to me if it did," he told her. "I know what's in your heart."

"You have to believe me, Zachariah," she said. "I told you I would never betray you like that."

"I believe you, Mylene. It's all right."

While she believed his words, she could not escape the guilt she still felt. Nothing happened this time, but would she be able to escape the temptation a second time, especially since everyone would now believe something had happened between her and Frederick?

At one-o-clock, Mylene walked through the house once more, making sure she had accomplished all her planned tasks. Satisfied she was leaving the place in good shape she went into the bedroom and undressed. She laid out her clothes neatly on the bed, and as she headed into the bathroom, she grabbed her lipstick. She filled the tub, holding her hand beneath the steaming water to be sure it wasn't too hot for her. Once it was full, she went to the mirror and stared into it, wondering what she should say, if anything, to somehow explain what she was about to do. Nothing she could think to write seemed appropriate, so she settled on words from the Scriptures and scrawled them onto the mirror using the lipstick. Finished, she set it aside and picked up Zachariah's straight razor.

She stepped into the tub and lowered herself into the water. Staring skyward, she repeated the words she had written, "Into thy hands I commend my spirit," then fell into total darkness. She remained in the dark for a very long time, until she lost all sense of herself.

When she again found her path to the light, she acquired a new name, Rebecca Jean.

Early one Saturday in May 2008, Rachel and Claire climb into her Jeep Cherokee and hit I-75 South. A little over two hours later, they pull up in front of a moderate-sized, cottage-style house, which was once painted an off-white color, but which now has a dingy brown tint to it, the paint chipping in some places, with vines climbing the walls. The yard is mostly dirt, with some gravel spread around, though in spots, dandelions dot the surface. Messner's black Chrysler LeBaron sits in the driveway and remnants of a white-painted fence still circle the yard, but the gate is missing, and many slats are broken or fallen over. Except for the car and the curtains in the windows, the house seems abandoned.

They exit the Jeep and for the first time since she was sixteen, Claire steps onto the walkway and faces the house where she spent her childhood and early teens.

Rachel stops beside her and runs her hand over Claire's back. "Are you ready?"

"No, but we're here now."

She leads Rachel to the door where they can hear the sounds of a television blaring from inside. Finding the screen locked, Claire pounds on it and a moment later, Selma peers out at them from behind a curtain.

Claire holds up her hands and shouts, "You knew we were coming."

Selma goes to the door, opens it enough to unlatch the screen then retreats into the house without appearing at the door or inviting them in. Claire sighs and holds the screen for Rachel and follows her in. At Selma's prompting, Claire latches the screen and closes and locks the door.

The interior is much the way she remembers it, though not as neatly kept up as Claire recalls. Stacks of newspapers line one wall, and the few lamps barely illuminate the interior. A thirteen-inch black and white television — a new addition — sits on a stand in the corner, facing toward the middle of the room, broadcasting, with the sound turned way up. A tray sits by the couch with empty plates and glasses stacked on it. Though she knows he's been dead for more than five years, Claire can still sense the presence of Zachariah in the house.

Selma, frailer and more wrinkled than Claire remembers her, is seated in the center of the couch, watching as the pair advances into the room. They stop, and Rachel clasps her hands in front of her.

"Mrs. Messner — Selma — I want to thank you again for agreeing to meet with us."

"Don't see what it's going to accomplish, but what else do I have to do with my time?"

"Clare has some questions that hopefully you can answer for her," Rachel says. "Perhaps you have some things you want to say to her as well."

"Claire," Selma says in a harsh tone. "I'm not sure I even know who that is."

Claire starts to say something, but Rachel puts up a hand to stop her and says, "Do you have any questions for me, Selma?"

"Yeah. I do. Why are you here?" Selma says.

"I'm here to make sure you two don't kill each other in the process." Rachel looks around at the house and says, "This is a nice place you've got here."

"Nice place?" Selma says. "Look out my front door. See that big ol' development over there? It missed my property line by fifty-two feet. Fifty-two feet and I'd be down in Florida, rolling in cash right now.

"Still, it's yours," Rachel says.

"Mine. Yeah." Selma says. "This property might get me forty, fifty thousand on the market. I got Zachariah's pension from Bickering; that ain't much. I got what little insurance money there was, along with Social Security. So, what exactly do I have left?"

"You have a remarkable daughter," Rachel says, indicating Claire. "Doesn't she count?"

Selma shakes her head. "Not in my estimation."

Claire smiles and nods, then pats Rachel on the shoulder. "Looks like you've got your work cut out for you, Rachel." She steps away and indicates the interior. "Let me give you a tour. We can start with the storage closet in the back where they locked me up and she beat me with coat hangers."

"There we go," Selma says. "Figured it'd be like this."

Rachel touches Claire's arm. "Claire, I know this place brings back lots of bad memories for you, and we can talk about them, but maybe we want to start out a little slower."

"Whatever," Claire says. She retrieves two chairs from the dining room and places them near the couch and sits in one.

Rachel points to the television. "Okay if I turn this off? It would make it easier to talk."

"Fine by me," Selma says. "I just keep it on for background noise."

Rachel turns off the television and sits. "I want to lay out some ground rules. We're not here to judge, or to blame."

"We've come to the wrong house," Claire says.

Selma snickers.

"Excuse me," Rachel says, looking at Claire. "I repeat, we're not here to judge or lay blame. It's okay to call BS, though, if you don't find a response sincere. If a subject is too uncomfortable, we can move on."

"Yeah, yeah," Selma says, waving her hand. "There's nothing I can't talk about. What do you need to know?"

"Why don't we start by getting to know you, Selma? Anything you want to share with us about your history?"

Selma considers this. "Okay, I don't want to talk about me right now. Move on to something else."

"That's one," Claire says, to no one in particular.

Rachel looks at her then shifts so she's facing her. "Claire, is there anything you want to share with Selma?"

"Like what?" Claire says.

"Maybe how you feel about being here or what you hope will be accomplished," Rachel says.

"Oh, share my feelings," Claire says. "That's a great idea."

"That's kind of why we're here," Rachel says.

"I'm sorry, Rachel, I know you want to help, but I am not going to sit here and discuss my feelings with her. If she doesn't understand how her actions affected me, nothing I can say will help."

"I don't want to talk about that with her either," Selma says.

"We're not going to get very far if the two of you don't want to talk about anything," Rachel says.

"Ask her about Frederick," Claire says. "That's why we're here. I'm still waiting for her to give me the information she promised me years ago."

Rachel turns to Selma. "What do you say, Selma? Acceptable topic?"

"Frederick I'll talk about," Selma says. "You want to know about him, then you'll need to know about Mylene."

"Mylene?" Rachel says, glancing at Claire.

"Messner's first wife," Claire says. "I mentioned her to you but couldn't remember her name at the time."

"So, you knew her," Rachel says to Selma.

"Course I did," Selma says. "Mylene's mama was Bessie Porter, my aunt. We was first cousins."

Claire sits up. "Cousins? Why haven't I heard this before?"

"You don't know the Tuckers," Selma says. "Most of 'em lived in Hawkinsville when you was around. Couple of Mylene's sisters are in Tifton now from what I hear. Oldest has a family in Cordele. They all fly planes. Mylene was the youngest like me. We was raised together."

"None of this was ever mentioned in the house when I was a kid," Claire says to Rachel. "If I hadn't spent time with Alvin's family, I wouldn't have even known Mylene existed."

"That's just the way it was," Selma says. "Once she was gone, she was gone."

"What can you tell us about her?" Rachel asks.

"Anything you want to know," Selma says. "We was as close as two people could be. More like sisters. She didn't tell me she was going to kill herself, though."

"Did that surprise you?" Rachel says.

"Not really," Selma says. "She knew I'd have told someone if I'd known." She points to the mantle. "That's us up there. Only picture I got left of her."

Rachel rises and retrieves the photo. She looks at it, then takes it to Claire, who immediately sees the resemblance between the two teenaged women. Mylene is radiant and has a pleasant expression on her face, while Selma seems awkward and uncomfortable. Though their features are very similar, they just seem to work better on Mylene. Claire hands the picture back to Rachel, who replaces it.

"When we was in school, Alvin used to say I was the Mylene somebody put through a blender," Selma says.

"How did Messner end up with someone like that?" Claire says to no one in particular.

"At the time, I didn't understand why Mylene loved him," Selma says, "but it was because he showed her something that he never showed anybody else, his real self."

"If it was anything like what he showed me, she would have run screaming from him," Claire says to Rachel. "When I saw him as an adult, I realized he was just a small, old man and there was nothing to be afraid of."

"Right. You figured him out," Selma says. "He scared everybody and as long as they was afraid of him, he had power over them. But with Mylene, he wasn't afraid to let down his guard."

"What did you see in him?" Rachel asks Selma. "Did you love him?"

"Not really. Never did."

"Then why was she with him?" Claire says to Rachel.

"Why not?" Selma says. "I was never anything. Once Mylene was gone, nobody loved me or cared about me. But when I became Mrs. Zachariah Messner people took me seriously. Daddy, Alvin, everybody treated me different. I was just like Mylene."

"Was that important to you?" Rachel says.

"Got me out of Daddy's house," Selma says. "I knew the only reason I was with Zachariah was because I looked like Mylene. He never made a secret of that. Frederick was the same way, only he couldn't admit it. They was both the same kind of men, shallow, small-minded, but Zachariah never tried to pretend he wasn't. Frederick did."

"What did Mylene do?" Rachel says. "Did she work?"

"Not after she was married," Selma says. "Didn't need to. Zachariah made a good living."

"Yeah, he foreclosed on people's farms for Bickering Financial," Claire says. "That was another strike against me growing up. Having a parent everybody hated."

"They hated him because they didn't want to face up to their responsibilities," Selma says. "They took out those loans because they wanted to live on somebody else's dime and when things didn't work out and it came time to pay, they just expected somebody to forgive them like Mr. Carter always did. Well Zachariah didn't forgive. They all knew that and resented him for it."

"He and Frederick were always at odds," Claire says. "They hated each other."

"Frederick didn't like Zachariah but that didn't stop him from calling every time one of his customers couldn't handle the easy payment terms at that furniture store," Selma says. "He knew most of those people couldn't afford the debt, but he also knew he could lay it all on Zachariah when things went South, so he just doled out the cash like it grew on trees and everybody loved him for it."

"Ask her why Frederick never got married," Claire asks.

"You just did," Rachel says. "Selma?"

"Frederick didn't get married because Frederick didn't want to get married," Selma replies. "It's why Mylene didn't consider him. People were already whispering about him bedding everybody else's wives."

"Like you?" Claire says harshly.

"Claire!" Rachel says.

"I only did what was expected of me," Selma says to her.

Rachel puts up her hand to stop Claire from responding. "What do you mean expected of you? Did Messner tell you to go to Frederick?"

"What do you think?" Selma says. "I wasn't going to let the situation kill me like it did Mylene."

"What's she talking about?" Claire says.

"What situation do you mean?" Rachel asks.

"They was married nine years," Selma says. "She had one miscarriage and after that, she didn't get pregnant again. Mylene is the only one out of all her sisters who never carried a child to term. Put two and two together. You got one man can't get his wife pregnant. You got another man who's not above taking advantage of a married woman, who's still holding a torch for the man's wife."

Claire sits back in her seat. "He wanted her to have an affair with Frederick."

"I can't swear that he did," Selma says, "Mylene wouldn't talk about that with me. But when I didn't get pregnant after that first year, Zachariah just said, 'Go see Frederick.' He didn't have to say it twice."

Claire looks at Rachel. "So, the only reason I exist is for him to get revenge on Frederick. Is that what you're saying?"

"He didn't want you," Selma replies. "He wanted a boy, like that Robinson kid."

"You said there were others," Claire says. "Who were they?"

"There was lots of women, going back a long time, but you was the only two kids as far as I know," Selma says.

"So, you kind of lied about that, too, eh?" Claire says.

"That's judgmental," Rachel says.

"Tip of the iceberg. I believe those are the words she used," Claire says to Rachel. "I'm being accurate."

"It's still judgmental," Rachel says. "We're not here to judge."

"Then let me rephrase," Selma says. "You was the only two kids I knew about for sure. Robinsons weren't the only ones who left the church, though. I guess some who left may have just suspected. Back then, there wasn't any sort of test to take."

"Messner claimed there were more," Claire says. "At least he implied it."

"If he said it, it was probably true," Selma says. "He knew everybody's business. If he implied it, who knows? He manipulated people. Didn't talk about it with me one way or the other."

"So, just to clarify, Messner wanted you to have an affair with Frederick to produce a son, is that right?" Rachel says.

"Zachariah wanted a boy he could make into the perfect Christian warrior. That's all he ever talked about and prayed for. If you'd been a boy, I'd have had me a nice life. Instead I got you."

"And you punished me for it the whole time," Claire says.

"You say you were punished," Selma says. "You can probably count on one hand the times Zachariah did anything to you."

"He didn't need to, did he?" Claire says. "You were violent enough for the two of you."

"I think we need to dial this back a bit," Rachel says.

"Zachariah was strict, but he mainly left you alone," Selma says to Claire. "He never once went to your room at night, did he?"

"Small favors," Claire says.

"No. Hold on," Rachel says. "Did your father do that, Selma?"

Selma drops her eyes to the floor. "Alec Porter was a violent man and a mean drunk. Even Alvin acknowledged that. It's why Alvin went in the army right out of school."

"Then he abused you both," Rachel says.

"Beat us both," Selma says. "Visits were just me. The less use Daddy had for you the worse he was, and he never had any use for me, until—"

She stops and puts up her hands.

Rachel eyes her closely, then says, "Until?"

"What I'm saying is, I had the deck stacked against me from the start," Selma says. "Zachariah ended up being my only way out."

"You exchanged one hell for another," Claire says. "Sentenced me along with you."

"You was always reading them books, going to that girl's house," Selma says. "What'd I have? Just these four walls."

Rachel looks at Claire who's shaking her head. "Claire, consider your response."

Claire glances at Rachel then says, "You spent all day here by yourself. Any time, you could have walked out, and taken me with you."

"And go where?" Selma says. "You think Frederick would have been some kind of savior to you? That he would have helped either of us?"

"You didn't even try," Claire says.

"Let me tell you about how much James Frederick cared about

you," Selma says. "He never once asked me if you was his. Not once. Until you grew up that one summer, he hardly took notice of you at all unless you was bugging him about something."

Claire considers this, trying to recall specific times this might have been true. Selma continues.

"When the Robinsons left the church because of him, other people talked about it, but he acted like he didn't even know the Robinsons all that well. The man thought he was God's gift, like nothing could touch him. I'd go over there and when he was done with me, he'd just say, 'You can go on home now, Selma.' Every time."

"He made me feel like I mattered when I was a kid," Claire says. "Always told me he loved me. That's way more than you ever did."

"You think he loved you because he paid some attention to you once in a while, gave you candy? He gave all the kids candy. They called him the Candy Man."

Claire looks away. "We did, didn't we."

"After you was born, it took him nearly a year just to figure out your name was Christine and not Carolyn. You know why? Because he didn't care. Maybe he told people he cared about them, but he really didn't. He never did. He was just like that with Mylene, too."

"In what way?" Rachel says.

"Right after she lost that baby, he was right there, badgering her. Telling her 'hey, wouldn't happen if you was with me'. Tore Mylene apart. Then, for her husband to be in favor of her going to that man, who's done nothing but torture her for as long as she's been married? That's why she killed herself. That's why."

Rachel looks at Claire. "It definitely could have triggered it."

"You want to know why I didn't go to Frederick," Selma goes on, "tell him about you? Because he would have denied it. He never took responsibility for the trouble he caused people."

"I always believed he was basically a good man who was led astray," Claire says.

"You didn't lead Frederick astray. He was already like that," Selma says. "When he hung himself, Zachariah thought it was the Lord's judgment on him. An eye for an eye; a life for a life."

"Mylene," Rachel says to herself.

"Other people sure didn't think it was the Lord," Claire says. "Jodie told me what people were saying after I left."

"People blamed us because they couldn't accept that the good deacon James Frederick was a monster," Selma says. "He smiled at people; called folks by their first names; looked them right in the eye and shook their hands and then he took advantage of them. I doubt he killed himself because of what he did to you. He just couldn't face the consequences."

"You knew what he was like and you gave me to him," Claire says. "And when I tried to get away, you gave me back."

"What was I supposed to do?" Selma says. "At the time, I thought it was either you or me and it wasn't going to be me."

"I was sixteen years old," Claire says. "I didn't understand anything about how the world worked. I believed Frederick when he said I was there to cook and clean house. The whole time you knew who he was to me. Did you hate me that much?"

"You think I hate you? I don't hate you. I just never loved you."

Rachel touches Claire's shoulder. "You need a break?"

"It's nothing I haven't known for a long time," she says.

"Just so you know," Selma says. "I wasn't mad at you for calling Zachariah to come get me in Atlanta. I just didn't think you'd ever do it. The whole way home, I just sat, staring out the window with a big ol' smile on my face thinking, 'That's my girl!'"

"I am nothing like you," Claire says.

"You're tough like me. The difference is you fight. Only time I ever saw Zachariah laugh was when he heard you put Frederick in the hospital. He wanted a warrior and he got one."

"You went back to Messner," Claire says. "You stayed. Why was that?"

"After I got back, we made a deal. He'd leave me alone, let me have my life, do what I wanted. All I had to do was stay here and look after him until the end. I didn't have a problem with that. I had a roof over my head, a car when I needed it, maybe a little money when it was all over. I didn't have nothing else to look forward to so why not?"

"Alvin said Messner blamed Mylene for not having children," Claire says. "If he loved her so much, why would he do that?"

"I told everybody I blamed her for not giving him children, but that was a lie. He never blamed her. She was the only person he ever truly loved. When he lost her, he lost the only decent part of himself. I got whatever scraps were left."

"Then how did he end up with you?" Claire says.

"I'm the twisted up Mylene, remember?" Selma says. "Couldn't have her, he'd settle for the less perfect copy, I guess."

"You started to say something before, Selma," Rachel says.

"Your father never had much use for you until. Until what?"

"Until he borrowed a lot of money from Bickering and couldn't pay it back," Selma says.

Selma sits quietly on the couch and watches as her father paces in the front room of the small frame house where she's lived her entire life. As usual, he has been drinking since before breakfast, and has a can of beer in his hand as he moves around the room. Weighing on his mind is the twelve hundred dollars he owes to Bickering Financial, now in the possession of Obadiah Carter. All morning, Selma has moved carefully around the house, not wanting to incite her father's anger and he has mostly ignored her, with the exception of his barking out a demand for breakfast around eight a.m.

It has been four months since Mylene was laid to rest in the cemetery outside their church and Selma still can't believe her cousin would take her own life in the manner she did. The two had always been close, and even though Mylene was the more popular of the two, she always found room in her life for Selma. When she married Zachariah Messner and quit her job at Walker Groceries, she recommended Selma as her replacement, and the two talked almost daily.

Selma had noted a change in Mylene's normally cheery disposition a day or so before Mylene killed herself, but Mylene never mentioned to Selma what might be behind it. Usually when one of them had a problem the two would eventually confide in one another and talk it out, which Selma expected they'd do in this case. The news of Mylene's death hit Selma hard; she constantly wondered if there was something she should have noticed.

Sometime around ten-thirty, a car pulls into the gravel driveway and stops, then footsteps are heard on the front porch, right before a dark figure appears at the screen door and knocks. Alec takes a long drink from his beer, draws in a deep breath, then lets it out slowly.

"Come on in."

Zachariah Messner enters. Since the funeral he's grown a full beard. On numerous occasions since then, Selma has caught him staring at her.

"Morning all." He focuses on the beer in Alec's hand and the edge of his mouth curls slightly. "Nothing like a few cold ones to start the day, eh, Alec? I imagine you've been expecting me."

Alec looks away from Zachariah. "I have."

"Guess there's no need to stand on ceremony, then," Zachariah says. "I believe there's a sum of money you owe to our benefactors up at Bickering. Any chance you might have scraped that up since your visit to see Mr. Carter last week?"

"I have not," Alec says. "Which you already know. Crops didn't come in like I expected. Times are tough, Zachariah."

"That they are," Zachariah says.

"I don't guess you much care about that. I heard about your visit to the Nelsons on Monday."

"A lot of folks thought they'd be doing better than they are," Zachariah says. "On the other hand, a man cannot reap what he does not sow. Compared to others, your field seems awfully barren for harvest season, Alec. What'd you really do with all that money?"

"Let's just get on with it," Alec says. "I know what's coming."

Zachariah moves his eyes around the room, lingering a moment on Selma.

"I realize I'm not a very well-liked presence in the community," he says. "Somebody has to settle the accounts, I suppose." He moves to the dining room table and pulls out a chair. "But maybe things aren't quite as dark as they seem, Alec. Perhaps there's a way for us to help each other."

"What are you talking about?" Alec says, moving toward the table.

In response, Zachariah sits and removes a roll of hundred-dollar bills from his shirt pocket. He begins counting out a stack on the table. "One, two, three, four, five, six, seven, eight, nine, ten, eleven, twelve." He waves his hand over the stack. "There you go. Twelve hundred dollars. All that's standing between you and total ruination, Alec." He holds up a finger then counts out two hundred more which he lays beside the stack. "Here's an extra two hundred to sweeten the deal. That's yours to keep, Alec. Mr. Carter doesn't even need to know about it."

Alec wipes his forehead. "What do you want, Zachariah?"

Once again, Zachariah turns his eyes toward Selma, this time settling on her. Alec looks at her a moment, before the meaning comes to him. He chuckles.

"Looks like you're worth something after all," Alec says to her. "Go on. Get your stuff."

Selma stares at the floor. "Daddy told me to go, so, I went and packed my bags and left with Zachariah. A week after that, we was married."

"Oh god," Claire says.

"I wish there was something I could say to that," Rachel says. "I'm sorry. For all it's worth."

"When Daddy died two years later, he left what little he had to Alvin. I didn't get a thin dime despite all I did for that man."

"No wonder you never talked about him," Claire says. "I don't blame you."

"I still visit Daddy's grave, but I don't leave flowers," Selma says. "I spit on it. Curse his memory. I hate that old man."

"If it means anything, Alvin hated him too." Claire looks away and shakes her head. "But whatever you went through doesn't justify what you did to me, and it never will."

"I think she knows that, Claire," Rachel says.

"Yeah, I do," Selma replies. "Maybe if you'd been Mylene's, she'd have looked after you better."

"I'd say that's an absolute certainty," Claire says.

"You wanted to know the story," Selma says. "That's the God's Honest Truth. Every word of it."

Rachel clears her throat, and looks between Selma and Claire, "Do you have anything else you want to talk about?"

Selma shakes her head.

Claire says, "I think I've heard enough."

Rachel considers this and nods. She rises. "Thank you again, Selma." She looks at Claire and points to the door. "I'm going to trust you two with a little time alone to say anything you wouldn't want to say in front of me. Try to keep it relatively peaceful." She exits.

Claire and Selma sit, staring at one another.

"Did Alvin ever tell you how Mama died?" Selma finally says.

"He said it was a car accident."

Selma shakes her head. "They was coming back from Macon. Daddy was driving drunk, as usual. Ran off the road and hit a tree on forty-one. Mama was thrown through the windshield."

"It's a horrible way to die."

"Thing is, that's not what killed her. She was still alive. Laying there, probably calling out for help. There was Daddy. Not a scratch on him."

"Did he try to help her?"

"No. He just sat there on a stump and finished drinking his liquor while Mama bled to death."

"No. Alvin didn't tell me that. I think I understand why. Did your father get in trouble?"

"He knew the judge. Let him off with just reckless driving."

Claire shakes her head.

"It don't matter," Selma says. "He got his in the end."

"What do you mean?"

"You ask anybody who still remembers him, they'll tell you Alec Porter died alone in his home after hitting his head when he fell while he was drunk," Selma says. "But that's not how it happened."

"What happened to him?"

"He did fall and hit his head. But he wasn't alone. Not at the end, at least."

"You were there?" Claire says.

"Daddy was always calling the house. Wanting me to come over and help him with something or find something or fix him something to eat. I went over that day and found him lying on the floor in the kitchen. Blood all over. He looked up at me and said, 'Selma. Help me.' He was drunk. I walked over, looked at him and said, "You hurt? You can't get up?' He nodded then asked me to help him again and I said, 'Look at me. Take a good look. Because the next time you see me, it's going to be in hell.' I went into the other room and got a chair then sat there and watched him. It took a couple of hours, but he finally stopped moving; stopped breathing. I got up and left. Few days later, one of his neighbors called Alvin to say they found him there. I never said a word to anybody. Not until now. Whenever I do get to hell, I hope the first thing I see is Alec Porter roasting over a fire. If there's a line for barbecue, I'm damn sure getting in it."

"Why'd you stay?"

"I just wanted to be sure he was gone."

Claire shakes her head. "I don't buy that. Why did you stay?"

Selma looks down. "I stayed — I stayed, because as much as I hated him, nobody deserves to die alone."

"Why are you telling me this?" Claire says. "Why now?"

"Figured I should tell somebody. Might as well be you."

Claire considers this.

"Then since you're being so honest, answer me one other thing. What did Messner say to Frederick when he went to see him during my emancipation hearing?"

"Told him about you for one," Selma says.

"What else?"

"Zachariah said we weren't going to cover for him. We sent you there to cook and clean, not to be his sex slave and he couldn't prove otherwise."

"That was a lie and you knew it."

Selma shrugs. "It worked."

Without saying anything further, Claire rises and returns the chairs to the dining room, then starts toward the door.

Selma rises and steps in front of Claire holding up a hand to stop her. "Listen. I know you don't owe me, but I want you to promise me something. Even if you don't mean it, I want to hear you say you promise."

"What is it?"

"When you hear it's my time, could you try to be there if possible? You ain't got to be nice to me. Just try to be there."

Claire starts to reply, but then stops and considers it a long time. "I'll do what I can."

Selma acknowledges this. "I wish things had been better — for both of us."

Claire nods. "Take care of yourself, Selma."

"Always have."

Claire exits to the porch and finds Rachel leaning against the Jeep, looking away from the house, deep in thought. Claire takes out her phone and dials a number.

"Hey, Jodie."

"Christine! I hope this means you're nearby."

"Yeah, I'm in town. You up for a little company this afternoon? There's someone I want you to meet."

"Of course. Come on by. I'll put out a party platter," Jodie says with a laugh.

"You think you might be able to rustle up Ernie Robinson and his family?"

"I can try," Jodie says.

"Great. We need to make a stop first, but we'll be over in about half an hour."

Claire puts away the phone and heads to the car.

Rachel looks up at her and says, "I honestly don't know if we accomplished anything here. I feel like I let you down."

"We may not have accomplished what you wanted, but I learned a lot and it helped." She gives Rachel a quick hug. "I just called a friend and she's expecting us in half an hour." She heads around to the driver's side. "But first, let me introduce you to Christine."

Shattered

Annabelle Collins has been having a particularly good Fall. Halfway through her senior year at Spelman College in Atlanta, she anticipates doing well on her finals and is looking forward to track season, for which she'll start training after the holidays. A star athlete on the relay and 1500-meter teams, there's been much buzz about her attending tryouts which could lead to a slot on the 1992 Olympic team. The youngest daughter of a busy minister in the African Methodist Episcopal Church, she's always met most challenges with energy and enthusiasm.

In terms of emotional connection, Annabelle is closest to her older brother Alfred, currently stationed in West Germany with the Air Force. She was hoping he'd be able to come home for the holidays, but he's re-enlisted and is being assigned to Japan. She continues to have a contentious relationship with her sister Avis and doesn't find her youngest brother, Avery — now the tallest in the family — to have much mutual interest in topics that concern Annabelle.

Some years after Aaron became pastor at Edgewood AME, he was appointed a Presiding Elder by the Bishop to fill a sudden vacancy. This necessitated moving out of the church parsonage, but also meant he wouldn't be changing congregations. The family settled into a nice house a few streets over so Avery wouldn't have to change schools. They remain active at Edgewood, where Aaron even returns to the pulpit on occasion.

As she's gotten older and acquired more diverse knowledge from her wide-ranging studies at Spelman, Annabelle has become much less assured in the faith that surrounded her since infancy. Alfred, who has been studying Buddhist teachings, has been her primary support, encouraging her in exploring her spirituality to discover what she truly believes. She feels she can't talk to her parents and certainly wouldn't confide in Avis, who was very critical the few times Alfred tried to explain Buddhism to her.

Tonight, Annabelle has been invited to a holiday party at a teammate's apartment in Marietta. She heads over to the family home hoping to borrow her mother's 1990 Miata. Living on campus and utilizing public transportation, she hasn't needed a car full-time; and anyway, her father has encouraged her to save up her money. But given the unusually large sprawl of Atlanta, using public transportation — let alone saving money while doing it — isn't easy, especially for a socially active college senior.

At the house, Maxine grills Annabelle on details of the party. "Who's going to be there?"

"Most of my teammates," Annabelle replies. "Probably other friends."

"But you won't know everybody?"

"Maybe," Annabelle says. "It's a party, Mom. People are going to drop by."

"Have you driven in Cobb before?" Avis chimes in.

"Not a lot," Annabelle says.

"I hate going there," Avis says. "If you're not going to the mall it's very confusing to get around. Everything's a super-highway."

"I have directions," Annabelle says. "It's in a subdivision. They drew me a map. If I get lost, I'll pull off and call."

"I think you should let us know when you get there," Maxine says.

"Mom, I'm not going to call you when I get to the party. I'm not ten."

"She's right, Maxey," Aaron says. "She's an adult. If something happens, she'll let us know."

He goes to Annabelle, puts his arm around her and says, "You have a wonderful night, Sweet Pea."

Maxine considers this. "Well, okay. But I want a full tank of gas when you bring the car back, you hear?"

"Sure, Mom," Annabelle says.

Maxine takes out the keys and Annabelle retrieves them and gives her mother a kiss.

"Watch out on 41," Avis says. "People are crazy out there."

"Yes, Mother Avis," Annabelle says. She pats Avis on the shoulder as she passes.

"You'll see," Avis says.

Annabelle loves driving her mother's Miata. While it's not a convertible — a moot point because it's December — it's small and sporty and Annabelle enjoys opening it up on the road when traffic isn't too heavy. Tonight, the traffic on the top end of 285 is moderate, and she cruises along between seventy and eighty, zipping around cars with the radio blasting "I'm Your Baby Tonight".

The directions she has to the apartment complex have her getting off near Cumberland Mall and following Cobb Parkway to a complex in Marietta. As she sits at the light, she glances at the map she's been given and verifies she's where she needs to be. The light changes and she takes off.

She's hardly into the intersection when the driver's side window shatters inward and her upper body is violently thrown sideways as the door crumples toward her, accompanied by the sound of metal on metal. Her perception becomes tenuous flashes, red light all around her, sounds of police radios, the sensation of being hoisted into a vehicle, someone repeatedly calling out her name, then she fades out completely.

After this, she can't tell what's real or a dream. Through the fog, she sometimes hears her father's voice, sometimes her mother, sister, or younger brother, but she's not sure where they are, or if they're actually present with her. She has no sense of time.

Finally, the fog clears, to the sounds of beeps and people talking. She opens her eyes to find herself in a hospital bed, hooked up to monitors. Avis is seated nearby, staring at her, but when Annabelle opens her eyes and struggles to say something, Avis jumps up, runs to the door, and calls to someone in the hallway then goes to Annabelle's side.

"Annabelle, can you hear me?" Avis says. "Do you know who I am."

"Avis," Annabelle says. "Where am I? What happened?"

Avis takes her hand. "You were in an accident. A drunk driver hit you. You've been in a coma ever since."

"How long?"

"Two weeks and three days," Avis tells her.

"Finals," Annabelle says.

"Don't worry about that," Avis says. "The school knows what's going on. Your coach and teammates have been here just about every day to check on you."

"I need to get up. Help me up."

"That's not a good idea. The nurse should be in shortly. She'll help you."

"Help me up." Annabelle tries to push herself up with her legs but finds she can't. "What's going on, Avis? Why can't I feel my legs?"

Avis looks away from her. "I wish Dad hadn't gone home. I didn't want to be the one to tell you."

"Tell me what?" Avis won't face her. "What is it, Avis? Just say it."

"I'm so sorry, Annabelle. Your spine was damaged in the accident. The doctors don't think you'll ever walk again."

About a month after the Challenger incident in January 1986, Alfred Collins withdraws his application to flight school (already stalled due to his lack of cockpit experience) and accepts an assignment as an air traffic controller in Wiesbaden, West Germany. Four years later, after he learns his unit isn't needed for service in the Gulf War, Alfred re-enlists and is assigned to Yokota Air Base in Japan.

One afternoon, at the local Buddhist temple he has taken to frequenting, he recognizes a young woman as a civilian employee at the base. He decides to practice the Japanese he's been learning by asking her out for coffee. After listening to his pitch, she chuckles and, in English, with only the hint of an accent, replies, "If you are trying to pick me up, you'll need to work on your pronunciation."

"That bad, eh?" Alfred says. "I haven't been studying long."

"That is obvious. What is it they say?" she replies. "Practice makes perfect."

"Maybe I need a tutor," he says. "Know anyone?"

She introduces herself as Chizuko Tanaka and explains that, in addition to her work on base as a Japanese instructor, she also teaches English at a nearby college.

"You're certainly better at English than I am with Japanese," he says.

"I have found that's true with most of the Americans I've met," she replies. "Does the offer of coffee still stand?"

Over the next year, they decide to marry — and begin working out her immigration status.

Following Alfred's discharge from active duty late in 1996, they head to Atlanta with sons Aaron Riku and Genzo Abel. Chizuko is expecting their third child. They purchase a large home in Avondale Estates; Alfred finds work as an air traffic controller at Hartsfield. Chizuko, bilingual proficient in five languages, becomes a translator with the state's Division of Family and Children's Services.

As they're settling in, the neighbors from across the street, Jack and Nancy Standridge, come over with several platters of food and other necessities.

"Moving is so hectic," Nancy tells them. "There's always something you forget."

After they've eaten and gotten acquainted, Jack takes them

around and introduces them to the rest of their neighbors, many of whom watched from porches and out of windows as the family moved in. Meeting them eases a lot of tension for the young couple, and while not everyone welcomes them warmly, most are cordial enough to form the basis for what will develop into solid friendships. The Standridges, in particular, become the family's first and closest friends in Avondale Estates.

Returning to Atlanta provides Alfred with his first opportunity to fully reconnect with his sister Annabelle since the accident which robbed her of the use of her legs. When he's been home on furlough, Annabelle hadn't wanted to spend time talking about how the accident affected her, and Alfred didn't want to pressure her. Now that he's closer-by, Annabelle seems more open to discussing the challenges she faces in re-establishing her independence.

Early in 1997, Alfred and Chizuko welcome their daughter, Midori Avis. Alfred initially wanted to name her after Annabelle, but Chizuko lobbied for Avis, since it's also his mother's middle name, and that of a great-aunt — thereby honoring three generations of the family. Aaron insists that Midori be baptized in the church, and, though neither Alfred nor Chizuko regard themselves as Christians, they decide that it's better to bend on this than to cause an unwelcome stir in the family. Avis and Annabelle are asked to be Midori's godmothers; Avis's agreement comes with lots of advice on how the child should be raised.

While Atlanta is gearing up for the 1996 Olympics, Annabelle decides she's sufficiently independent to get along without the watchful eyes of her parents and is tired of their constant inquiries as to when she's planning to return to Spelman to complete coursework for her degree. She's also not happy with their insistence on her attending church with them. Even before the accident, Annabelle was questioning her faith. Since she's been paralyzed, what little belief she had has evaporated and she's finding it harder to pretend otherwise for her family's sake.

The congregation has a tradition called "the laying on of hands" where parishioners who feel moved by the Spirit can come forward and "bless" members who've been designated as "sick and afflicted" due to circumstances in their lives. Once a month, when this ceremony is performed, someone always wheels Annabelle down, despite her pleas to her father not to make her part of it. Aaron is sympathetic, and tries to intervene;

but, far more often than not, the well-meaning congregants ignore his and Annabelle's requests not to include her. Sensing Annabelle's discomfort, Avis suggests she wheel herself into the vestibule or the women's restroom shortly before the ceremony. Avis accompanies her and waits with her until it's over.

"I don't understand why this bothers you so much," Avis says. "The church has been doing it the whole time we've been here."

"I'm not sick or afflicted," Annabelle says. "I don't want those people putting their hands on me."

"Those people care about you," Avis says.

"They pity me. That's not the same."

Annabelle successfully completed rehabilitation about a year after her accident, gaining quite a bit of mobility using her chair. Some tasks are manageable using nothing but forearm crutches. She's insisted on fixing her own meals to gain experience navigating the kitchen, and has started taking MARTA to get around town, rather than arranging her schedule around her parents' or sister's availability. She's been making money part-time as a medical transcriptionist, and her employer assures her there's plenty of work for her to go full-time.

Searching classified ads in Creative Loafing, she finds a notice for a one bedroom on the first floor of a building in Decatur which seems to suit her needs. The building isn't far away, and rather than sort out MARTA's schedule, Annabelle wheels herself into the living room, where Avis is watching a talk show.

"Are you busy?" Annabelle asks.

"No. Why?"

"I need you to take me someplace."

"Where?"

"Decatur."

"Why do you need to go there?"

"I just do, okay?" Annabelle says. "Can you take me?"

"Ask Mom or Dad."

"I don't want to wait for them to get back. Plus, I don't really want them to know about this just yet."

Avis sits up. "You want me to take you to Decatur, but you don't want Mom and Dad to know about it. What's going on, Annabelle?"

"Nothing. Just something I need to look into."

Avis throws up her hands and sits back on the couch.

"I'm not taking you anywhere if you're going to be secretive about it."

"I want to see an apartment," she says.

Avis sits up again, this time sliding to the edge of the sofa and switching off the television. "An apartment? You're kidding, right?"

"Why not? My physical therapist said there's no reason I couldn't learn to live on my own."

"Mom and Dad aren't going to allow that."

"Mom and Dad don't get a vote in this," Annabelle says. "I'm an adult. I'm not under anyone's care or guardianship. I can make my own decisions."

"Yeah. Bad decisions," Avis says. "Nobody's going to rent you an apartment."

Annabelle lifts the paper from her lap. "They will." She hands the paper to Avis and points to the ad. "Look, it's on the first floor and it says the building is accessible, and they have a non-discrimination policy."

"This is probably the dumbest idea you've ever had," Avis says. "What's wrong with living here? You're with your family. There are people around if you need something."

"Right. Watching everything I do. Commenting on all my choices. I'm tired of it."

"We're not that bad."

"Look, will you take me or not? I can always call MARTA and have them send the accessibility van over."

Avis rises and retrieves her car keys. "Okay. I'll take you. But this is a mistake. You'll see that when we get there."

"Maybe so, but at least I tried."

The apartment is an efficiency, with an attached kitchen and doors large enough for her to maneuver in her chair and the location is easily accessible to downtown Decatur. The building has a ramp and, as they're waiting to talk to the manager after touring the unit, Annabelle notes a man entering with a service dog.

"See?" she says. "He gets around okay."

"He can walk," Avis replies.

The leasing manager outlines the monthly rent and associated fees and Annabelle calculates that it's within her budget. Despite Avis's warning that their parents won't approve, Annabelle signs the lease and starts making plans to move.

That night, Annabelle is not surprised when her parents call her into the living room for a conference, despite not having informed them yet.

"Avis couldn't keep her mouth shut, could she?" Annabelle says.

"Were you planning on running any of this by us?" Maxine says. "Seek our approval for this move?"

"I'm almost twenty-seven years old, I don't need your permission or approval," Annabelle says.

Maxine starts to respond but instead looks to Aaron for support.

"You're right, Annabelle," he says. "You're old enough to make your own decisions. But have you really considered what this would mean? Are you sure you're independent enough to live on your own?"

"No. Probably not," Annabelle says. "But I'm never going to be if I don't get out and learn. Maybe in a few months, I'll call you to come get me, and then you can say I told you so. But I need to find out."

Annabelle moves a few items into the apartment in order to take possession of it a week or so after signing the lease and begins the slow process of moving out of her parents' home. She inherits furnishings from her family and orders some items from a local department store, some of which need to be assembled. She enlists Avery's help in getting the items set up properly.

She's been using MindSpring to connect to the Internet. Once her phone is connected, she sets up DSL service through them and gets back online as Lady Midnight, her handle since 1994. Aside from church, interacting with people on the Internet has been Annabelle's primary social outlet.

One of her more consistent acquaintances is a fellow in his last year at Case Western Reserve University in Cleveland, who goes by Atomic Punk at Netcom. Annabelle first encountered him in 1995 on a Usenet news group Atlanta General, where he inquired about apartments in the Metro area, stating that he was thinking of moving to town once he graduates. From there, she gets to know him via several religious and cultural groups, where she finds him to be an outspoken critic of organized religion, and the resources he cites provide Annabelle with sufficient focus in formulating her opinions on it.

They move from posting online to communicating via email, and Annabelle learns his name is Roscoe, or, more commonly, Scoey Delahunt. They begin a significant correspondence and Roscoe introduces her to many resources online with which she's not already familiar. When he arrives in town just as the

Olympics are wrapping up, he invites Annabelle to have lunch, but she's reluctant at first.

"Hey, it's just lunch, okay?" Roscoe says. "I don't have any ulterior motives."

"It's not that," Annabelle replies. "It's just that, in person, I may not be what you're expecting."

"Please. Wait until you get a load of me," he says. "You'll be the one running for the hills."

"Maybe not running," she replies. She tells him about her confinement.

"So, we'll find someplace accessible," he writes back. "Maybe with a patio."

When they finally meet at a taco place near her apartment, Annabelle is surprised to see he's a short, balding man with thick, horn-rimmed glasses, who appears much older than his stated age of mid-twenties. The image she's formed of him from his online persona is much more dashing and cavalier. After a few minutes of conversation, though, the personalities they cultivate online begin to shine through and they become friends in real life. Roscoe is working as a computing consultant and continues to be a good source for finding resources on the Internet, and Annabelle finds herself becoming hooked.

When Avery graduates high school, he's offered a basketball scholarship to UCLA, which he accepts. On the advice of his father, he insists that he be guaranteed four years of school whether or not he plays all four years. This proves to be fortuitous late in his second season, when he blows out his right knee during a game, ending his athletic career. He goes on to get a degree in film and television production and starts doing rap and stand-up around Los Angeles under the stage name Lil Ace. Over several years, he works himself up in the clubs throughout California.

He's offered a minor speaking part in a film called Strike Force, which is cobbled together using footage of Arnold Schwarzenegger from an earlier film that was shelved. The lead actress became a household name on a sitcom and her agent demanded more money, which held up production. By the time the dispute was settled, the actress's career had cooled, and Arnold was no longer available for reshoots, so the film was recast around the available footage.

It turned out to be a huge boost to Avery's career. In his one major scene, he makes the most of his opportunity, seamlessly improvising an extensive conversation with Arnold by walkie talkie, which garners lots of attention from the industry, making Lil Ace the breakout star of the film. To date, he's never actually met Arnold though most who've seen the film believe them to be best friends.

The attention he garners in the immediate aftermath of the release of the film, leads to him getting a comedy special on HBO, and occasional hosting gigs in the clubs, though not quite headliner status. His agent has also mentioned the possibility of developing his own sitcom for the Fox Network, with no firm commitment on the part of the network. While on the West Coast, he's dabbled in many different religions and philosophies, from Scientology to Nation of Islam, without really committing to any of them. Whenever his parents or siblings question him on it, however, he claims it's all for publicity and that his core beliefs have not changed.

Once she's away from her family, Annabelle stops attending services at their church. She's deliberately vague about her reasons, implying she's going somewhere else, hoping to avoid telling her parents her true reasons for not being there. After repeatedly quizzing her about what she's doing Sunday mornings, Aaron and Maxine decide to pay her a visit unannounced.

"What are you doing here?" she asks when they show up at her door.

"We were led to believe you were attending services at another church," Aaron says. "Is that not the case?"

"I never said I was," Annabelle replies. "I only said I was doing something else."

"Sitting here alone all morning?" Maxine asks.

"Not always."

"What's this about, Annabelle?" Aaron says. "You've always enjoyed attending services at the church."

"I enjoyed seeing friends and interacting with people," she says. "I haven't gotten much out of the spiritual aspects in quite a while."

"Why am I only just now hearing about this?" he says. "Is it because of the healing ceremony?"

"That's uncomfortable for a different reason," Annabelle sighs before continuing. "The truth is, I've changed. I'm not connected to the spiritual side anymore."

"Not connected? What does that mean?" Maxine turns to her husband. "You were raised in the church young lady. What do you mean you're not connected?"

"If you're having a crisis of faith, talk to me," offers Aaron. "We can pray about it."

"Prayer isn't going to help," Annabelle says. "I'm not having a crisis. I have no faith."

"Annabelle, what are you saying?" Maxine looks at Aaron. "What does she mean by that?"

"I think you should consider your words very carefully, Annabelle," Aaron says. "This isn't a subject to take lightly."

"Lightly?" Annabelle is incredulous. "You don't think I've thought about this? Worried over it? I didn't just wake up one morning and decide, 'Oh, now I'm going to stop believing.' I've been wrestling with this since high school."

"Why didn't you come to me?" Aaron says. "You don't think I've dealt with doubts before? I've had them myself."

"Listen to me," Annabelle says. "I don't have doubts. I may have had doubts at one time, but not anymore. I'm pretty assured in how I think now."

"That's ridiculous," Maxine says. "This is because of your accident, isn't it? God's dealt you a rough hand and you're ready to turn your back on him."

"This has nothing to do with my accident," she says. "I was already moving in this direction before that. At the time, I felt the accident only confirmed what I already felt."

"The Lord has a purpose for you, Annabelle," Aaron says. "It's in times like these that he reveals his plans for us."

"When the accident happened, I asked myself over and over what purpose was served by confining me to this chair," Annabelle says. "Taking away the life I'd known." Aaron starts to respond but she wheels herself closer and doesn't let him get his words out. "I felt like God abandoned me."

"Annabelle don't say that," Aaron says.

"I'm not just saying it, Daddy," she says. "I believed it. I felt it. When I looked inside myself, there was nothing. No grace. No assurance. Just emptiness."

"You should have come to me," Aaron says.

Annabelle wheels herself away from them. "And said what? My God, my God, why have you forsaken me?"

"Job was tested," Aaron says. "He never lost his faith."

She turns back. "I don't think Job is the best example here."

"Don't you speak that way to your father," Maxine says. "We taught you better than this."

"Right," Annabelle says. "The God you taught me to believe in would never abandon me like that. I get that. I managed to put the accident, the wheelchair, the changes I've had to undergo in context. It wasn't some cosmic plan, just an incredibly flawed human being who caused all this. But I didn't come to that realization with prayer or turning things over to the Lord. The answers came from within me."

"We shouldn't question how the Lord works his miracles," Aaron says. "We wait for his plan to be revealed."

"Yeah, which is a glorified way of saying, 'Let's just wait and see what happens,'" Annabelle says. "What is the point of believing in an entity that can do whatever it wants whenever it wants, and we're not even allowed to ask why?"

"The Lord loves us, Annabelle," Aaron says. "Loves you. Even through the hardships, he's there for you. You've endured troubles no young woman should ever have to face, but that's no reason to turn away from the Lord."

"I told you, I came to terms with all that. It was coming to terms with it that finally opened my eyes. I stopped looking at everything as part of some divine plan and instead saw it as the random happenstance it is. The outcome is no more guided by an unseen hand than a scoop of ice cream that's fallen on the street and is sliding aimlessly down a hill. Once I realized that, I saw that there's no purpose, no plan, no reason. I finally let myself believe that the god you taught me to believe in doesn't exist at all."

"How dare you," Maxine says, then looks at Aaron, who's shaking his head.

"That is not the answer, Annabelle," Aaron says. "That's just wrong and you know that in your heart."

"You say it's not the answer," she replies. "Do you even know what the question is anymore? Because if you don't, you and I don't have much left to discuss."

Aaron starts to reply, but instead turns away, throws up his hands and moves toward the door. Maxine looks after him, then goes to Annabelle.

"Annabelle, you apologize to your father," she says.

"No. Mama. I won't."

"Annabelle!"

"Maxine, let's go," Aaron says.

"Aaron, we can't leave it like this. You need to talk some sense into her."

"No, Maxine. If I stay any longer, I'm liable to say something we'll all regret. I think we each just need some time for reflection."

Aaron exits. Maxine looks at Annabelle and angrily shakes her head, then follows him out.

A little over an hour later, someone starts pounding on the door. Avis's voice comes from outside.

"Annabelle! You open this door. Let me in there right now."

"Round two." Annabelle opens the door and Avis storms in. "I was expecting you sooner."

"This is all just a big joke to you, isn't it?" Avis says as she enters.

"I don't think any of this is a joke," Annabelle says.

"Dad has been sitting on the back porch for over an hour, just staring into the yard," Avis says. "He has the Bible in his lap and hasn't opened it once. He just sits there, shaking his head."

"I knew it wouldn't be easy for them to hear. It got a little more heated than I'd wanted."

Avis circles the living room then turns and throws up both her hands.

"What is wrong with you? You've always been his favorite. How dare you treat him like this. You're breaking his heart."

"If you think that it was easy for me to look into our father's eyes and tell him I no longer believe in his god, then you don't know me at all, Avis."

"Frankly, I'm beginning to wonder." She circles the living room again. "You need to apologize. Tell him you were wrong."

"I wasn't wrong," Annabelle says. "It might not have been the best way to tell him, but he needed to hear it. They both did."

"Does it even matter to you what this could do to our family?"

"I'm being honest. In the long run, that'll be a good thing. You all need to see me for who I am. I won't lie about it any longer."

"I don't even know why I came over here," Avis says. "You're impossible to talk to about anything."

Avis leaves.

Later that night, Annabelle receives a call from Alfred.

"I've got to tell you, Annie, I was worried about telling Mom and Dad I'm a Buddhist. You definitely took the heat off me."

"You're welcome," she says. "So, who gave you the news, Mom or Avis?"

"Avis. She said Mom's too angry to talk about it."

"She came to see me, too."

"She mentioned that," he says. "How are you feeling?"

"Not great. I know it had to happen sooner or later, but I wish it could have gone better."

"They weren't going to be happy either way," Alfred says.

"I know. I wish I could say they caught me off-guard, but I've been expecting this ever since I stopped going to services. I know what I feel, or don't feel, but putting it into words they'd appreciate was a different matter."

"I'm here if you need me," he says. "Call anytime."

"Thanks, Alfie."

Annabelle anticipates being able to talk to her parents once they've had time to cool down and consider what she's told them. Before that can happen, though, a few weeks later, Maxine collapses at church and the doctors who examine her at the hospital state she's had a massive stroke, which leaves her in a persistent vegetative state. Aaron asks to be relieved of his responsibilities with the church so he can be with his wife.

Though she initially doesn't say anything directly to Annabelle or Aaron, Avis is certain the stress surrounding the situation with Annabelle contributed to her mother's medical condition. Over time, she becomes more vocal about this when talking to Alfred or Avery. She and Annabelle grow apart as a result.

In February of 2001, Aaron suffers a heart attack and is declared dead on arrival at Grady Hospital. The family comes together for his funeral. Though Avis remains distant from Annabelle, she makes every effort to be cordial and consoling when they're together.

Nothing is said at the time, but a few months after the funeral, Alfred approaches Annabelle about taking their mother off life support. The doctors have assured him that Maxine will never recover, which Aaron knew but could never bring himself to give the instructions. Annabelle agrees with Alfred that their mother should be at peace, but both know Avis will not support the decision. Avery, who has lived on the West Coast since college, has not been sounded out on the idea, and neither Alfred nor Annabelle know how he'll respond. Alfred calls a meeting with Avis and Annabelle at the family home to discuss it.

"I am absolutely opposed to this idea," Avis tells them. "This is the woman who gave each of us life and she shouldn't be discarded."

"We're not discarding her," Alfred says. "If I thought there was any chance that she'd come out of this, I'd do everything humanly possible to make it happen."

"It's been four years, Avis," Annabelle says. "If there was any sort of miracle going to happen it probably would have happened while Dad was still around."

"Of course, you would be in favor of this," Avis says. "Neither of you have any faith."

"I have never stopped hoping she'd show some improvement," Annabelle says. "At a certain point, we need to be realistic."

"Blaming us isn't going to make this situation any easier, Avis," Alfred says. "The doctors all said it was just a matter of time. Mom ignored the warnings about her blood pressure and could never remember to take her medicine. Dad was always bugging her about it and she still forgot."

"The stress probably hastened it," Avis says.

"I am tired of you laying this all on me, Avis," Annabelle says. "Mom would be in the same shape now even if I had remained quiet. I wish we could have talked about it, but I don't regret telling Mom and Dad."

Alfred steps between them. "Look, this isn't helping. We need to come to a decision. Dad nearly went broke keeping Mom on life support. I think he was leaning toward removing her, but just couldn't let her go."

"I hope you're not saying she isn't worth the expense," Avis says. "That's just heartless."

"Stop twisting our words, Avis," he says. "She's worth every effort to heal her, if she could be healed. The doctors say she can't."

"We need to bring Avery into this discussion," Annabelle says.

"Good idea," Avis says. "I wonder how quick he'd be to pull the plug on our mother."

"I left a message for him earlier," Alfred says. "I thought we'd have heard from him by now, but the woman I spoke to at his place said he's performing and may be out late."

Avis wastes no time in calling Avery once she's home to advocate for keeping their mother on life support and ask for his help, but Avery won't commit over the phone. She refuses any further meetings with Alfred and Annabelle until all four siblings can be together under one roof. Avery calls Alfred to let him know he's flying in over the weekend, and Alfred sets up another family meeting.

When Avis arrives, the conversation immediately becomes heated with Avis refusing to yield on her position and resuming her attacks on Annabelle. Alfred tries to mediate between them, but Avis attacks him as well, all the while pleading with Avery to side with her to save their mother.

"There's no brain activity at all?" Avery asks.

"None," Alfred says. "That's been consistent since before they transferred her to the nursing facility."

"Have any of you ever gotten a reaction from her when you've been with her?" Avery says.

"I haven't," Annabelle says. Alfred shakes his head.

Avery looks at Avis, who seems deep in thought. "What about you, Avis? You're sure she's still there."

"I don't recall," she says.

"Then I'll take that as a no," he replies. He indicates a file sitting on the coffee table. "This is the doctor's statement?"

"Yes," Alfred says. "Not just her regular doctor, but two others who've examined her."

Avery nods and sits to review the file. When he finishes, he rises and goes to Avis. "Sorry, Avis. I agree Mom's not coming back. As much as any of us wants this, it isn't going to happen. She needs to be with Dad."

"I can walk into court tomorrow and put a stop to this," Avis says.

"Nobody wants that Avis," Alfred says. "Please don't make this harder than it already is."

"Hard?" she says, tears brimming in her eyes. "It doesn't seem very hard for any of you."

Annabelle wheels herself toward Avis. "If I thought there was so much as a distant possibility that she could get better, I'd go with you to court to file those papers. She died a long time ago, Avis. We're just prolonging her death."

Avis rises and walks to the window and stares out for a long time.

"Do whatever you need to do. I won't try to block it." She turns to face them. "You will all be called to account for this one day."

Annabelle starts to respond but Alfred shakes his head. He rises and moves toward Avis but stops a careful distance from her.

"Thank you, Avis," he says. "Let's all meet there on Friday. I'll talk to the nursing home and take care of the arrangements."

"Fine," Avis says. Without further discussion, she collects her things and leaves.

Friday, at the nursing home, after meeting with the doctor, the siblings assemble outside Maxine's room. After a bit of discussion, they decide to each spend time with Maxine alone to say whatever they want with no time limit placed on them. Alfred suggests Avery go first, followed by Annabelle, then Avis, then him. Everyone agrees.

Avery enters the room and sits beside the bed. "Hey Mom. Sorry I haven't been around so much lately but living on the West Coast makes it hard to get over here. I just want to let you know that I appreciate all you and Dad did to make sure I turned out okay. Things are starting to happen for me out in L.A. and none of that would have been possible if you hadn't raised me right. I've missed having you around." He takes her hand in both of his. "I really hate saying goodbye, but you taught me that we'd all be together again someday, so rather than goodbye, I'll just say, 'See you later.' Love you, Mom."

He rises and kisses Maxine on the cheek then goes out and nods to Annabelle.

She goes to the bed and lays her head on Maxine's shoulder. "Mama. There's so much I wish I said to you when we could still talk about it. I know it's too late, but I am so sorry for any distress I caused you and Dad. I'm not sorry for being who I am and believing what I believe, but I'm sorry I didn't handle telling you better. I never imagined we'd have so little time. I don't know where you are now, or if Dad's with you, but I do hope you're at peace wherever that is and that all your pain has ended. I promise you I will use whatever time I have left to try to be the person you taught me to be. I'll always be your little girl."

She buries her head against Maxine's shoulder and cries. When she's finished, she rolls back out into the hallway and gives Avis a smile. "Your turn."

"Mom?" Avis says when seated beside Maxine. "Please Mom. If you're still there; if you can hear me, do something. Move your eyes or squeeze my hand. Just something to let me know and I'll put a stop to all of this. I've always tried to do whatever was expected of me. I've always tried to be what you wanted me to be. I just need your help." She lowers her head as her tears begin to flow. "Mom. I wish, just once, that you'd showed me you appreciated all I tried to do for you; for Dad. I never knew if you cared for me at all. We argued so much. But that doesn't matter. You give me just the slightest sign and I'll fight them all for you. We'll beat them, but you have to let me know." She waits a long time. "Okay, Mom. I guess you're tired. I'm tired too. I understand. Just know I love you. I'll always try to be what you expected me to be."

Avis rises and goes back into the hallway without acknowledging any of the others.

Alfred goes into the room and sits beside Maxine. He takes her hand, kisses it, then closes his eyes and sits with her for twenty minutes without saying a word. Finished, he rises, kisses her on the forehead, then picks up and presses the nurses call button. When the nurse answers, he says, "We're ready."

He goes to the door and motions for his brother and sisters to join him. A few minutes later, the doctor enters with a nurse. He explains to the family what's likely to happen and asks Alfred to sign a form, which he does. Avis stands at the foot of the bed, with Alfred between her and Annabelle. Avery steps beside Annabelle and puts his arm around her shoulder. Alfred tells the doctor to proceed.

The doctor turns off the respirator and for a few moments, nothing changes. The heart monitor continues to register a regular beat. Avis bows her head and starts saying a silent prayer while Alfred, Annabelle, and Avery keep their eyes on their mother. Then the heartbeat becomes irregular, and, at last, goes flatline. Avis, her head still bowed, says, "No."

The doctor checks Maxine's vitals. He looks at the clock and turns to the nurse. "Time of death, nine forty-two p.m." To the family, he says, "I'm sorry for your loss."

The doctor exits. The nurse turns off the monitors, then tells everyone, "Take as much time as you need." She leaves.

Avis is standing at the foot of the bed, weeping silently. Alfred moves to comfort her, but she puts up her hands to stop him and walks out of the room without speaking to any of them. He turns to Annabelle and Avery.

"I don't really feel like now is the best time to be alone, so you're both invited over for as long as you want to stay."

"What about—?" Annabelle says, looking after Avis.

"I'll try calling her," Alfred says. "But she probably just needs some space right now."

Though it's late when she gets home, Annabelle calls Roscoe, who, she knows, is a night owl.

"September 8th, 2001 may not rank as the worst day of my life, but it's definitely in the top ten," she tells him.

"Listen, tomorrow I'm going over to 7 Stages with Aileen to see a show. She's the woman I met at Dragon Con last year."

"Yeah, I met her, remember?"

"Oh, yeah. Well, Aileen wants to have dinner with the Stenographers beforehand. Why don't you join us?"

"If you don't think I'd be in the way," she says.

"Not at all," he says. "Aileen was just saying she'd like to spend more time with my friends."

"Okay then. I'll meet you in Little Five," she says. "I sure hope 2001 doesn't get any worse."

"You and me both," he says.

The following Tuesday, 11 September, Avis stops in at the leasing office of a storefront in downtown Duluth. She's finally decided to follow a calling she's felt since her father's death and start a small congregation from which she hopes to minister to the needs of the community. Earlier in the year, through online courses, she was ordained as a minister in an Apostolic fellowship. It's her second visit to the office, the first being the previous day when the woman behind the counter said they were out of the proper forms. Avis rings the bell and, receiving no acknowledgement, leans forward and sees the attendant glued to a television.

"Hello?" Avis calls to the attendant.

"Oh, sorry," the woman says. "I was watching the news. A plane crashed into the World Trade Center."

"This morning?" Avis asks.

"Yeah, they're not sure if it was taking off or landing or where it even came from."

She turns the television around, and they watch from the counter. As they do, a second plane hits the South Tower.

"That's not an accident," the woman says. "Are we under attack?"

"I don't know," Avis says. "Whatever it is, it's not good."

The woman breaks down. Avis goes over and turns off the television and puts her arm around the woman. "It's okay. Things will be okay."

"I'm scared," the woman says. "What's going to happen?"

"Listen to me," Avis says, taking her hands. "This is very frightening and confusing. I don't know what's going on or what's going to happen. But the Lord has a plan and we're a part of that. If you trust in his wisdom, you can endure whatever the world throws at you."

"I'm not a very religious person," the woman says.

"That doesn't matter," Avis says. "God hasn't given up on us. It's times like these he shows us his love and concern."

"I'd like to believe that."

She starts to cry again. Avis takes the woman in her arms and comforts her.

"It's all right. Mother Avis is here."

Through Roscoe, Annabelle learns about The Frantic Feminist, a blog maintained by Rebecca Asher, who Annabelle also knows as a reporter for Creative Loafing. Rebecca's bold and free-wheeling style of writing impresses Annabelle, and she anticipates each new entry every few days. Rebecca divides the blog into four main topics, posts on general feminism, which she publishes on Wednesday, reviews of shows or openings and recommendations, she typically posts on Monday, film reviews, which appear on Friday, and general topics she posts intermittently, as ideas occur to her.

Annabelle frequently contributes to the discussion threads, and on numerous occasions, she and Rebecca have exchanges. When Annabelle tries to get Roscoe to introduce her to Rebecca, however, she learns his girlfriend had a falling out with her, and he's no longer speaking to Rebecca out of solidarity.

"Aileen doesn't approve of me reading the blog either," he tells Annabelle, "but usually doesn't make a big deal about it."

Roscoe tells Annabelle that his colleague at work owns a place in Kirkwood, which she's selling so she can move to Midtown. He informs her that the house has certain features left over from the previous owner which would make it ideal for her, such as a ramp and extra wide doors. Annabelle has considered owning a home but wasn't sure she'd be able to afford the payments. She agrees to take a look and checks into her financing options and learns she'll easily qualify through her credit union. The payments will be less than what she's paying for rent, so she contacts the owner and makes arrangements to see the house one weekend.

Kirkwood isn't far from her apartment, but she needs to coordinate buses to find one that goes by the property. Around three, she rolls herself up the front ramp and rings the bell. She's met by a woman who looks to be in her mid-thirties.

"Dr. Walker," Annabelle says and introduces herself.

"Leah," she replies as they shake hands.

"Roscoe gave me the story on the place," Annabelle says. "I do like the ramp."

"Yes. I thought about taking it out but haven't had time to do much renovation around here, other than the obvious."

"It sounds like it will meet my needs, but I wanted to get a feel for the place."

"Perfect," she says. "Scoey probably mentioned it's a private sale. I have my broker's license, so it's not listed currently. You get first refusal."

"Wonderful. I did want to verify that the price Roscoe quoted me was accurate. It seems rather low for this area."

"Yes. If this place was fully renovated, I would be asking a lot more, but as I say, I haven't invested much into fixing it up, beyond paint and some minor repairs, so I'm selling it as is for slightly more than I paid for it."

"Sounds good. It's definitely in my price range and seems like a great investment."

"You know a deal when you see it," Leah says. "Let me show you around."

"If this isn't my business, just say so," Annabelle says as they start the tour, "but are you connected to that development firm that's building all the McMansions around town? I believe it's called Walker, too."

Leah chuckles. "It's my father's firm. But I am not otherwise connected. This is my house, not theirs."

The house is a two-bedroom, two bath, brick unit with a small studio in the basement that has a bathroom and a kitchenette. Annabelle appreciates that otherwise there are no stairs, except from the back deck to the yard; and even then, as Leah takes her out the front to show her, the yard is readily accessible from the driveway. Leah describes the neighbors as "friendly, but they keep their distance" and says traffic isn't too bad, even on weekends, but that there are several bars and other businesses nearby. Annabelle particularly likes the iron security gates on the front and back doors, which Leah had installed.

"I can definitely meet your asking price," Annabelle tells her when they're talking in the living room after the tour. "My credit union wants an inspection."

"No problem," Leah tells her. "I expected they would."

Annabelle gives her the contact info on her loan officers and Leah agrees to get in touch with them about the closing. The sale goes through quickly and by late 2005, Annabelle is settling into her new home.

One morning in December, Annabelle calls up the page for The Frantic Feminist and notices it has a black background. Rather than Rebecca's acerbic prose, there's a note from Steven, Rebecca's brother, informing readers that Rebecca was killed in a car accident in late-November. Annabelle joins the chorus of readers posting condolences, and receives a brief boilerplate note of thanks from Steven.

Roscoe informs Annabelle that he and Aileen, have decided to get married, and Annabelle is among the friends they're inviting to witness the ceremony at the DeKalb courthouse. On the morning of the wedding, she makes arrangements to get to Decatur, where she encounters the most unusual wedding party she's ever witnessed. A number of Aileen's friends work in the entertainment industry and come in elaborate costumes they've designed for Dragon Con or Renaissance fairs, and more than a few are well-adorned with tattoos on much of their visible skin. Roscoe is wearing a plaid sports coat with chinos and a dark polo shirt, and Aileen has on a white mini dress with black, knee-high boots and is wearing a crown of silk flowers. After the ceremony, they adjourn to a nearby T. J. Bailey's for the reception.

Twenty-three-year-old Paul Searcy, the man responsible for Annabelle's accident, was the son of a prominent business owner in Kennesaw, Georgia, who was driving drunk when he ran a red light. Police estimated he was traveling around fifty miles an hour when he T-boned the Miata at the driver's side door. He had not attempted to slow down going into the intersection, and Annabelle's body took the brunt of the impact.

Annabelle had no contact with him, except on the day of his sentencing, when he faced her from the witness stand, and repeated several times, "I'm sorry. I'm really sorry." He seemed genuinely upset, but Avis, who was in the gallery that day, was convinced it was mostly an act for the courtroom. At the time, Annabelle was still recovering from the news she'd never walk again; emotionally numb from the whole experience, she sat, stony-faced throughout the display.

Her father had lectured Paul, telling him to get right with God and use his time behind bars to straighten out and learn to make amends for the suffering he had caused. Paul received fifteen years, but Avis mentioned on the way home that he'd probably get out earlier on parole.

"His family's probably going to take care of that," she said. "Rich white folks look out for their own."

Annabelle had never checked to see if any of this was true. The less she thought about Searcy, the happier she was. In the time since the accident, she had all but put him out of her mind completely.

Which is why she's surprised when she answers a knock at her door and finds herself face to face with him one afternoon. After a brief standoff, she admits him, giving him only ten minutes to explain himself. He struggles with his thoughts.

"I've had a lot of time to think the last fifteen years. I guess now that I'm here, the words are a little hard to come by."

"Time is short," is Annabelle's only reply.

Paul removes a photo from his pocket which he holds out for Annabelle to take. It's a college photo of her that Aaron gave Paul after he went to prison to remind him what he'd done.

"Like I could ever forget," he says.

When she presses him to get to the point, he tells her, "I've wished there was some way I could make it up to you, but I realize nothing I do is going to be sufficient."

Annabelle shakes her head and sighs loudly.

"This is some sort of twelve-step thing, right? Where you go around asking for forgiveness from all the people you've hurt? Sorry, Paul. I'm not in a very forgiving mood."

"I don't want your forgiveness, or your pity. You hate me and I don't blame you for that."

What he says next catches her completely off guard.

"I took your life away from you. I'm here to offer you mine."

Paul explains that he's offering to devote the remainder of his life making amends to her, for as long as she chooses to have him around. While she's considering all of this, Paul looks at his watch and rises to leave, thanking her for listening to him. As he moves toward the door, Annabelle is struck by how he's kept his word, agreeing to leave as she's asked him without any prompting from her. Still very wary of his intentions, she decides to put him to the test and agrees to let him work on a project for her, putting in a ramp from the back deck to the yard.

A few days later, when he shows up to start the job, Annabelle does all she can to avoid him. She's relieved to see that the avoidance is mutual. Building materials were delivered that morning, and other than checking in to let her know he's here, Paul has not attempted to interact with her at all. From the living room, she can hear the sound of sawing and hammering, but she suppresses for as long as possible the urge to check on his progress.

At last, when she hears a lull in his work, she wheels herself out to the deck and is surprised by the progress he's made. He's already framed out the rise and is constructing the surface.

"Afternoon, ma'am," he says.

"Wow. You've made more progress than I expected," she says. "It looks good."

"Yes, ma'am," he says. "I'm not sure I'll get it all done today but should be able to wrap things up by tomorrow at the latest."

"How are you at wiring?" she says.

"I've had some experience," he says. "Are you talking about electrical or speaker wires?"

"Speakers," she says. "Though I could probably use electrical too. I want to have music throughout the house."

"I can do that," he says.

"Let's talk when you finish the ramp," she says.

As he finishes each project, Annabelle thinks of something new for him to tackle. A lingering question remains for her and finally, one afternoon, she asks him to join her in the living room.

"Why are you doing this Paul? What's this all about?"

"We talked about it," he says. "I told you—"

"I know what you said. But what compelled you to come here? Did you find Jesus or something? Make me understand this."

"It wasn't because I found something, ma'am," he says. "It's because I want to lose something."

"What do you mean?"

"When I first went to prison, I wanted to kill myself. I figured I didn't have anything to contribute. I just screwed everything up all the time, hurt good people. Like you. Then I met this other fellow who changed my thinking."

"Changed? How?"

"He taught me that it wasn't my body that needed to die. It was how I saw myself, how I thought about things, my personality, attitudes."

"Death of the ego. Alfie — my brother, Alfred — has talked

about that. It's a concept in Buddhism."

"Yes ma'am. It's part of the steps on the Path."

"The eightfold path. You're following the Path to Enlightenment."

"Yes ma'am. I don't know if I'm doing it right, because I'm kind of making it up as I go along, but from what I've learned, it's not a destination, but a journey."

"That's how Alfie describes it."

"When I looked inside myself, I learned that I always thought everything was about me. What I wanted. What I needed. But it's not. It's about being part of a bigger picture."

"Being at one with the universe."

"Yes ma'am. When we finally get it right, the cycle stops, and we cease to exist."

"Nirvana. The end of all suffering; the conclusion of the cycle of death and rebirth."

"Yes ma'am. When I heard that, I thought it's sounded pretty good."

"Why did you come to me?"

"I had to stop running away from my past. From all the bad things I did and all the people I hurt. Most of them wouldn't talk to me anyway. My family cut me off a long time ago. So, I came to see you, because you're probably the one person I hurt the most."

"You said you didn't want my understanding or forgiveness."

"I meant that. I don't deserve it. I shouldn't want it anyway. That's my ego speaking. I'm here because it's the right action, right motivation. What I do, how long I stay, that's all out of my hands. When you tell me to leave, I'll go, and I won't ask any questions either."

"Thank you for telling me this, Paul. I think I'm starting to understand a little better."

"Yes ma'am."

Once she's gotten past her initial reticence at having Paul around her home, Annabelle finds him to be a very useful person. In prison, he pursued many interests, and this has resulted in his becoming a jack of all trades, with a little knowledge on a wide variety of topics, including carpentry, electronics, and computers. He also occasionally worked in the prison cafeteria and is a very good cook.

"Paul, do you know anything about blogging?" she asks.

"We didn't have access to post on the Internet, but the trustees could view stuff under controlled circumstances," he says.

"I've been wanting to set up a site," Annabelle says. She has a thought. "Hold on. I know someone who blogs."

That night, she calls Roscoe.

"What's the best site for starting a blog?"

"Depends on what you want," he says. "Ease of access, visibility, subject matter. I can give you details about the site I use, but also make a list of some of the better platforms I've seen, so you can compare."

A few weeks later, after reviewing some of the sites Roscoe recommends, Annabelle goes online with, "The Midnight Hour" using her handle "Lady Midnight". On it, in addition to posts about herself and her experiences navigating the world, she shares her thoughts about religion, politics, and human rights. Using some of the tricks Roscoe has taught her, she's able to get the word out, and before long, she forms a steadily growing community of followers. Users are drawn in by her variety of topics, her straightforward and concise method of communicating, and her consideration of opposing points of view without being denigrating or insulting.

As she finds her voice on the blog, Annabelle starts to examine other aspects of her life. For a long time, she's thought about going back to school to pursue an advanced degree. The thought also occurs to her that there's no reason she shouldn't be able to drive and goes online to investigate cars equipped with hand controls for people in her situation. With each step she takes, she finds herself beginning to reengage with the world.

Axe Man

Edward Abraham Branch, III carried on the fine tradition of Branch men playing football at UGA. His family called him "Ned" to distinguish him from his grandfather, "Big Ed" and his father, who was still called "Eddie, Jr." despite the elder Edward being dead since Ned was a boy. A quarterback, Ned had a wealth of natural talent, and, as such, had not been much in the habit of working very hard in high school despite — or perhaps because of — his winning record on the field.

When he arrived at the University, he spent his first year mostly on the bench, developing a work habit that would, eventually, earn him a starting spot on the team. His coaches recognized him as a solid, if not stellar player, who could be depended upon to go the distance, and elicit enough occasional brilliance to pull out the wins. About the time he gained his starting spot, Ned married his high school sweetheart, Lindsay Maddox. Lindsay accompanied Ned to UGA where she was taking classes in banking and finance. They decided to forego starting a family until their studies were behind them.

Ned's attendance at UGA had been cast in doubt, when a local girl, Charlotte Sanger, identified him as the father of a child she was carrying. Charlotte was considered a mousy little thing, who was mostly known for singing in her church choir, and for being the sister of that guy who'd been caught fooling around with the married son of the pastor at their Baptist congregation. She also had some weird disorder that caused her to repeat things people said to her, earning her the nickname Echo at school. She'd befriended Ned and Lindsay their senior year, which led to her unexpectedly being named Homecoming Queen.

Not wanting to involve the family in any messy controversy, Eddie, Jr. called Ned's coach, Harold Ricketts, into his office at the car dealership, and impressed upon the coach a need for him to handle things. Coach Ricketts started a whisper campaign to shift responsibility away from Ned and onto a teammate, which worked so well, the other boy's family insisted he marry Charlotte, but she snuck off in the middle of the night one evening, leaving behind no word as to where she was headed.

Eddie, Jr. owns and operates Branch Motors (*Your Branch office!*) in Dublin, Georgia, the largest population center near where he and his family have lived for generations. They specialize in big American vehicles, mainly General Motors trucks and autos, and most of their revenue comes from leasing fleet vehicles to Bickering Textiles — a wholly-owned subsidiary of Bickering Plummet in Atlanta — which employees nearly the majority of the local population, second only to the agricultural plant, also a client of Branch Motors. Owning a virtual monopoly has given Eddie, Jr. much prestige and influence in the community, but he forever feels he's in the shadow of his attorney father, who'd served for a couple years as a state legislator in the 70s. Eddie, Jr. has hustled to fill his father's enormous shoes ever since Big Ed's death in 1988.

Eddie, Jr. and his brothers — Clement, Earl, and Polk — all played for The Dawgs. Eddie, Jr. had been a fullback, warming the bench for most of his freshman and sophomore years, and finally earning a few starts late in his junior year. He was an uninspired and undistinguished player who only went out for the football team because his father said he had no choice. He spent far more of his four years there drinking beer and chasing coeds, activities he found much more to his liking, careful to be sure he never crossed any lines athletically or academically, that might endanger his position on the team, and thus with his family.

He was a fair to middling student in his chosen major of business administration, learning only enough to guarantee he'd know how to hire the right people in whatever profession his family deemed worthy of him pursuing. Socially, he was the life of the party, always with a fun anecdote or joke that left his listeners thoroughly entertained. He combined this with a friendly smile, a firm handshake, and an easy-going disposition, making him difficult to fluster or anger — much unlike his father, who could fly off the handle at a moment's notice.

In the aftermath of the Charlotte Sanger situation, once she had fled the scene, Eddie, Jr. heaved a sigh of relief. He remained wary, however, of the implications of an unseen, unstable young woman, and a pregnant one no less, skulking around in the shadows and plotting her revenge on his son. He called Coach Ricketts in a few days later, for a full debriefing.

"So, you don't know where she's gotten off to, do you Coach?" Eddie, Jr. said then swiveled toward the wall and placed his right index finger to his head. "Hmm, let me think on this a minute." He suddenly spun back around with his finger in the air. "Ah, here's a thought. Where's that fruitcake older brother of hers?"

"Couldn't tell you," Ricketts said. "Ain't thought about that boy since all that mess with the preacher's son."

"Well, while you've been scratching your head, I've been conducting some research," Eddie, Jr. said. "It may interest you to know one of our top mechanics is a fellow by the name of Dexter Sanger, who just this past Fall was the escort of this year's unlikely Homecoming Queen."

"You don't say," Ricketts said.

The intercom buzzed. Eddie, Jr. picked up the phone, listened, and said, "Thank you, Noreen. I'll buzz you when we're ready." He looked back to the coach. "And that young man is sitting right out there in the reception area, as we speak."

"Get him on in here, then," Coach Ricketts said.

"Not so fast, Hal," Eddie, Jr. said. "I'm going to need you to go hang out in the showroom while we conduct our business. I'll have Noreen come get you if I need anything else."

Disappointed, Coach Ricketts rose as Eddie, Jr. buzzed his receptionist. As Dexter entered, Eddie, Jr. said to the coach, "Thank you again, Coach Ricketts. Branch Motors is proud to continue its support for the team." He rose to shake the coach's hand and, seeing Dexter, he said, "Well, look here. I believe this is one of your former players, isn't it?"

Both Coach Ricketts and Dexter looked confused. Dexter said, "No, sir. I thought about it, but that's about the time my Daddy died. I had to go to work after school."

"My mistake, then," Eddie, Jr. said. "You just got that athletic look about you."

Eddie, Jr. dismissed Coach Ricketts and invited Dexter to have a seat.

Dexter is a solid, compact man, with just the earliest hint of a spare tire showing. His personnel file states he lives in Dublin with a wife and two daughters and lists his religious affiliation (*Optional*) as "Baptist". Under "Personal Information" it lists that he's a guitar player, who sometimes plays with a band in honkytonks around the region.

He went to work for Branch after he graduated high school in 1991, and completed his certification in GMC automotive maintenance, and since has gotten high marks on his yearly evaluations. His supervisors mostly refer to him as a "quiet and efficient worker". For this particular meeting, he was still wearing his purple Branch Motors polo shirt and baseball cap, with the bill pulled down to just above his eyebrows.

"How you doing, Dexter?" Eddie, Jr. said.

"I'm all right, Mr. Branch," Dexter replied. "I hope there's no problem or nothing."

"Not at all, not at all," Eddie, Jr. said. "Just wanted to spend some quality time with a quality employee."

"Uh, okay," Dexter said. He remained rigidly seated.

"How are things going for you down in the service bay?" Eddie, Jr. continued. "Anything I can do to make your time here more to your liking?"

"Things are going okay," Dexter said. "Workload's pretty even. I don't have any complaints."

"Good to hear, good to hear," Eddie, Jr. said. "How's your family getting along? That wife of yours — ah — Carrie Ann. She treating you right?"

"We're getting along okay," Dexter said. "It's always challenging with young kids in the house."

"Of course," Eddie, Jr. said. "Say, you've got an older brother, haven't you? Brian, I believe."

"Yes sir," Dexter said.

"What's that old boy up to these days?"

"I reckon he's still living in Atlanta," Dexter said. "That's where he was last time I talked to him."

"You don't stay in touch?"

"Not really," Dexter said. "He's got his life; I've got mine."

"Ain't a thing wrong with that," Eddie, Jr. said. "What about that sister of yours, Charlotte? Think she's gone up there to be with him?"

"That'd be my guess, yes sir," Dexter said.

"Atlanta's a good place to get lost," Eddie, Jr. said. "I'm hoping you might be able to help us guarantee she'll stay lost."

"I'm not sure I understand what you mean," Dexter said.

"I'm just suggesting that if you were to hear any rumblings about her headed back in this direction, you might could give me a heads up. That's all."

"I reckon there won't be any harm in that," Dexter said.

"I'm glad we have an understanding, Dexter," Eddie, Jr. said. "And if there's ever anything, and I mean anything that might make your time here at Branch more rewarding, you just let me know, and ol' Eddie, Jr. will take care of it personally."

"I appreciate that, sir," Dexter said.

Eddie, Jr. dismissed Dexter, feeling he had secured the family's legacy at UGA. About forty minutes later, he remembered Coach Ricketts was still waiting in the show room and picked up his phone.

"Noreen, would you please tell Coach Ricketts he can stand down?"

"What's that mean?" Noreen replied.

Eddie, Jr. shook his head. "That means he can go on home. Thank you, Noreen."

When Dexter arrived home that night, he phoned his mother at the truck stop. "You were right, Mama. Eddie, Jr. called me in this afternoon."

"Well, I hope you told him what he wanted to hear," Amelia said.

"I let him believe we're on the same page," Dexter said. "If you talk to Brian or Charlotte, tell 'em the Branches won't be a problem."

Brian Sanger came to Atlanta in 1991, when the Braves went from being lovable losers to the powerhouse team they'd become throughout the nineties. He found himself caught up in the fervor surrounding the team and after watching them win the World Series in '95, decided that watching baseball wasn't enough for him. He researched and found a city league in Atlanta, and within a few years of discovering his love for the game, found himself out on the field, where he developed into a decent shortstop, with a .315 batting average.

While in the city leagues, he befriended Lee Raines, a data analyst with Bickering Plummet, who, though working one floor down from Brian's department, has never worked with Brian personally. The year after Brian moves to Avondale Estates, Lee forms a team in the DeKalb County leagues called The Peaches, comprised of gay and transgender male players, and invites Brian to join the team. Since Lee is a shortstop, Brian moves to centerfield, where his strong right arm becomes a major asset to the team.

At first, the other teams have quite a time making fun of The Peaches, some calling them The Sissy Boys, along with a lot of less polite names. Lee, captain of the team, stresses the basics of the game and insists on teamwork from day one. Standout players are expected to mentor those less accomplished, and, at team meetings, everyone has a say, regardless of his place on the team. Practice is mandatory, and anyone who misses more than two without a valid excuse, is dropped from the roster. Despite the work involved, the first rule is for everyone to have fun and enjoy the camaraderie.

When they take the field for their first game, the jeers of the opposing teams' fans — prompted by the team's peach colored uniforms, and practice of singing popular songs during warmups — are soon silenced, as they show themselves to be fierce competitors. By the end of their first season, the team has garnered quite a few fans. They hold their first end of year awards soirée, catered by teammate Hector Rivera, and at the end of their third season, they invite the other teams in the league to join them. It quickly becomes one of the highlights of the season, along with the preseason mixer the league sponsors.

The star pitcher for The Peaches is Stan Markham, an expressive man the team calls "Swish". Other teams derisively referred to him in that manner when he started with the team, due to his mannerisms off the field, but the team now maintains that the name represents the sound his pitches make when they go past the batter. Few in the league look forward to playing the team when Swish is on the mound. A very flamboyant personality off the field, when he suits up and takes the mound, he's deadly serious, with a thousand-yard stare that chills the blood of even the most fearsome of batters. His fast ball has been clocked as high as 100.5 MPH, and his change-up has yet to be hit by an opposing player. His reflexes are lightning quick: once, he caught a line drive, spun about, threw out the runner at third and was halfway back to the dugout before the batter even realized the inning was over.

Being the chief male influence in his family, Brian sees it as his responsibility to be a father figure to his nephew, Ishmael. Step one, after basic caregiving, is fostering Izzy's interest in baseball, taking him to games, player appearances and training camps, and teaching Izzy the finer points of how to hit a ball and field. When Izzy shows an interest in pitching, Brian asks Swish to give the boy some pointers. Izzy shows a talent for it and picks up everything he's taught quickly. Swish helps Izzy cultivate his fast ball and changeup and makes some suggestions on how to deliver a slow curve. Swish notes that Izzy can pitch just as well with his left hand as with his right and encourages Izzy to develop the talent. Charlotte decides against letting Izzy play little league, however, worrying that his studies might suffer — she recently had to cut back on his musical practice for the same reason. She eventually relents: if his study habits improve, he can try out for the team in high school.

In the Fall of 2000, Ned and Lindsay, expecting their first child, move to Suwannee, in the Metro Atlanta area. It's mostly for Ned's career: now a fourth-round draft pick for the Falcons, he's beginning his tenure as the backup quarterback. It's here the couple confirms what became of their friend, Charlotte, as they discover that the singers who've been invited to perform the National Anthem at the season opener are Charlotte and her brother, Brian, now under the moniker Echo.

The team does not interact with the opening duo, but Lindsay finds herself in the Skybox with them, and after a few awkward moments, during which she meets the boy Charlotte introduces as her son, they reconcile, and Lindsay promises to have the family over to their home. When Lindsay tells Ned of the encounter, he's secretly relieved to learn Charlotte did not name the boy fully after him, as he has no desire to be the father of Edward Abraham, IV.

Ned finally meets the boy when Charlotte, Brian, and Izzy visit a few weeks later. In their discussions leading up to the visit, it was decided that they weren't going to hide the fact that Ned is Izzy's father from the boy, but when they introduce Ned as such to Izzy, he takes it in stride, being far too young to realize the implications of it all, and he's never really lacked for "father figures".

Izzy turns out to be an energetic child, with a natural curiosity about the world around him, and no shyness toward new people. He and Ned hit it off immediately, and Brian and Ned spend an hour or more chasing him around the yard and playing catch with him. Lindsay and Charlotte watch them as they chat on the back deck.

After the meeting with Izzy goes well, Ned and Lindsay discuss the possibility of Ned formally acknowledging Izzy as his son. Lindsay voices no objections, though she is concerned the timing might overshadow the arrival of their child, who, they've learned from the ultrasound, is also a boy. Ned agrees to discuss it with the team's legal counsel, and to bring Charlotte into the discussions before they go very far.

"One thing we both need to agree on," Lindsay says, "your family stays out of the loop until everything's settled."

"Way ahead of you, Linz," Ned says. "The last thing we need is them mucking around in the situation."

Lawyers for the team outline the process of acknowledging paternity, but caution Ned that he should confirm with a DNA test that he is Ishmael's father. Ned doesn't believe Charlotte will appreciate this step, since he believes she's telling the truth about Ned being the only man who could be the father but agrees to at least broach the subject with her. Officials with the team express concerns over the publicity such a move might bring.

"Is there really a pressing need to take this step at this time?" one of the player reps asks.

"I'm just getting started with the team," Ned says. "My profile will only get bigger the longer I'm here."

"That is true," another says.

"Charlotte isn't likely to cause much of a stink unless she feels she's being disrespected," Ned says. "Or if someone's trying to cause problems for Ishmael."

"I don't see a problem with it," the players rep says, "just so long as it's done with as little fanfare as possible."

"Understood," Ned says.

Lindsay insists that she be the one to approach Charlotte with the idea, since the two of them get along a bit better than Ned and Charlotte. As it turns out, Deanna Savage, the mother of the family Charlotte's living with, is a social worker in Gwinnett County, and is well-acquainted with the process. Charlotte arranges a meeting with Deanna where she and the Branches can discuss the matter in more detail.

Deanna's a lively woman, who's naturally inclined to hug someone on a first meeting, but usually asks first to make sure it's okay. She outlines all the requirements and implications of the step Ned wants to take.

"The team's legal counsel suggested getting a paternity test," Ned says, glancing toward Charlotte to gauge her reaction.

"Test, test, test. For what? Look at Izzy. Anybody can see the resemblance."

"No, actually, it's fairly standard in this type of case," Deanna says. "A court would order one anyway. It would help to establish Ned's claim as Izzy's father."

"Father, father, father, father. It's not going to change anything, but if you say we should, I'm willing to do it."

"The lawyers also outlined how I go about amending Izzy's birth certificate," Ned says.

"I suppose you'll want him to have your name, too," Charlotte says with exaggerated seriousness.

"That's up to you, Charlotte," Ned says.

"No. I don't mind him being a Branch," she says.

Deanna recommends several attorneys who specialize in family cases, and after further discussion, Charlotte petitions for a name change for Izzy, to Ethan Ishmael Sanger Branch, substituting her father's first name for Ned's, since Ned is finally taking responsibility for his son.

Before any of this can take place, Lindsay goes into labor, and delivers a healthy baby boy, who she and Ned name John Isaac, though, from the start, they nickname him "Ike". Izzy is thrilled to hear he has a baby brother, and though Ned's family is disappointed the child isn't named after his father, they otherwise welcome his arrival.

Shortly after Ike's birth, Charlotte receives the results of the DNA test, which yield no surprises, and Ned completes the Paternity Acknowledgment form, has it notarized, and sends it off to Vital Records. Over the next several years, Ned and Lindsay have two daughters, Ansley Mae, and Emily Kaitlyn. While Ishmael remains with his mother, he makes frequent visits to the Branch household and gets along well with his step-mother and half-siblings, in particular his brother, Ike, who looks up to Izzy.

A year and a half into his contract, Ned, who's being considered for a trade to Buffalo, gets his first and only start, in an away game against the Dolphins. He leads the team to a respectable 34-13 score, but in the final drive of the game, he gets tackled hard by a defensive end, just as he's completed a long pass for a touchdown. The momentum of the opposing player, along with the angle Ned hits the ground, combine to give him a serious head and neck injury, which proves to be career-ending.

Fortunately, Lindsay had the foresight to ensure Ned has good personal injury coverage, over and above what the league provides; plus, she's been very prudent in investing his considerable guaranteed earnings. Once Ned is on his feet again, he's offered a position as a reporter and the weekend sportscaster for Action News, and as a color commentator for a local sports radio station. A large insurance company in Atlanta hires him as a spokesperson, and he becomes a fixture in the community as a local celebrity, speaking to churches and civic groups.

One congregation that always welcomes him is Apostolic Awakening a conservative evangelic church led by "Mother" Avis Collins. Mother Avis promotes herself as a black conservative, and over the decade since starting her ministry, has begun taking stances against gay marriage, extra-marital sex, race mixing, and government entitlements. She grew up in a mainstream Methodist congregation, but became a fundamentalist following a fallout with her siblings from the deaths of their parents.

Her church promotes "family values" and "economic empowerment;" in practice, their philosophy is a curious mixture of feeding the homeless while criticizing them for a lack of initiative, promoting Jesus's teachings, while encouraging church goers to become entrepreneurs, and welcoming members of all races, just so long as none of them try to intermarry. Apostolic Awakening boasts a growing congregation of nearly four hundred parishioners, and their services are a rousing mixture of amplified Gospel, warm, welcoming fellowship, and fiery rhetoric delivered by Mother Avis.

Over the years, even though he does not always support the church's positions on social issues, Ned and Mother Avis become good friends. Noting his popularity in the community, officials with both political parties send out feelers to gauge his interest in running for local or county government, but Lindsay puts her foot down and insists Ned not consider running for office while the kids are small, so as not to expose them to the grind of a political campaign. She tells him she may support it in the future, however, when the children are older.

When Charlotte moved to Atlanta, Deanna and her husband, Emanuel, known as Manny, welcomed her as one of the family. Manny helped Charlotte get a job with the Forestry Service after Ishmael was born, and the Savage kids have always treated Izzy like a little brother. As they became old enough, Derek and Gloria would watch Ishmael whenever Charlotte was at work or out at a gig. Charlotte loves the Savages as much as she does her own family, and especially enjoys the jams at the house, where musicians from all over play together until the wee hours, which she and Brian continue to attend after they move to Avondale Estates.

Charlotte's job with the Forestry Service has earned her the title of "the Snake Lady." She has never been afraid of snakes, and, as a child, studied and handled them, though in civilian life, she typically observed the poisonous snakes from a respectful distance when she encountered them, and didn't try to pick them up. As an adult, she has immersed herself in every detail of their care, feeding, proper handling, venom, and treatment for bites. Using her employee training benefits, she registered for night classes at Mercer's Atlanta campus, eventually earning a degree in zoology, with a concentration in herpetology, and now, regularly gives talks at schools, churches, civic groups, nature centers, and scout troops, on how to interact with reptiles found in the environment. A popular feature of her talks is when she handles copperheads, cottonmouths, or rattlers.

She's been bitten by every type of snake at least once whilst working in this capacity, so regular injections of antivenins against the most common types of snakes in her area is a common precaution. Each one comes with differing levels of severity, from copperheads (whose bite causes immense pain and swelling in adults, but usually not death) to Eastern Diamondbacks, which are the deadliest type of snake found in Georgia. She's also become the person everyone in her neighborhood calls if a snake shows up.

Most of what she deals with near her home are garters or brown snakes. But occasionally, a copperhead will come along, and Charlotte has put the word out to contact her when in doubt, and not engage or harm the snake unless immediate personal safety is an issue, or unless someone gets bitten. She is especially notified in those cases, sometimes at odd hours of the day or night. While most of the local snakes are not dangerous to humans, they can be scary when they suddenly pop up, and even non-venomous bites aren't exactly fun. Whenever she's outside, Charlotte has taken to wearing high top, military-style boots, reinforced in the areas most vulnerable to a strike. She's passed along to Izzy and Brian the same level of respect and caution in dealing with the environment.

For her talks, Charlotte usually spends half her time outlining the typical types of creatures found in the area and shows slides of some of the species she's dealt with in the wild. Always nearby are the cages with the live reptiles in them; there's always a reaction whenever the rattler makes its distinctive sound. She always saves the dangerous snakes for last, and usually limits the time she handles them, both for her protection and to lessen the stress on the snake. There's always an assistant with her, who'll have a snake around his or her neck, and Charlotte often walks around with non-lethal reptiles, to give people the opportunity to touch them, or see them up close depending on comfort level.

When she's ready to bring out the poisonous snakes, she recites a list of rules, which include cautioning people to remain seated, to not approach her, to take no flash photos, to avoid sudden movements, and to never attempt to handle such a snake on their own. At those times, her assistant puts away the other snake, and assumes a watchful stance between her and the audience. They also make sure that the assistant, usually a young man, stands in front of her and a few feet away to point out features of the snake while Charlotte handles it. That way, if anyone should ignore the rules, the assistant can act as a buffer.

Consequently, Charlotte is a popular guest whenever it's Ishmael's turn to a bring a parent to class for career day. She never brings lethal creatures with her on informal visits to the school, focusing more on educating the children on the type of reptiles they'll most likely encounter, and instilling in them a proper respect for the environment and the creatures who live there. She brings common reptiles, such as Anole lizards, whilst enlightening kids on fascinating facts, like how the lizard can detach its tail to escape a predator and grow a new one.

Suffice it to say, she's not fond of snake-handling religions, which, in addition to endangering humans, will also sometimes mistreat the snakes. While the church she and her family attended when she was growing up was a mainstream Baptist denomination, Charlotte has cousins who are Pentecostal, and part of their worship involves snake handling. Once, while visiting them as a child, Brian dissuaded her from handling the snakes; but also told her, if she was moved to do so, she should use the same basket as the pastor, as those were most likely to have been milked beforehand. What frightened her most about the experience was not the presence of the snakes, but what she perceived as the out of control fervor of those handling them.

Her expertise has brought her in contact with the Apostolic Awakening Fellowship, which, in recent years, sometimes uses "serpents" in presentations during their worship services. Her visits with them are always in an official capacity, and when dealing with them, she frequently has to hold her tongue, given the church's outspoken views against homosexuals. Despite this, she has found the pastor, Mother Avis, sincere in her interest in properly housing and handling the creatures, and her desire to not harm them in the practice of their faith. Only senior congregants with the proper training are allowed to interact with the snakes, and they are kept a safe distance from others in the worship services.

After learning the pleasant young woman from the Forestry

Service, who sometimes repeats the things people say, is also a singer in a band, Mother Avis mentions the possibility of them performing at the church. Not certain Echo's music would fit with the church's stated mission, Charlotte leaves a copy of one of their albums for Mother Avis to review. The topic is never again raised when Charlotte is visiting.

Ishmael Branch enters the hallway at Tucker High School where his home room is, and strides toward his locker. At fourteen, he's already over six feet, taller than his uncle Brian, though with his head and shoulders slumped, as usual, it's not always easy to tell. Looking at his well-worn jeans, motorcycle boots, and Neil Young T-shirt under a knotted-at-the-waist flannel shirt, one might imagine he's a grunge rocker from Seattle in the early '90s, rather than a high school freshman in Tucker, Georgia in 2011. A backpack is slung over one shoulder, and the hard case he carries houses an expensive Martin acoustic guitar. His hair is styled in dreads and, even at his young age, he's managed to grow a thin mustache with a soul patch.

Halfway to his locker, he passes Midori Collins, leaning against hers, intensely staring at her cell phone while she texts. Without looking up or otherwise acknowledging Ishmael, she pushes away from the locker and falls into step with him. Midori is at least a foot shorter than Ishmael, with black, frizzy hair and a deep olive complexion. He and Midori have dated since seventh grade, but they've been friends since his family moved across the street from hers while he was a child.

In addition to going out, they play music together and have performed as a duo at school recitals since they were young children. When they perform together, she stands at the mic and either recites her original poems or sings and plays the flute, while he accompanies her on an acoustic guitar or mandolin. Her voice in this context, is a sweet soprano with an ethereal quality to it. When she performs with the occasional bands they join, she takes on more of a Riot Grrl or noise rock style that's been compared to Miho Hatori or Kathleen Hanna. In addition to her original songs, she's known for performing covers of Patti Smith, Yoko Ono, and Cibo Matto. Academically, her favorite subject is chemistry.

"I guess you have band practice after school," Ishmael says.

"Hmm," Midori says in an affirmative manner.

"If you're up for vegetarian, Mom invited you over for dinner," he goes on.

"Sounds good," she says without looking up.

"Is that Jordan?" he says.

"Pics from the Cake show at Variety Playhouse," she says.

They stop at his locker and he sets the guitar case down and swings his backpack off his shoulder and onto the ground.

"Got your English homework?" she says, still engrossed in her phone.

"Of course," he says.

As he's switching out the books in his bag, a group of guys, led by Jeff Chambers, a pitcher on the baseball team come around the corner. Seeing Ishmael, one of the guys says, "Hey, it's the Axe Man."

Since the case for the Martin is too large to fit in a locker, whenever Ishmael has it with him, he has to carry it around from class to class. This has prompted certain of his older classmates to refer to him as the "Axe Man".

"Hey Axe Man, you going to let me play your guitar?" Jeff says. The guys with him start to snicker.

"This guitar is worth more than that car you drive," Ishmael says.

"Mommy buy it for you?" one of Jeff's cohorts says.

"No," Ishmael says. "A friend gave it to me for my birthday."

Another of the guys says to Midori, "Hey, is your uncle really Lil Ace?"

Midori rolls her eyes and looks at her phone. "Of course." She makes several finger swipes then holds it up, with a photo of her with her uncle Avery. "That's from last Thanksgiving."

The group looks at it and one says, "Whoa!"

Discussing this among themselves, the group starts to move on. Ishmael calls after them. "Hey, Jeff, when are tryouts?"

"Why are you asking about tryouts?" Jeff says. He holds up his right hand and flutters his fingers. "You want to be like me, Axe Man?"

"So what? You throw a baseball," Ishmael says. "I can throw a baseball."

"Think so?" Jeff says. "Tryouts start Monday."

Once the baseball players are gone, Midori says, "You're really trying out for the baseball team?"

"Why not?" Ishmael says. "Mom agreed my grades are good enough."

"Why would you want to be on the team with those assholes?"

she asks.

"To show them I can," he says.

The following Monday, Ishmael arrives at the field for tryouts. An assistant coach has one list for the returning players, and a sign-in sheet for newcomers. Jeff Chambers is standing near the dugout as Ishmael heads over to the area designated for infielders. He calls out, "Hey Axe Man, where's your axe?"

"Today, I deal in strikes," Ishmael says.

Coach Lloyd Murdoch introduces himself to the new players. He's a man in his early forties, trim and well-built, wearing a cap, a team T-shirt, with an unzipped warmup jacket over it, with the sleeves pulled up. He gives a short talk about his team philosophy, then tells the players to take their desired positions on the field. He points to Ishmael. "What are you here to try out for, son?"

"I'm not your son," Ishmael says, which elicits a look of surprise from the coach. "I'm here to pitch."

"All right, then," the coach says, amused. "I see you brought your own glove. The mound is yours."

As Ishmael walks to the mound, the coach puts on an umpire mask and moves behind the plate. He indicates the catcher. "Jerry's your catcher." He signals to a large guy with a bat, who's approaching the plate. "Ron here's our best hitter. Let's see if you can get a few by him."

"No problem," Ishmael says. He takes some signals from the catcher, then goes into his wind up, and releases the ball. The batter swings, but the only sound is the pop of the ball hitting the catcher's mitt, followed by the catcher howling as he rips off the glove and grabs his hand.

"Damn!" he screams. "Put some heat on that one."

The coach takes off the mask and walks over and picks up the ball. He shakes his head. "Right down the middle, Ron. You couldn't hit that?"

"Hit what?" Ron says.

Coach Murdoch picks up the mitt and places it on his hand. "Take five Jerry. Go ice that hand." He tosses the ball back to Ishmael. "Let's see you do that again."

He crouches down, and nods to the batter, who returns to the plate. Ishmael winds up and delivers several fast balls. Ron manages a foul tip and a line drive straight back to the pitcher, which Ishmael bobbles a bit getting out of his glove, but just misses getting to first in time. This time, as he throws the ball back, the coach says, "You got speed, no doubt about it. Show me some finesse."

Ishmael nods. This time, his pitch is slower, but wobbles erratically in the air and curves away from the batter. Murdoch dives sideways to make the catch then stands with the ball in his glove. "Where'd you learn to throw a knuckleball?"

Ishmael shrugs. "My uncle took me to a clinic with Phil Niekro once."

"Just once?" the coach says.

He has Ishmael run through his pitching repertoire and Ishmael shows him his slow curve, changeup, and slider. Ron connects with several pitches, but overall Murdoch is highly impressed by what he sees. He notes the best and worst of Ishmael's pitches, mentally taking notes for improvement.

Afterward, he asks, "Are you as serious about baseball as I hear you are about playing your guitar?"

"Yes, sir," Ishmael says.

"Welcome to the team," the coach says, extending his hand.

As Ishmael walks off the field, Jeff Chambers says, "Good arm, Axe Man. You're going to have to show me that knuckleball sometime."

Ishmael nods with a smile. "Maybe, someday."

When Ike learns Ishmael has made the baseball team at school, he bugs Ned about taking him to see his brother play. Ned's work schedule usually prevents him from being available for weekend games, so it isn't until Izzy is pitching relief in an afternoon game, while the Braves are out of town, that Ned finally has time to take the whole family over to Tucker one Saturday. Ishmael gets called in around the seventh inning and handles himself well enough to stay until the end, allowing only one fly ball to shallow center, which the shortstop handles. Afterward, the Branches head over to the house in Avondale Estates. It's the first time in a while that the whole family has visited the Sangers at their home, and Ike spends a good deal of time in the back yard, feeding the chickens and quizzing Ted about being in the Army.

John Isaac Branch takes more after his mother's side of the family than his father's, and by age eleven, is average height for his age, stocky, and has so far demonstrated none of his father's athletic prowess, showing no real ability in football, baseball, or soccer. A very friendly young man, he's regarded as scholarly and bookish, joining the Chess and Audio-visual Clubs. When he comes home one afternoon, announcing his interest in getting involved in a sport, Ned's hopes are raised, only to discover the sport is fencing, but Ike takes to it with a passion and exhibits a real talent for it.

Ned's family back home, especially Eddie, Jr., is constantly telling Ned he needs to "toughen that boy up" but despite their criticism, Ned and Ike get along well and Ned is determined to let Ike chart his own course. While he has no interest in playing, Ike enjoys watching football and baseball, and loves the frequent trips he takes with Ned and Ishmael to see the Braves, Falcons, and Hawks, especially since his father can often get them into the player areas with his press credentials. An avid reader, Ike enjoys mystery and true crime books, and can often recall minute details of the cases he's read about. (Lindsay, who otherwise encourages Ike's sundry interests, has cautioned him against talking about especially gory cases at the dinner table. Doing so upsets his sister, Ansley — especially when younger sister Kait, who takes after Ike, joins in.)

Ishmael does his best to support Ike's athletic pursuits, and he and Midori get Charlotte to drive them to one of Ike's fencing matches one Sunday. Ike greets them at the tournament wearing his chest protector and breeches. He explains that his chief weapon is the foil (though, in his excitement, forgets to explain exactly what that is) and lets them know where in the lineup he's scheduled, then heads back to be with the team. Charlotte, Midori, and Ishmael sit with Lindsay and Kaitlyn, and Lindsay explains that Ned and Ansley are at a father/daughter outing with her Sunday school class.

Ishmael finds it difficult to follow the matches, some of which are over before he's had time to really get into the action. Each competitor makes a few passes, then someone gets a hit and the action stops for a moment. When Ike's name is announced, Ishmael and Midori lean forward to pay closer attention. Ike acquits himself well, but his competitor wins the match. Afterward, though, he's upbeat, focusing on a couple of good hits he made.

Ned's out of town for the game where Ishmael makes his debut as a starter, and Charlotte has to work, so Brian brings Swish and Lee Raines to the game to provide moral support. Ishmael starts out well, pitching five shut-out innings and showing good control and confidence on the mound. With two outs in the bottom of the sixth, he suffers a few jitters when he gives up a base hit, then quickly falls behind the count with the next batter and seems to founder about, taking longer than average to ready himself. Murdoch senses his pitcher is in trouble and signals to the bullpen for a reliever to start warming up.

When his next pitch goes high, making the count three zero, Ishmael shakes his head in frustration, then pulls off his glove and drops it beside the mound. Murdoch calls from the dugout, "Branch, what are you doing?"

Ishmael ignores him, flips the ball into his left hand and takes his ready position from the opposite side of the mound. The catcher looks confused at first, but gives Ishmael several signals, until Ishmael sees the sign he likes. He then delivers a sizzling fast ball that breezes past the batter, who swings, but way too late. Murdoch says, "Lord o' Mercy" and those in the dugout rise and press against the fencing to get a better look. Ishmael sends two more fast balls by the batter to end the inning then picks up his glove and heads off the field.

As he's headed into the dugout, Murdoch stops him and says, "Why didn't you tell me you could do that?"

"You didn't ask," Ishmael says.

The following week at practice, Ishmael begins working with the pitching coach to cultivate this skill.

Early in 2011, Ned tests the waters on a run for the House of Representatives. Hearing of his intentions, Mother Avis promises him the full support of Apostolic Awakening and invites him to attend a "traditional values summit" the church is planning for the square in Duluth for the Spring to help build up his profile among potential voters. The man Ned has tapped to run his campaign, Lonnie Jenkins, is a bulldog of a conservative political consultant, with a buzzcut hairstyle, a firm handshake, and a straight-forward, intense manner of dealing with those he serves. Lonnie agrees it's a good idea to keep Ned's name fresh in everyone's mind, even if it's just as a local celebrity and not an official candidate.

As speculation mounts that he'll seek office, a problem that dogged him during his time with the Falcons resurfaces. Throughout his football career rumors followed Ned around that he has an illegitimate son, which Ned has neither confirmed nor denied. Lonnie thinks the best way to address that is to get the topic out there but control how people interpret it.

Ike invites Ishmael and Midori to the event and Lindsay picks them up from Doraville MARTA station the morning of the rally. For Midori, it's a chance to see her aunt Avis up close. While she's always been close to her Aunt Annie, Avis has been estranged from the family since Midori was a child. She has brought a homemade lunch, with a paring knife to slice up the tomatoes, carrots and cucumbers from her family's garden. Ike, Midori, and Ishmael spend the morning wandering around the grounds until early afternoon, when the speakers are ready to start. Ned is scheduled later in the afternoon.

The trio works their way into the lively crowd and settle about fifty or sixty feet from the stand. Mother Avis comes to the podium and welcomes everyone with a rousing come to Jesus speech, which gets the crowd pumped up. She introduces Lonnie Jenkins, who's represented as a close friend of Ned's, who came to talk about his career on the field and off. He highlights Ned's work in the community, and calls him a great husband and father, then takes on a more serious tone.

"Now I know some of you have heard the rumors floating around about some of the skeletons in his closet, and let me say, even if they're true, it doesn't take away from the kind of man Ned is," Lonnie says. "We all have those youthful indiscretions in our past we'd rather not have to be reminded of, am I right?" The crowd roars with approval.

Midori looks at Ishmael, who's becoming agitated as the speech goes on.

Lonnie continues, "He's only human. For instance, what's a typical red-blooded man supposed to do, say, when some little honey starts shaking her tail in his face? Chasing him around like some," he pauses and chuckles, "well, considering the crowd, I'll say some little female dog in heat?" Once again, the crowd reacts heartily.

"He's talking about your Mom," Ike says.

Ishmael reacts angrily. "That bastard!" Midori grabs Ishmael's arm to prevent him from rushing the stage, then takes a leftover tomato from her pack and hands it to him. He looks at it. "What am I supposed to do with this?"

"You're a pitcher," she says. "Pitch."

Ishmael grins and nods, then gives the tomato a good squeeze, and rushes forward as he yells, "My mother's not a whore, you asshole." He hurls the tomato like a fastball at Jenkins, which hits him squarely in the face. Jenkins falls back, disoriented, then collapses onstage. The crowd seems stunned, then some start booing. Some who are nearby grab Ishmael to prevent him from getting away.

"Whoa!" Ike says. "Took him right out."

Midori turns to Ike. "Get out of here, Ike. Find your Mom." He nods and disappears into the crowd. Midori goes to assist Ishmael, leaping into the middle of the men holding him swinging her fists.

Pandemonium ensues, with Mother Avis, mistaking the remnants of the tomato for blood, loudly shrieking, "Lord help us!" as members of her security detail hustle her off the stage. Others, accompanied by county police, head into the crowd to intercept Ishmael, who, with Midori's help, seems about to escape from the people trying to detain him. Officers surround them, and both are handcuffed. One of the guys in the security detail takes Midori's pack and removes the paring knife and holds it up to show the officers. Reporters gather as they're being led away and start shouting questions at Ishmael and Midori.

"My name is Ethan Ishmael Branch," he yells at them. "Ned Branch is my father. You want confirmation? Here I am."

The police take Ishmael and Midori to county headquarters. Ike finds Lindsay and reports what happened, and she phones Charlotte and Midori's family. About an hour later, Alfred shows up at headquarters to retrieve Midori.

"The officers say they're not sure what you did, other than fighting with those people, which I told them was self-defense, so they're releasing you to my custody," he tells her. "They were concerned about the knife, but since you had vegetables in the bag, I convinced them you didn't mean any harm with it."

"I don't want to leave Ishmael here," she says.

"Ishmael is in a whole mess of trouble, young lady," Alfred says. "The man he assaulted is pressing charges. He could be looking at some serious jail time. Some of the witnesses are calling him a domestic terrorist."

While they're speaking, Mother Avis arrives to give her statement. Seeing Alfred, she walks over, but maintains several feet of space between them.

"Alfred," she says with a nod. "I didn't expect to see you here. It's been a while."

"Avis," he replies, coolly. Indicating Midori, Alfred continues,

"We're still living in Avondale. I'm here to pick up my daughter — your niece, Midori. Remember her?"

"Hello, child," Avis says, shooting a quick glance in Midori's direction.

Noting the tension, one of her assistants hurries over. "Mother Avis is everything okay?"

"Everything's fine," Avis says.

Alfred waits for Avis to say something more and when she doesn't, he says, "I'm her brother. This is her niece."

"Oh," the assistant says and starts to move away. "Well, I'll just—"

"No, no. That's quite all right," Avis says. "We're done here."

She leads the assistant away.

"So that's Aunt Avis," Midori says.

"That's Avis," Alfred says.

Charlotte arrives and speaks to Alfred about what happened. At Midori's insistence, Alfred agrees to stick around for moral support. Charlotte talks to the sergeant to get a full report and find out how much trouble Ishmael's in.

Avis sees her and walks over. "Miss Sanger. It's a nice surprise to see you here. I trust all is well."

"Well, well, well. Everything will be fine, Mother Avis, when I can walk out of here with my son."

"Are you referring to the young man who disrupted our rally?" Avis says.

"Yeah, I think so. He's my son, Ishmael," Charlotte says.

Avis puts her hand on Charlotte's shoulder. "I'm afraid he's going to be in some trouble. But, if there's anything I can do to lessen it, I'll try."

"Try, try. Thanks, Mother Avis."

Ned arrives and, seeing him, Charlotte marches over and glares at him. "Fix this!"

"And a pleasant afternoon to you, too, Charlotte," Ned says. He acknowledges Avis.

"Charlotte, Charlotte, Charlotte — don't make a joke out of this, Ned. You need to call off your goon. Police say he's pressing charges. I don't blame Izzy one bit for what he did, if what I've heard from your other son is true."

"Yeah, sorry about that," Ned says. "That wasn't part of his scripted remarks. It may not be that simple, but I'll see what I can do."

Ned goes over to where Jenkins, his nose bandaged, is giving a statement. "How you doing, sergeant? Wonder if I might have a few words with Mr. Jenkins?"

The sergeant seems a bit star struck at seeing Ned then nods and steps away, after getting Ned to autograph his notepad. Ned takes his seat and leans toward Jenkins. "Lonnie, I'm going to need you to drop the charges on this."

Jenkins looks at Ned in disbelief. With much difficulty he says, "That maniac hit me in the face with a tomato and called me an asshole."

"You are an asshole, Lonnie," Ned says. "That's why I pay you. That maniac is my son, okay. From what I hear, you went a bit off-script and said some nasty things about his Mom. That was not part of the strategy we discussed. Trust me when I say, if you think he's a terror, you don't want to have to deal with Charlotte." He nods his head toward the seething woman several yards away. "It took all I could muster to keep her from coming over here and pleading her case in person."

Jenkins looks in her direction and suddenly seems a bit frightened. Even with this, it takes quite a bit of convincing on Ned's part, including the offer of a generous raise and an extended vacation to anywhere Lonnie wants to recuperate, just so long as he leaves right away.

Ten or fifteen minutes later, Ned's back with Charlotte. "Lonnie's been contained, and Avis is willing to have a talk with her security detail and will do what she can to spin the situation with her congregation, but the police are still saying they take potential terrorism very seriously and may go ahead and charge Ishmael anyway. If so, it could become a federal case."

"Case, case, case. Handle it. Or I'm going to hit the airwaves tonight with the whole story. That wouldn't sit very well with the voters in your district I imagine."

"I imagine not." Ned takes out his phone and dials a number. "Hey, Judge Bartholomew, Ned Branch here. How you doing? I'm doing fine; thanks for asking. Listen, I've got a situation over here at the Gwinnett Police, and I need to see if you could work a little magic with the district attorney for me."

Ned steps into an empty interrogation room and closes the door. Twenty or so minutes pass before he emerges and gives Charlotte a thumbs up. "Izzy's going to need to apologize and swear never to be caught brandishing tomatoes in Gwinnett County again, but I managed to get the state's attorney to classify this as a protest which went awry, not a terroristic act. It took some convincing to get him to see a tomato as free speech, but it's all good."

Charlotte nods then points at Ned. "You tell that employee of yours that if I hear he's made any more statements about my character, a tomato will be the least of his worries."

"I think he got the message," Ned says.

Sometime later, Ishmael is brought out, accompanied by an officer. Charlotte hurries to him and hugs him. She takes him over to Avis, introduces him, then pokes him in the ribs with her elbow, and says, "Apologize."

Izzy does as he's told.

"So, this is Ishmael," Avis says. "Arise, lift up the lad, and hold him fast with your hand; for I will make him a great nation." Rubbing his right arm, she goes on, "You have quite an arm, young man. Please don't ever come to anymore of our rallies."

"No problem there, ma'am," Ishmael says. "I'm done with politics."

Avis turns to go and along the way stops to say to Ned. "Mr. Branch, please stop by the church on Monday. We have a lot to discuss."

"No doubt," Ned says. "I'll see you around three."

"That will be fine," she says.

Ned goes to Ishmael and Charlotte. "Izzy, I understand what motivated this, but there was a better way to handle it."

"You're probably right," he replies.

"Now's obviously not the time but sounds like we have a lot to talk about," Ned went on. "I've got some explaining to do myself."

"I agree," Charlotte says. "You need to keep this quiet. I don't want to hear either of our names on the news."

"I'll do what I can," Ned says with a sigh.

Since it was a local church gathering with political overtones, none of the news stations sent camera crews, except Channel 46, which had the correspondent do some local color reporting early on then sent the crew to cover a pile-up on 285. Reports from those on the scene about the disruption become almost impossible to corroborate. The public relations fellowship at Apostolic Awakening issues a statement to the press that some protesters crashed the gathering and were handled and that contrary to rumors, no one was injured in the incident.

Ned's office releases a statement in support of "every American's right to protest, so long as it's peaceful" and Lonnie Jenkins leaves for an extended vacation out of state. Parishioners who claimed to have captured video of the incident disavow all knowledge when reporters follow up with them, and instead complain their religious freedom is being violated by the inquiries. Within forty-eight hours, no mention of it appears on local or national news.

The following Tuesday, Ned, accompanied by Lindsay and Mother Avis, holds a press conference to confirm that when he was a teenager, he had a relationship with a classmate he refuses to name to protect her privacy, and that the relationship resulted in the birth of a son. While he regrets the circumstances, he is not ashamed of the boy and he and the mother are still "good friends" and that "she's a fine person and an excellent mother".

One reporter with the Fox affiliate, acting on a tip, attempts to nose around at the Sanger residence in Avondale Estates, but as he steps onto the porch and before he can even ring the bell, the front door flies open, and Charlotte kicks open the screen with a Louisville Slugger over one shoulder. "Is there something I can help you with?"

The reporter flees and is never seen in the vicinity again.

Coach Lloyd Murdoch is a native of Savannah, Georgia, where his older brother, Anthony, taught him the basics of fielding and hitting. His father's job caused the family to move closer to Atlanta halfway through his time in elementary school, and Lloyd played baseball and ran track at West Georgia College, earning degrees in Physical Education and Biology, which he teaches at the schools where he's been employed. He's remained close with his brother, a big bear of a man who enjoys camping and hunting and works as a physical therapist in Tucker. A life-long bachelor, Lloyd enjoys barbecue, having a few beers with friends after work, and action-adventure films with Jason Statham. He takes his commitment to the young men he coaches seriously, and often uses his free time after school and on weekends to drop in at players' homes to learn more about them and get to know their families.

One Saturday, he heads over to a house in Avondale Estates, where Ishmael Branch is said to live. So far, Murdoch has yet to meet Ishmael's mother or father, though this isn't out of the ordinary, since some parents are too busy to attend games. He's heard Ishmael's mother sings with a band in addition to her full-time job. Rumors around school have indicated Ishmael was somehow connected to an incident at a church gathering in Gwinnett, and Murdoch wants to be certain Ishmael isn't just the target of a bullying campaign, since there's been almost no word in the press beyond a few, early, contradictory reports about the incident, which disappeared quickly from the news cycle.

Murdoch rings the doorbell, and a moment or so later, a young woman, seemingly in her early twenties, who seems familiar to Murdoch, answers. She's wearing no makeup, so Murdoch can see her freckles, and her long, light-red hair is braided into corn-rows. She's wearing a mid-length flannel house dress, with long sleeves, which she's rolled up to above her elbows. He recalls seeing her in the stands at games, and, noting a resemblance to Ishmael, Coach Murdoch assumes she's related, though Ishmael has never mentioned having a sister.

"Can I help you?" she says through the screen door, which she doesn't unlock. Her attitude seems guarded to Murdoch, and her voice bears traces of an accent Coach Murdoch recognizes from the Savannah area.

"Hi, I'm Coach Lloyd Murdoch from Tucker High," he says. "I'm here to see Mr. or Mrs. Branch."

"Branch, Branch, Branch," the young woman repeats, while tilting her head slightly left. She shakes her head and sighs in frustration. "What's Izzy done now?"

"Excuse me?" Coach Murdoch says.

"Izzy," she says. "My son. Ishmael. He's the only Branch lives here. I'm Charlotte Sanger."

Coach Murdoch stares at her in surprise. "Ah. You're Ishmael's mother. I apologize, ma'am. I'm coach of the baseball team. This is just a courtesy call. Ishmael is not in any trouble — as far as I know. I phoned yesterday and spoke to your husband, perhaps?"

"Husband, husband. That'd be a trick, considering I've never been married."

"I believe it was Brian," Lloyd says. "He sounded kind of busy and didn't mention exactly how he's related. We didn't talk long."

"Yeah, he's my brother," she says, as she unlocks the screen. "He's the other adult here." She opens the screen for him. "Come on in, Coach." Lloyd enters, and Charlotte closes and locks the door behind him.

"Sorry if I sounded a little suspicious," she says. "We've had some unwanted visitors the past few weeks." She motions for him to follow her. "We're in the kitchen."

Coach Murdoch notes she's wearing high-top, military boots with her knee-length dress. As they walk, she says, "The last time a high school coach visited me at my house, I almost ended up married."

"I'm sorry?" he says.

"Don't worry about it," she says as they enter the kitchen, Lloyd looks out through the large picture window and notices an older black man in the yard, tending to several chickens in a coop and stops to watch him. Charlotte notes his interest and glances outside. "That's Ted. The Chicken Man."

"Yes. Chickens," Lloyd says.

"He's a veteran," Charlotte says. "Comes from down around Statesboro near where we're from. His family owns a poultry business down there, so he helps us out with them. He's mainly retired but does some plumbing and electrical contracting for us."

Lloyd nods. "Statesboro. I thought you sounded like folks from that region. My family's originally from Savannah. We moved to Austell when I was in elementary school."

Charlotte motions to the table. "Small world. Have a seat, Coach." She goes to a door, opens it, leans in and yells, "Brian, we got company. Coach Murdoch."

From below, a man's voice answers, "Oh, yeah, he called yesterday."

"You don't say," she replies.

"Claire was here," Brian replies. "We were mixing the album."

"Album, album. Whatever."

"I'll be up directly," he says.

She closes the door and retrieves a coffee cup from the table and fills it. "Can I offer you some coffee, Coach? Just made a fresh pot."

"Yes, ma'am," he says.

She retrieves a cup and starts to pour. "Need any room for cream or sugar?"

"No, ma'am," he says.

"Man after my own heart," she says as she brings both cups to the table. She sits across from Lloyd. "Tell me something, Coach, how old a man are you?"

"I'm forty-one," he says. "Why?"

She nods. "Yeah. Well I'm thirty-two. No need to call me

ma'am. Charlotte's fine, or Ms. Sanger if you want to keep it formal."

"Not a problem, Charlotte," he says.

"Charlotte, Charlotte. Got you a wife at home?" she continues, with a bit of a smile.

"No, I'm happily unmarried, as they say," he replies.

"Probably just haven't met the right woman," she says with a wink. "Assuming that's what you're looking for."

"You assume correct," he replies.

There are footsteps on the basement stairs, and a moment later, a tall man with dark blonde hair which Lloyd guesses is Brian enters, wearing shorts, a tank top and flip-flops. He gives Lloyd a close look as he strides across to the table.

"Coach — Murdoch," he says, extending his hand. "Your name just registered with me. Are you related to Tony Murdoch?"

"He's my older brother," Lloyd says as they shake hands.

"I see the resemblance," Brian says. "He's the catcher on my baseball team. The Peaches."

"You're on The Peaches," Lloyd says. "You guys are a damn good team. A lot of great teamwork. Wish I had more opportunity to catch some games."

"Yeah, others in the league started out calling us The Sissy Boys," Brian says. "Now they call us division champs."

"I would not refer to my brother as a sissy boy," Lloyd says. "Certainly not to his face."

"Definitely not," Brian says. "Greatest shock for a lot of the other teams was finding out how many of their former teammates are gay."

He pours himself a cup of coffee and joins them at the table.

"Tony was very happy to find a team where he didn't feel like he had to hide that," Lloyd says.

"He talks about you enough," Brian says. "Definitely appreciates your support."

"I had some problems when he first came out, but I got over it," Lloyd says. "End of the day, he's still the big brother who defended me from the neighborhood bullies growing up and taught me how to field."

"Field, field, field." Charlotte takes a sip of coffee, then leans on the table. "The Coach here is from Savannah." Brian acknowledges this. "What's on your mind, Coach?"

"As I said, it's mainly just a courtesy call," Lloyd says. "But there have been some rumors circulating around school about

Ishmael's involvement in some sort of incident in Gwinnett a few weeks ago and I thought while I was here, I'd ask about it, just to be sure people weren't spreading stories about him."

Brian and Charlotte exchange a glance and nod. Charlotte says, "Yeah, that kind of got hushed up." She and Brian fill Lloyd in on Ishmael's background and the events at the rally.

"Then Ishmael is the son Ned Branch mentioned at his press conference," Lloyd says.

"Yeah, mentioned," Charlotte says. "I told him to keep our names out of the press. Enough about that. I don't suppose you came here to get mucked up in our family's politics. Let's all get to know one another."

They spend the remainder of the morning into the early afternoon talking, comparing notes about where they came from, and having a bite to eat. Ted joins them at one point, and Lloyd recalls visiting the family's poultry business once with his school. They spend several minutes discussing the Braves prospects for the season. Toward the afternoon, Ishmael comes in, accompanied by Midori Collins, and says, "Hey, Coach. What are you doing here?"

"Just getting to know your family a little better," Lloyd says.

Ishmael introduces Midori, then says to Charlotte, "Riku and Abe want to go to Stone Mountain. Is that okay?"

"What's going on at Stone Mountain?" Charlotte asks.

"Nothing," Ishmael says. "They just want to hang out. Maybe climb the mountain."

"No rallies or gatherings?" she asks.

"Of course not," he says.

"Not, not, not. Are you taking food?"

"Mom," he says with a sigh.

"Okay, I guess that will be fine," she says and kisses him on the cheek. "Have fun."

Ishmael and Midori leave.

Lloyd glances at his watch. "Oh. I have to be at my brother's in an hour."

Charlotte walks him back to the front door.

"I think I'm starting to have a better understanding of Ishmael," the Coach says.

Once they get to the porch, they take a long time saying their goodbyes and Lloyd seems hesitant to leave.

"There something else on your mind, Coach?" Charlotte says.

"Sorry if I'm being forward but would you like to have dinner some evening, Charlotte?"

"Dinner, dinner, dinner." Charlotte gives him a smile. "What you got in mind, Coach?"

"I know a great barbecue place near Clarkston. The ribs are excellent."

"Sorry, Coach, I'm a vegetarian," Charlotte says.

Lloyd lowers his head. "Ah. Not a problem."

She touches his arm. "Tell you what, why don't you let me take you to dinner?"

Lloyd perks up. "I'd like that."

"You got my number," Charlotte says. "Ring me up in a few days. We'll see what transpires."

One afternoon, after practice, Ishmael is changing in the locker room along with Ron, Jeff, and some other players.

"Hey Axe Man, I heard the coach is dating your mother," Jeff says.

"Yeah, he is," Ishmael says. "Couple of weeks now."

"That's weird," Jeff says.

"What do you mean, weird?" Ishmael says. "She's still young."

"No, I mean, just having him around," Jeff says.

"I'll get used to that," Ishmael says. "I'm just glad to see my Mom getting out. She works all the time or is performing."

Another player asks, "What does she do for work?"

"She's with the Forestry Service," Ishmael says. "She goes around to places and talks about reptiles."

"Like the Snake Lady?" Ron says.

"Yeah, she is the Snake Lady," Ishmael says.

"Your Mom's the Snake Lady?" Jeff says.

"She came and talked to my scout troop one year," Ron says. "Best guest we ever had."

The Martin guitar is sitting beside Ishmael on the floor. One of the other players indicates it and says, "How 'bout playing something on that guitar?"

Ishmael takes out the guitar. "Any requests?"

"How about Stevie Ray?" Jeff says.

Ishmael starts playing Scuttle Buttin'.

"Oh, yeah," another teammate says, then sits on a bench and starts tapping out a beat. The rest gather around to hear Ishmael.

For Thanksgiving that year, Charlotte and Brian invite their family from down South, and other friends and family from the area as well as any neighbors who might not have plans. The event has been described as informal and people are encouraged to stop in as they can with assurances that there will be plenty of food.

Brian invites some of his teammates from the Peaches, who drop in at different times throughout the day and Claire brings Rachel Lawson and Steven Asher and mentions some other friends might stop in. The Collins family is also hosting a get together and extend their welcome to anyone who wants to drop into their house as well as the Sangers, so there's a steady stream of visitors back and forth.

Charlotte won't allow meat to be cooked or stored inside the house, so Brian has a freezer on the back porch stocked with beef, poultry, and pork, all of which he cooks on a grill. Since Charlotte has been dating Lloyd, he's been contributing to Brian's supply —all of the above plus the occasional fresh venison he gets from Tony during hunting season. Tony's hunting is one of the few sore spots between him and Charlotte, who otherwise enjoys having him join the family on hiking or camping trips. Brian, Lloyd, Ted and Tony have the grill fired up well before the first guests arrive with a nice variety of meats. The only exception Charlotte makes to her "no meat" rule is for her mother, who always brings a cooked turkey or ham; Charlotte lets her warm it in the oven.

Since many of those in attendance are musical, the afternoon erupts into an impromptu jam session. Izzy plays guitar with his uncle Dexter, Manny, and Gloria Savage, and he and Midori perform with her on flute and singing. Charlotte teaches everyone some shape-note songs she's been working on, then hustles them into the basement and has Claire record them. Charlotte also insists she and her sisters, Emma and Beatrice record themselves singing harmonies which she and Brian can include on an upcoming album. Dexter lays down some guitar tracks for a song Brian's writing and their mother Amelia plays the pedal steel guitar. As is the custom with the Savages and their jams, Brian and Charlotte invite their non-family guests to spend the night if they don't feel like driving. The music goes on for hours.

Toward the end of the evening, Charlotte and Lloyd corral everyone in the living room for an announcement which most have been expecting.

"I don't think it's any secret Lloyd and I have been an item,"

Charlotte says. "Well it's official. He's asked me to marry him and I can't think of a good reason not to."

Charlotte's family welcomes Lloyd and Tony as in-laws. Ishmael, who already has one extended family, congratulates his mother and future stepfather.

Rain Maker

Leah Walker is seated in the reception area of the office of David Cairo (pronounced Kay-ro), an Atlanta venture capitalist who has doled out close to a billion dollars to entrepreneurs in recent years. She's been working as an independent contractor with firms around town starting in late-2001, after finishing up work on her second doctorate — in Internet and Web Security — from Georgia Tech. To drum up business, Leah hacked into the web servers of several of Atlanta's top companies, gathering facts which she used to compile dossiers on ways the companies could protect their Web assets. Her approach met with mixed reactions, with several companies threatening litigation and a few CEOs complaining to her father about the break-ins. Bickering Plummet, however, had been impressed enough to put Leah under contract to help them sort out their online security. She's also been working with them on contracts with the IRS and FDA.

While working with Bickering, Leah learned of the site where the government announces requests for proposals to perform work for them. Between assignments, she found an announcement from the National Security Agency (NSA) looking for a firm to develop methods for protecting the phone system in the event of a terrorist attack. A special stipulation is that the contract must go to a minority-owned or woman-owned business. That same day, Leah logged onto the Georgia Secretary of State's website for corporations, and registered "L. J. Walker Security, LLC" and then set out to secure financing.

In the mid-1990s, Cairo, an Atlanta native, like Leah, founded Cairo Enterprises, which he took public in 1997, during the high-tech boom that was transforming the economy. Overnight, he became a multi-billionaire, both exciting and confounding the business elite in the city. Due to his unorthodox style of management, Cairo has a strained history with the Buckhead business community — in particular, her father, Paxton.

Given this history, Leah is wary of dealing with him. On more than one occasion, while still CEO of his own firm, Cairo had been openly critical of Walker Development, Paxton's company, barely concealing his contempt for its role in transforming Atlanta from what Cairo termed "a quaint Southern city" into "a monstrosity of glass and steel with no soul or charm." Leah has heard such criticism about Walker Dev throughout her life, particularly after becoming an adult, but Cairo made it personal, going so far as to compare Paxton to General Sherman.

She arrived at 12:45 for a 1:00 appointment, and it's now 1:23. When she came in, the receptionist, Tracey McIntosh, buzzed Cairo to let him know Leah was here, receiving acknowledgement and thanks from Cairo. About twenty minutes later, she buzzed him again, and this time, her entreaty was met with a terse, "Acknowledged."

Tracey, who appears to be in her early-fifties and of mixed race, with — if Leah had to guess — a generous portion of Chinese or Korean as part of the mix, has been chatting with Leah.

"My husband is an electrical engineer and his firm contracted with Walker Development in the 80s," Tracey says. "We met once when you were a teenager."

"Really?" Leah says. "Where was this?"

"We were invited to Paxton's Christmas party one year. I believe it was just before your family moved to Lawrenceville."

Leah nods. "1985. I met a lot of people that year, Andrew Young, Marvin Arrington, Sam Massell."

Paxton's Christmas parties, which served the duel function of thanking his staff for a job well done and advertising his business, were once considered "must-attend" events on Atlanta's social calendar each year. Invitation-only, those who were included always found themselves among the elite politicians and business owners in town. The events came to an abrupt halt the year after Leah's mother died and Paxton retired from the day-to-day operation of his business in order to raise Leah's sister, Alyssa.

"I was so sorry to hear when Melinda died," Tracey says. "I didn't know her well, but she was always such a sweet lady."

"Yes, she was," Leah says.

Tracey looks at the clock and says, "If he doesn't call you in soon, I'll go in and drag him out."

Leah acknowledges this. "Don't worry about it. I didn't expect this to be easy."

The intercom buzzes, and Cairo's voice comes through the speaker. "Tracey, I have this nagging feeling that I have an appointment scheduled."

Tracey looks up at Leah, shakes her head, then punches the button. "L. J. Walker is still waiting to see you. Her appointment was for 1 p.m. She's been sitting here since a quarter 'til."

"L. J. Walker?" Cairo replies with a note of surprise in his voice. "You don't mean Leah Walker, do you? Dr. Leah Joanna Walker, Ph.D.?"

"Yes, Mr. Cairo," Tracey says.

"Why was I not informed of this?" Cairo says.

"I've notified you twice that she's here," Tracey says.

"This is outrageous," Cairo says. Movement can be heard in his office, then his door flies open. He appears, then throws both hands over his mouth, wearing a look of consternation.

The man who greets Leah appears to be in his late-thirties to early-forties with brown, shoulder-length hair that's pushed back from his face without the benefit of a comb. He's dressed in jeans and a buttoned down, striped, Arrow shirt, untucked, with the sleeves rolled up, and looks like he hasn't shaved in a few days.

Cairo fixes his gaze on Leah. "Dr. Walker, my deepest apologies for this appalling oversight." He goes to her, bowing deferentially, "If only I had known you were waiting."

Cairo spins about and points at Tracey, and, in mock outrage, says, "Clean out your desk, Tracey. You're done here."

"Yes, Mr. Cairo," she says blandly, and begins removing items from her drawers. Catching Leah's eye, she twirls her finger beside her head, and mouths, "Crazy."

"Please, please, Dr. Walker," he says, indicating his office. "Please join me in my office."

He leads Leah into his office, closes the door, and indicates the chair in front of his desk. "Make yourself comfortable, Doctor." As he moves behind his desk, he goes on, "Now, do you go by Dr. Walker or Dr. Doctor Walker?"

"Doctor's fine," Leah says with a bit of a sigh. Although to his credit, it had been a whole week and a half since she'd heard that one.

Cairo sits and folds his hands on the desk. "You understand, Doctor, that I'm taking quite a risk in meeting with you, given that litigation is still pending against you from a certain soft drink manufacturer in town."

"We're in a cooling down period," she says. "Which is all I'm at liberty to say on the matter at this time."

"The pause that mediates," he says dramatically. "I must say, Doctor, your exploits have been very thrilling to follow. Bickering's IT chief almost lost his job over the whole affair, and all you did was play a few parlor tricks on them."

"In retrospect, I probably should have handled a few things differently."

"Bet Daddy Leroy didn't take it well, did he?" he says, using Paxton's hated first name.

"He was a little annoyed. I got called on the carpet by him after he had to field some calls. But, to his credit, he told them they should hire me."

"Speaking of dear old Dad, I must say, I was very surprised to see you'd scheduled an appointment with me. You're not upset that I compared your father to Sherman?"

"Actually, I thought that was pretty funny — and kind of justified."

"Damn right it was." He leans forward and points at her. "Because of your father, we don't have the Fox Theater anymore."

Leah shakes her head. "That wasn't Dad."

"It wasn't?" Cairo says.

"No. That firm was a coalition of two groups that called itself The Fox Development Corp. Walker Dev only did some renovations for them in the 80s. Dad did want to level Rhodes Hall, but the backlash from the Fox put a stop to that."

"Oh, right," he says, "the hunk of junk. Forgot all about that."

"Wait. You owned Fox Tower in the late-90s. That's how Bickering ended up with it. Why are you complaining?"

"Not buying that building wasn't going to bring the Fox back. Besides, it's the tallest building in the city, and I got it for a song after the management group went bankrupt. At least I had them restore the Egyptian Room on the mezzanine."

"True," Leah says. "That was a nice touch, I'll admit."

They both sit and consider this a moment. Finally, Cairo sits up and says, "Oh well, enough pleasantries. Why are you here? Daddy Leroy wouldn't cough up enough funds for you?"

"I didn't ask my father for money," she says. "I don't discuss my business plans with him."

"He doesn't know you're here, does he?" Cairo asks. Leah shakes her head. Cairo claps his hands together and says, "He is going to go ballistic when he hears about this."

Leah rolls her eyes. "Probably."

"That, alone, will earn you a seat at the head of the class," he says. "How much do you want? I'll cut you a check this instant."

"Don't you want to see my business plan first?" Leah says, lifting her briefcase into her lap.

"No need for such trivialities. I know you've done your homework." He puts his feet up on his desk and says, "They don't hand out a Ph.D. from Tech or MIT for participation. I'd estimate that watching the fallout from this would be worth at least five hundred thousand."

"Glad to be able to provide you with such entertainment, but that's way more than I need," Leah says.

Cairo waves dismissively. "Nonsense. It's a drop in the bucket. You'll need space, furniture — computers. You need to show you can walk the walk. People pay more for the illusion of competence."

"That's how you wowed them wasn't it?" Leah says.

"Idiots. Every single one," he says. "Paying us millions of dollars to 'establish our web presence' when all they had to do was hire a few high school kids with some HTML coding under their belts."

"I still can't believe you got away with it," she says. "The World Wide Web was the greatest cyber-swindle of all time."

He removes his feet from the desk and swivels around, then leans on the desk. "Let's cut to the chase, shall we? You're here because you want to compete for the NSA contract, but you don't want it to look like Daddy's buying it for you as a graduation present."

"I wouldn't put it like that," she replies, "but yes, I do want that contract."

"How much of your soul are you willing to sell for it?"

"Did you really just ask me that question?"

"As Bobby Zimmerman says, you've got to serve somebody," he says. "This is where we get down to the brass tacks and find out what L. J. is really made of."

"What exactly does that mean?" she says.

"I do my homework, too," he says. "The only reason you're sitting there is because you think I'll just cough up some cash to tweak Daddy Leroy's nose."

"That thought may have crossed my mind."

"Of course, it did." He shakes his finger at her. "You're very calculating — Dr. Rosales."

Leah is surprised. When she first returned from MIT, she worked for her father's company using her mother's maiden name so no one would discover her connection to Paxton. "Rosales? How do you know about that?"

His voice slips into a rustic Southern accent as he says, "Why you've been on my RADAR for quite some time little lady." He rises and returns to his normal voice. "You put forth this veneer of independence, man-tailored suits, avoiding Daddy's financing network, but when you got back to town and needed a job, where'd you turn?"

"You have done your homework."

"A Ph.D. from the Massachusetts Institute of Technology would open any door you needed open, but you just couldn't resist that legacy Georgia Tech enrollment, could you? Daddy got his master's there, so you had to do him one better." He circles her. "All these years and you're still trying to prove yourself worthy of his affection."

Leah becomes annoyed and says, "Is this all part of your usual screening process or am I getting an extra dose of abuse?"

"Oh yes," he says, "I've been aware of you for quite some time, L. J. Don't think it didn't cross my mind to take a crack at the attractive daughter of one of my fiercest rivals."

Leah starts nodding. "Here we go. I wondered when it was coming."

"You want my money, you can have as much as you need, but everything comes with a price." Cairo goes to the window and motions toward the city's skyline. "All this I will give unto you if you will but bow down and worship me."

Leah shakes her head. "I knew it was a mistake coming here." She picks up her briefcase, rises, and starts to leave.

"Oh, Dr. Doctor, are you really going to walk away from all this opportunity? What would Daddy Leroy say to that?"

Leah spins around. "You know — you sit there behind that desk in your jeans and sneakers and try to pretend like — like you're some sort of maverick. But you know what you really are? You're just like every other asshole I've ever had to deal with in this business — just a — just a wolf in casual dress."

"Some of my best friends are wolves."

"Crawl back into whatever hell you came out of. I don't need anything this much."

Cairo claps his hands together loudly. "At last! She makes an appearance. The warrior I was expecting would walk in here."

Leah gives him a curious stare. "What are you talking about?"

"Your reputation among the IT crowd is the stuff of legend," he says. "Do you have any idea what the men you work for grumble about you behind your back?"

"I doubt it could be much worse than what they say to my face."

"I hear what the law prevents them from saying to your face. Chief security officers indiscriminately using the c-word. Very ungentlemanly. Do you really think they just ran out of work on your last assignment for the FDA? The director himself threatened to cancel the entire contract if you stayed on."

"I suspected it was something like that," she says. "It wasn't my most pleasant work experience."

"And yet you do not change, and you will not compromise," Cairo says. "Know what I've hated about some of the women I had as supervisors throughout my tenure as a working-class stooge? They couldn't delegate. They'd give me a job and were constantly watching over my shoulder to make sure I was doing it the way they wanted it done regardless of whether or not the process affected the outcome. Of course, my view is probably skewed since most of my supervisors were women. There was one, though. Lisa Portnoy — Summers, now I understand. She was at Bickering when I worked there."

Leah nods. "She's still there. We've worked together."

"Too bad for her," he says. "She deserves better. Totally at ease wielding authority. Compassionate, but she could delegate."

"I've encountered my share of micromanagers, too," she says. "I'd say the split is more fifty-fifty male to female. And most of my supervisors have been men."

"But from all I've heard you do not micromanage — and when you tell someone to get something done you expect it to get done in whatever way is necessary. Pity the poor fool who tests you."

Cairo motions to the chair. "Please have a seat, Doctor. Let's start over, this time eye to eye, as colleagues." Leah hesitates, then takes her seat again. "Everyone's salivating over that NSA contract. Marty Devore at Bickering would sell his first born for a crack at it, but the government says it has to go to a minority or woman-owned business. Am I right?" She nods. "The government wants to see who'll give them the most bang for their buck."

"I assume you can tell me how to do that," Leah says. "What do you want from me in return?"

"Aside from ten percent of your revenue for the next five years, I want you to lose the know-it-all attitude," he says. "Nothing you learned at Wellesley, MIT, or Tech has prepared you for this, Doctor. Win this contract and every tech firm in the country will be lining up to lick your boots."

Leah sits back. "I'm listening."

"Good," he says. "The government is nothing but rules and regs. You play by their rules, they'll give you the keys to the kingdom. Fail, and you'll get filed away in their discard pile, never to be heard from again. What are the specs of the RFP?"

"It says they're looking to thwart cyber-terrorism. In particular, they want to protect the phone system in case of attack."

Cairo nods and sorts through some business cards. He takes one out and hands it to Leah. "Here's an individual who would prove very useful in such an endeavor."

She takes the card and looks over it. "Roscoe Delahunt? I know that name."

"You probably ran across Scoey at Bickering," Cairo says. "He sometimes manages their product support team when they don't piss him off. He knows more about hacker culture and phreaking than anyone I've ever encountered. His online address book alone is enough to get him investigated by every cyber terrorism squad on the planet."

"Perfect," Leah says.

Cairo pushes the intercom button. "Tracey, what are you doing right now?"

Tracey's voice comes back, with a sarcastic edge, "I'm cleaning out my desk as you insisted."

"Well stop that and come in here."

Tracey enters and presents herself to Cairo, who addresses Leah. "Avert your eyes, Dr. Walker, for you are in the presence of true greatness. Tracey helped Bickering Plummet win twenty-two government contracts, totaling over five trillion dollars."

"You don't say," Leah says.

"Marty Devore didn't appreciate the asset he had, so I lured her away with a four-day work week and triple the salary just because I could. He still won't return my calls." He motions toward Leah. "Tracey, Dr. Walker here is hell bent on winning the NSA contract. I want you to teach her everything she'll need to know to get it."

Tracey nods to Leah. "Gladly. Provided you understand, I don't work on Wednesdays."

"Not a problem," Leah says. "What else?"

"What else do you need?" Cairo says. "Scoey can help you realize the scope of the work involved and Tracey can wrap it all up in a pretty little package for Uncle Sam."

"Won't I need staff?" Leah says. "Programmers, database people."

"No," Tracey says. "Personnel brings baggage and baggage equals costs. Costs are very bad if you're competing for contracts. You'll need a partner with a vested interest and a lot of funds but who can't compete on their own."

"Bickering Plummet," Leah says.

"Ding, ding, ding, ding," Cairo says. "Normally, they work with Guinevere Byrne on something like this, but she's an airhead who thinks the world is only six thousand years old."

"I know Gwen," Leah says. "She's very competent. I enjoyed working with her on the IRS contract she was managing."

"Trust me, NSA is way beyond her pay grade, and Bickering knows it," Cairo says. "So, instead, they're waiting for a savior to rise from these streets."

"How do you know they'd even want to work with me?" Leah says.

"You cracked their system and they gave you a job," he says. "You are a woman of science, my dear, and they know that. Doesn't hurt that you have a well-known name that's considered a cornerstone of the business community here."

"I guess I could always find something for Gwen to do once I have the contract," she says.

"Now you're thinking like the big boys," Cairo says.

"Please, don't insult me," she says. "Because of my father, I've had to smile politely and endure the condescending attitudes of his old boy network most of my life."

"You've got to think like them if you're going to beat them," he says. "Outsource all the costs. Makes accounting a breeze. You've filed with the state, correct?"

"L. J. Walker Security, LLC," Leah says. "Incorporated two days ago."

"Great," Cairo says. "Tracey, work your magic."

"On it now," she says as she rises, then turns to Leah. "Nice to be working with you." She exits.

Once she's gone, Leah says, "Now, about that half a million."

"What the hell?" Cairo says. "Make it a million. I can afford it."

"That's an awful lot of money," Leah says.

"Don't be ridiculous. I bet Daddy Leroy drops more than that on his dry cleaning."

"You seem to have a skewed view of how much he's actually worth," Leah says. "Granted, we weren't hurting for money."

"No, I bet you weren't," Cairo says. "Are you prepared to deal with the fallout once he finds out you took my money?"

"I doubt our relationship could get much worse," she says.

"My father was from South Georgia," Cairo says. "We didn't get along all that well either."

"He died before you went out on your own, right?"

"Yeah. Dad never saw any of this. He went to his grave thinking I'd never amount to anything more than just another corporate drone."

The intercom buzzes, and Tracey says, "Everything is set for next Tuesday. Have Dr. Walker stop by on her way out and we can discuss the details."

Leah rises. "How hard is it to get in touch with Delahunt?"

"I wouldn't be surprised if he's available right now," Cairo says. "When you meet him, you'll think I've played a massive practical joke on you, but he has much to teach, Grasshopper."

"Wow. So much to do," Leah says.

"Tracey can set up a time for the check signing and handle the press release. I can make sure Daddy Leroy gets an advance copy if you'd prefer."

She nods. "Yeah. I think this is one of those things it's best he hears from someone else."

Hardly anyone believes the truth behind the rise of David Cairo, but Roscoe Delahunt was there. He witnessed it all first-hand. And it was just as messy and disorganized as people have claimed. Cairo didn't so much engineer his success, as just kind of stumble into it but was good enough at selling the myth that enough people came to believe he was a genius. That's not how Roscoe remembers it.

Roscoe arrived in Atlanta just as the 1996 Olympics were winding down. Not much of a sports fan, he came more for the high-tech opportunities he anticipated in the wake of the Games than any curiosity about the event. At the time he graduated from Case Western Reserve University in Cleveland, Roscoe had been corresponding with a local resident, who he knew online as Lady Midnight, for nearly a year as he made his plans for his future. Her guidance on how to navigate the city proved invaluable to him when he arrived.

Once in town, Roscoe signed up with a temp agency who sent him out to short-term staffing assignments which usually never resulted in his being offered full-time work. While skimming the want ads during lunch one afternoon, he ran across an ad for Cairo Enterprises, described as "an Internet startup company looking for highly motivated self-starters" and promised "many positions available". Roscoe called the number to learn where to send his résumé and was instead told to report to an office downtown the following morning.

The office, on the third floor of a rundown former department store near Five Points MARTA station, was lined with folding card tables on which people had set up laptops. There was no defined reception area, and Roscoe entered, largely unnoticed by anyone. At last, he was approached by a somewhat disheveled man in his late-twenties or early thirties wearing jeans, a polo shirt and sneakers.

"You don't have pizza, so you must not be the delivery guy," the man said. "And you don't look like that goon who works with the building manager, so I assume our rent check didn't bounce."

"I called yesterday about a position," Roscoe said.

"Oh, right." The man looked around. "Let's see if we have any available computers."

"What exactly do you need me to do?" Roscoe asked.

The man looked confused. "Then you're not the person I interviewed on the phone."

"Roscoe Delahunt," Roscoe said, extending his hand. They shook hands. "Scoey."

"I remember now. Good to meet you in person, Scoey. I'm David Cairo. What would you like to do with our company?"

"What do you need?" Roscoe asked.

"Everything. Take a look around. You can see we're not that organized."

"I see that. I have my résumé, if that would help."

"Yes. Résumé. That sounds great."

Roscoe retrieved a copy from his satchel. Cairo gave it a close reading. "Wow. Looks like you know a little about a lot of things." He considered something. "How are you at support and Q&A?"

"I could definitely handle that," Roscoe said.

"Great," Cairo said. "Let me get you set up and as soon as we have something to test, you'll be in business."

"Then I'm hired?"

"Why? Do you have another offer?" Cairo said.

"No. This has just gone a little quicker than I thought it would."

"Like I say, we're sort of getting off the ground here," Cairo said. "Trying to drum up business before anyone realizes we don't really know what the hell we're doing."

"Got you." Roscoe chuckled. "What about salary?"

"Ah. Yes. You will need to get paid. Our financial expert is out just now. She can give you specifics. How does thirty thousand sound? I think that's reasonable. That's about what Bickering was paying me when I started."

"I can probably live with that to start," Roscoe said.

"Oh, it's also been suggested we do some sort of profit-sharing program as an incentive. I don't have details on that, but if it will sweeten the pot, there you go."

"Sounds good," Roscoe said.

Cairo extended his hand. "Welcome aboard, Scoey."

He guided Roscoe into the office in search of an available machine.

"Do I need to fill out any sort of application?" Roscoe asked.

"Yeah, we'll take care of all that when Helene gets back," Cairo said. "As I say, she handles the books."

Roscoe surveyed the confusion around him.

"I saw this was a startup," Roscoe said. "It certainly looks it. What are you hoping to accomplish here?"

"I can't speak for everyone on the team, but personally, I'm hoping to make a lot of money, so I won't have to work anymore," Cairo said.

"Okay," Roscoe said. "What does the company do?"

"Everybody's hot for the web these days," Cairo said. "No one knows why, but they all need to be on it." He pointed at an Asian man and a Latina woman seated at one of the tables. "James and Dolores are our programmers. You'll probably be working with them the most. I'll introduce you at the staff meeting." He motions toward a woman in a long dress, her hair in ponytails. "Kristy does the HTML, makes it all look polished and professional."

"So, you design websites," Roscoe said.

"Pretty much," Cairo said. "And if someone asks for something we don't do, we say okay, then either figure it out or hire someone who can." He chuckled. "We're sort of in the process of defining ourselves currently."

"Yes, you are," Roscoe said.

Within a year of that first meeting the initial public offering happened and the scant thirty-thousand-dollar salary Roscoe started with tripled and he became the manager of the support division. By then, everyone knew Cairo's name and he was routinely mentioned alongside Jeff Bezos, Steve Case and other purveyors of the "new economy". More importantly, Roscoe earned stock options which didn't make him a billionaire like Cairo but gave him the freedom to pursue whatever course he desired. Those shares turned into Bickering Plummet stock after the merger, and Roscoe went to work for them as an independent contractor.

Now his association with Cairo has brought him a new opportunity, and as he sits at his computer terminal in his home in East Atlanta, he's reading the doctoral thesis of someone he'll be meeting with that afternoon.

The doorbell rings and after a brief pause, his girlfriend, Aileen calls out, "Scoey, there's a strange woman here to see you."

"Right on time," Roscoe says, then calls back, "Does she seem extremely professional?"

"Extreme to the extreme," Aileen answers.

"Is it L. J. Walker?" he says, making his voice sound like a game show announcer.

"Yes!" Aileen replies. "At least, that's what she says."

"Lovely. Send her on back," Roscoe answers.

Roscoe remembers hearing Leah's name bandied about at Bickering Plummet but doesn't remember being on a team with her. He recalls there being some problems with one of her assignments, but it apparently wasn't enough for Bickering to fire her. She enters, wearing a dark, pin-striped suit with a deep blue blouse and carrying a briefcase.

"L. J. Walker," he says, extending his hand as he propels himself toward her in his chair, "Scoey Delahunt."

"Leah," she says as they shake hands.

"So, here to learn about hacking, are you?" Roscoe says. "From what I hear, you've been a rather naughty girl yourself lately."

"I figured you heard about that," Leah says.

"Who didn't?" he says. "It was all over the hacker forums. If you're interested, I can give you several reams of chatter from the newsgroups on everything they say you did wrong."

"I may take you up on that," she says. "It got my foot in the door at a lot of places."

"No Coke for a while, I'm guessing," he says.

She waves her hand dismissively. "I prefer tea anyway. I'm here to learn whatever you think I need to know."

"How much is Cairo fronting you?" he asks.

"Enough to get the job done," she says. "And then some."

He shakes his finger at her. "Ah, cagey. We can discuss terms once I have a better idea of the work needed." He rolls back to his desk. "Pull up a chair, let's get acquainted. I tried to see if I could get Mitnick on the line for this, but he's still restricted from talking computers at present."

"He'd definitely be a resource." Leah sets her briefcase on a table and selects a typing chair with no arms, sits, and rolls halfway to where Roscoe is seated.

"I had a look at the RFP after you called," he says. "You're going to be dealing with lots of proprietary information on this one. Secrets the telecommunications industry wants to keep under wraps."

"Yes, I had the same thought," she says.

"I figured." He clicks some icons on his desktop. "How do you want to play this? I can give you an overview of my skills, or I can crack something for you."

"I'd rather not start off our association by going to prison," she says.

"Tips and tricks then," Roscoe says and begins tapping the keyboard. Within seconds, several overlapping windows pop up on his monitor. He sighs in disgust and shakes his head. "Damn graphics card. One day, I hope we'll have the capability of multiple monitors."

"I'm hoping for holography," Leah says.

"Ooo, holodecks!" Roscoe says. "My favorite imaginary innovation. I downloaded some specs on a proposed working model a guy in the Netherlands posted looking for funding, if you want to see that."

"Let's stick to the present for now," Leah says. "Maybe later, though."

"Got it," he says. Several telecommunications sites appear in the windows he opened. "Telephony got much more interesting after they broke up Ma Bell. A lot more to worry about, but a lot of opportunity for an enterprising hacker."

"Like Mitnick?" she says.

"By the time he's back in circulation, the world will have passed him by," Roscoe says. "That's just how fast the industry is moving. Paulsen missed the rise of the Internet while he was behind bars."

"We live in interesting times," Leah says.

"Lots of moving parts to sort out," Roscoe says. "Hardware, software, network. Any one is vulnerable to attack."

"And yet, the most vulnerable is still the wetware," Leah says.

"Never underestimate the value of a harried temp when making cold calls."

He turns from the screen to face her. "Let's get this out in the open right away, so we don't have any misunderstandings. My way of working is to be fully in control of whatever project you hand me. I'm the expert and you need my expertise, and I'll expect that in writing from the get-go. I'm not someone who tolerates a lot of tinkering with the job requirements after the fact. One of the reasons I keep popping in and out of Bickering."

"Perfect," Leah says. "We'll get along well, then, once we've defined what I need you to do."

"All right then," Roscoe says. "Let's roll."

They spend several hours discussing the project and what will be needed. Aileen drops in at one point to deliver an antipasto tray with an assortment of deli meats, cheeses, bread, and vegetables.

"You two in here talking shop," Aileen says. "Leaving me to tend to the gardenias out back."

"Gardenias?" Leah says.

"Well, that's what it says on the packet," Aileen replies. "I don't have much of a green thumb. I just dump the seeds and see what sprouts."

"I'm guessing you'll have an interesting garden then," Leah says.

"All these bits and bytes just confuse me," Aileen says.

"Ha!" Roscoe says. He thrusts his thumb in Aileen's direction. "Don't let this one fool you. She's helped out with the wi-fi for Dragon Con more than once."

"Maybe I should offer you a contract," Leah says.

"I'm not into full-time employment," Aileen says. "I like to keep my time free in case a modeling or acting gig comes along."

"Where have you worked?"

"Mostly community theatre," Aileen says. "I do improv from time to time at The Comedy Factory."

"I dabbled in that when I was in Boston," Leah says. "Not my forte."

Aileen excuses herself. "I'll let you two get back to your computing mischief. Enjoy the finger sandwiches."

"If we get this, we're going to need people on the team who know their way around the less savory parts of the web," Roscoe says. "Fortunately, I know quite a few who'd like to get back to living normal lives instead of evading the Feds, so they may be open to helping out in exchange for certain considerations from Uncle Sam."

"Sounds good," Leah says. "I'm going to be working with Tracey McIntosh on some aspects. Truth be told, I'm probably going to steal her away from Cairo once I have a check in hand."

"She must be good, judging by how lamented she was at Bickering when Cairo hired her," Roscoe says. "She probably knows the government like I do the phreaks. With us on the team, this contract is a lock."

"Let's hope so," Leah says. She waves at the screen. "Show me some magic."

"Thought you'd never ask," he says. He taps on the keyboard and a few moments later, a site comes up with Arabic writing. "Welcome to the Saudi Ministry of Agriculture."

"Wow," Leah says. "What can you do here?"

"Not much if you don't want to start an international incident," he says. "We could take a look at some projections or budgets, though. Those aren't too secretive."

"This is the future," Leah says, pointing at the screen. "In my thesis for Tech, I predicted that cybercrime will be the racketeering of the new millennium."

"The next war will be fought with bytes," Roscoe says.

"That's from my thesis," Leah says.

"I downloaded a copy," Roscoe says. "You make some interesting points, but I think your timeline might be a little slower than what's actually happening."

"That's why I'm here," she says. "To bring myself up to the cutting edge."

"Then you're certainly in the right place," he says.

"Why don't you introduce me to some of your friends."

"Not a problem," Roscoe says. With a few clicks, a page pops up with Russian characters.

"Den of Thieves," Leah says. "Appropriate."

"You read Cyrillic," Roscoe says.

"Russian was one of my electives in college," she says. "A friend and I visited Moscow just after the Cold War ended."

In less than a minute, they're in a chat room, conversations streaming by incredibly fast in many languages.

"Hang on, I'll switch on the translator," he says.

"Don't bother," Leah says, concentrating on the screen. "I can handle most of the European languages."

"No, this is for me," he says. "I barely squeaked through Spanish at Case Western."

"A lot of data mining going on," Leah says.

"It is a den of thieves."

Roscoe points out several individuals, identified only by handles. "They'd be assets. Of course, getting them to show themselves will be a challenge."

"Then that will be among our top priorities," Leah says.

Tracey Whitaker started as an entry-level accountant with Bickering Plummet in 1975, fresh out of Georgia State University, where she majored in Business Administration. Her father was a Korean War soldier who, when wounded in battle late in 1951, met the South Korean nurse who would become her mother, while he was recovering at a hospital in Seoul. Not long after starting at Bickering, Tracey married Lowndes McIntosh, an electrical engineering graduate of Georgia Tech, who she met at church; and over time they had two daughters and a son.

Feeling her professional life was getting nowhere in the accounting department, Tracey availed herself of an opportunity to get on the team which put together the proposals for government work. Over time, she became adept at crafting the perfect combination of elements that won countless contracts for the company. As vital as she was to the success of these endeavors, her position allowed her a sufficient level of anonymity, and, other than her immediate coworkers and supervisors, only the most highly placed in the company knew of her work.

One morning, late in 2002, she was surprised by a knock at her office door.

"Good morning, Tracey, I'm David Cairo," he said, leaning into the office.

"Of course, Mr. Cairo. How can I help you?"

"I was wondering if I could pick your brain for ten or fifteen minutes. I have a project I'd like your help with. Can I buy you a cup of coffee across the street?"

"We could just close the door," she said.

"It's more of a personal project than a company one," he replied. "I'd rather not get into the details here, if you don't mind."

When Cairo Enterprises completed its merger with Bickering Plummet in 2001, Cairo gained a seat on Bickering's board of directors. Tracey was aware that the companies weren't a good fit with one another; neither was Cairo. Along with its treasure trove of proprietary Internet technology — much of which would be obsolete in a little over a year — and the deed to Fox Tower, which became Bickering's corporate headquarters, Cairo Enterprises brought with it a boatload of debt and an unwieldy corporate structure that Bickering found unworkable; very little of it survived the transition. As a result, Cairo spent a lot of time pursuing other endeavors, trying to find the next big thing to keep him occupied.

One such endeavor put him in New York in September 2001, where he was associated with a legal firm that was wiped out in the 9/11 attacks. While she did not know the details, Tracey has heard that some of the families of the victims felt Cairo was responsible for some element of the tragedy, loudly rebuffing his efforts to reach out to them. Following this, his behavior on the board became more erratic. He seemed to be no longer guided by the profit motive and had become a vocal critic of some of Bickering's under the table dealings. In particular, he had issued several calls for Bickering to divest itself of a Brazilian subsidiary said to be highly exploitative of its workers and was repeatedly voted down on the board.

It had not yet been made public, but Tracey had been hearing buzz around the office that Cairo had submitted his resignation, effective the first of January; among other things, this made her very curious about this project he was proposing. Once they were at a coffee shop down the street from Bickering's corporate office, she learned that he was planning to, as he would later phrase it, "extract a pound of flesh" as he left.

"I'm leaving Bickering, and I want to take you with me."

This caught her off guard. "Me? With whom you've never worked a day in your life. Frankly, I wasn't aware you even knew I existed."

"Everyone who's anyone at Bickering knows you exist," he said. "There's a short list of people upper management feels it can't live without and you're at the top of that list with five gold stars by your name."

"All right. You know what I do for the company," Tracey said. "Is that something you'll have a need for?"

"Not really," he said. "My days of begging coins from Uncle Sam are far behind me."

"Then what do you foresee me doing for you?"

"Whatever you want," he said. "You can write your own ticket."

Tracey shook her head and started to respond.

Cairo held up his hand. "Before you reply, here's something to consider." He slid a folded piece of yellow notepad paper to her.

She opened it to find a salary offer considerably more than she was making.

"This is nearly double what I'm making now," she said.

"I'm prepared to nearly triple it, if it will seal the deal. Beyond that, ask for anything you want. Holidays. Abbreviated working hours. The sky's not even the limit. I'll book the space shuttle if it gets you on my team."

"Your team?" She considered this. "Just so we're fully clear, you're offering me this salary to keep me from working for Bickering, correct?"

"That sounds about right," Cairo said. "Do we have a deal?"

Tracey shook her head. "I'll need to discuss this with my family."

"Fine by me," he said. He handed her his business card. "There's my private cell number when you're ready. You dictate the terms. You tailor the job to suit you."

A thought occurred to her. "If I ask for Wednesdays off?"

"You get Wednesdays off. It's as simple as that."

As Tracey suspected, Lowndes was supportive of the move, since it would mean a lot more money without the demanding schedule she currently had.

Her supervisors at Bickering Plummet were devastated when she tendered her resignation shortly thereafter and offered her a twenty percent increase in salary — nowhere near the amount Cairo was offering. Tracey said she'd consider it, then almost immediately refused. Her last day of work was 30 November 2002; the day before, the manager to whom she directly reported was hospitalized and placed on a 48-hour suicide watch. Tracey and Lowndes went on a Caribbean cruise for the entire month of December. In the wake of her departure, Bickering lost several big contracts to Lockheed and Northrop.

In the time since, she's come to regret the move, given that Cairo has little use for her talents. While she does maintain a tight ship and keeps track of the companies he's financing, she knows someone with much less experience could handle those assignments. Cairo tries to maintain the guise of needing her, but in truth, he doesn't have many day-to-day responsibilities himself, so Tracey finds herself largely scheduling his appointments and performing basic office management, fewer responsibilities than she had working in the accounting department at

Bickering.

On numerous occasions, she's expressed her frustrations to Lowndes about the lack of challenges working there and has contemplated early retirement, since she's sure Cairo would be very generous with a pension. All that changes, however, the day Leah Walker comes for her meeting. For the first time in a long while, Tracey sees a new opportunity forming and she's anxious to take advantage of it.

As she and Leah are discussing details about the meeting with Bickering after Cairo agrees to finance L. J. Walker Security, Tracey mentions she'd be interested in coming on board to help get things started. She learns Leah's already preparing to make her an offer.

On Wednesday, she heads to Midtown to meet Leah, who she finds seated outside the coffee shop at Colony Square. Leah's viewing office space, and Tracey offered her assistance in their conversation the afternoon before.

"I appreciate you meeting with me on your day off," Leah says as Tracey sits with her.

"Wednesday's the day my husband and I play Bridge," she says with a laugh. "But that's in the evening. When Cairo made his offer, I asked for the day off and he didn't even flinch."

"Good for you."

"No, good for him," Tracey replies. "It gave him immense pleasure to hire me away from Bickering. He was only slightly exaggerating when he said Marty was pissed. I keep getting offers to come back and every time I do, I show them to Cairo, and he increases my salary."

"You probably know where most of the bodies are buried at Bickering."

"Who do you think brought the shovel?"

"Working for Cairo must be an experience," Leah says.

Tracey shakes her head. "That's one way to put it. I've raised three kids. I never thought I'd have to raise another one at this point in my life. But it has its moments."

"I'd imagine someone like you would get bored with a job like that," Leah says.

"It started getting old after about the first month."

"I'm going to have all the challenges you can handle, if that's what floats your boat."

"Ah yes, let's talk about that," Tracey says. "I think we might make a good team. So far, I've been very impressed with how you've gone about your plans. Not many would be able to walk into the lion's den and come out unscathed."

"It was either that or deal with Dad's old-boy contacts who'd go on about 'little Leah' finally trying to make it on her own, along with all their tired clichés about what it takes to succeed."

"So, the real question is, when do we get started?"

"I think we already have," Leah says. "Shouldn't I make some sort of offer first?"

"I know how much you're getting from Cairo, remember? Don't discount your father's network either. Cairo's backing will change their attitude about funding you."

"Not to worry," Leah says. "I've planned on using them all along. I just didn't want to approach them. Once word gets out, I expect to be hearing from a lot of the old boys."

"A well-placed leak could get the ball rolling on that."

"I knew we'd work well together," Leah says. "What else do you need besides a salary that's probably nowhere near competitive to what you're already earning?"

"I love challenges, and this sounds like a great one."

"Well write down a number," Leah says. "You know what you're worth."

"We'll get to my compensation. NSA is small potatoes. I can get you all the government work you can handle and all the warm bodies Bickering has to spare, not to mention half a dozen other firms itching to subcontract."

"Perfect," Leah says. "What else you got?"

"I'll be your full-service, one stop shop," Tracey says. "Office management, bookkeeping, facilities. You make the top-level decisions and I make sure they get carried out. You'll never know I'm there and miss the hell out of me when I'm not."

"This sounds like the start of a beautiful partnership."

"If it will sweeten the deal, I'm fluent in French and Spanish and learned enough Korean from my mother to navigate without a guide when I've been there."

"Working proficiency in Korean but not bilingual," Leah says. "I bet Cairo's going to miss you."

"Half the time, the only reason I'm there is so he doesn't have to talk to himself all day. Besides, my youngest daughter is graduating from Berry College and needs a job."

"Think she can handle Cairo?"

"Angie was a babysitter in high school. She'll be fine."

"Do you handle contract negotiations? I want to bring Delahunt onboard."

"I'll get right on it," Tracey says. She rises. "But first, let's go find us an office, shall we?"

Leah lets Tracey take the lead in negotiating for office space, watching as she insists on an upper-floor office with a view of the skyline, and haggles over the price and renovation schedule — all the while deferring the final decisions to Leah, who outwardly acts like she needs to be convinced, while quietly agreeing with Tracey's suggestions.

"We need this space ready middle of next week," Tracey tells the leasing agent.

"That's a very accelerated schedule," the agent says.

"The space is empty, right?" Tracey says. "If we sign the lease today, there's no reason we can't get started tomorrow."

"Are you planning on bringing in your own team?" the agent asks. "Most of the crews we work with are booked until the fall. There's a lot of construction going on in Atlanta right now."

"No kidding," Tracey says. "When is there not? Hang on a sec." She takes out her phone and dials. "Glennis. Hi, it's Tracey, is Carlos available? Good, put me through."

She steps away from Leah and the agent.

"Ms. Walker, this suite is awfully large and one of our more expensive offerings," the agent says.

"It's Dr. Walker."

"My apologies, Dr. The upper floors are always in great demand. I could show you something on three or four that would be much more in your price range."

"You don't know my price range. I'm aware the upper floors come at a premium and that's exactly why I want one." She points to the window. "I prefer a killer view. The space? We'll fill it in."

Tracey rejoins them. "I just talked to Carlos Baron and he can have a crew here first thing in the morning."

"Carlos Baron?" the agent says. "We were told his firm is booked solid until the middle of 2006."

"He's available for us," Tracey says.

"Very well, then," the agent says. "If this suite meets your needs, we'll get the paperwork ready for you to sign."

As they follow the agent back to the elevators, Leah says to Tracey, "What do you want for a job title?"

Tracey considers it. "How about director of operations? I like the sound of that."

Paxton Walker is on the balcony of his condo in Buckhead, overlooking the intersection of Peachtree and Roswell Roads. A half-smoked Camel sits between the index and middle fingers of his right hand, and a rocks glass of bourbon (neat) is on a tray beside him. He's leaning forward in his chair, staring intently at the early evening traffic.

He moved here a few months after his youngest daughter went away to college in Carrolton. Alyssa had expressed concerns about his selling their home in Lawrenceville so soon after her departure, but he dismissed her entreaties, pointing out that the condo has a second bedroom for her to use when visiting. Despite the extra room, she rented an apartment nearby when she returned from her graduation trip to Europe.

He's a man of medium height, trim build, and an erudite Southern accent, slow and measured, as though he's given much more thought to each of his utterances than he actually has. Since his semi-retirement from his company, he's grown a beard and dresses in casual slacks, polo shirts, and loafers. While he went through the motions of retiring to raise Alyssa after his wife died in 1991, he never actually relinquished control of the company and still okays most of the decisions made by the board, setting aside several hours each day to be on the phone with his second in command. A pack-a-day smoker and moderate drinker, he's sometimes plagued by discomfort in his chest, indicative of a heart condition he's ignoring — which will end his life in a little over six years on the golf course he visits at least twice a week.

Paxton is the oldest son and second offspring of Moreland Walker, primary owner of Walker Groceries, a company which runs a chain of supermarkets throughout Georgia and the Carolinas. Paxton disappointed his father by pursuing his dream of being an architect and developer in Atlanta rather than taking over the management of the family business; but his decision was validated by his vast success, making him one of the major developers in his adopted hometown. Many of the buildings in downtown Atlanta and a number in Buckhead were either built by his firm directly or as a joint venture with other firms.

With the influx of individuals moving to town from the suburbs of Atlanta along with the already growing population, Walker Dev has shifted from commercial to residential designs. The firm has made a killing with houses and condo developments throughout town in the newly "rediscovered" neighborhoods such as East Atlanta and The Old Fourth Ward.

He hears the front door open and close and a few moments later, he senses another presence behind him. He doesn't alter his gaze but takes a draw on his cigarette, expels the smoke then shakes his head.

"I heard some rather interesting news today, Leah."

"I guessed as much," she says.

"My contact at the Business Chronicle called to alert me to a story that's appearing next week in their start-ups report."

"Did they list me as L. J. or Leah J.?"

"There is just no limit to the lengths to which you will go to get under my skin, is there?"

"Thanks, Dad, I'm excited about this new venture, too."

"It's all just one big joke to you, isn't it, Leah?" he says, finally turning to face her.

Whenever Paxton looks at Leah, he doesn't see his daughter, but rather his older sister Peg; and Peg never took him seriously, so he always feels like he's at a disadvantage. Leah doesn't just resemble her aunt: she's picked up a lot of Peg's attitude and mannerisms as well, particularly her brash manner of dealing with others — men in particular. The main difference is in how they dress. Peg rarely wore trousers or shorts, whereas Leah seems fond of them; and Peg had an affinity for scarves, which Leah rarely emulates. Also, Peg was a chain smoker while Leah was never more than a social smoker who gave up the habit in college.

"I'm getting a pretty massive startup check that says otherwise."

"What in the hell possessed you to go to that clown for financing?" Paxton says.

"It's what he does."

"Did I not make it clear to you that my network of financiers would be at your beck and call?"

"Right, and every dollar would have a string attached to it," she replies. "Cairo takes a hands-off approach to his financing."

Paxton remembers all too well the rise of David Cairo in the 1990s as do most of his colleagues in the Buckhead business establishment. No one knew for sure where he came from, though he claimed to be an Atlanta native; and his meteoric rise to fame and fortune left many confused as to what to expect from him. From the start, he displayed both a lack of concern for how business was accomplished in town, and a decided hostility toward the "old money" situated around Buckhead.

In particular, Cairo seemed to have a major bone to pick with Walker Dev and its role in transforming Atlanta into the modern, international city it became in the wake of the 1996 Olympics. For Paxton, the final straw came when word reached him that Cairo had compared him to General Sherman during a meeting of the Buckhead Coalition. Paxton wasn't present at the meeting and could never confirm exactly what Cairo had said, but as a multi-generational Georgian whose great-grandfathers had battled Sherman at Vicksburg and defended Atlanta under Johnston and Hood, he was incensed by the comparison.

"That man has never shown a bit of respect to me or to anyone else in this city. What he did to Herb Templeton was unforgivable."

"Herb? Oh, yeah. Felix's father. What was Cairo's beef with him?"

"No one knows." Paxton takes a drawl from his cigarette. "But once Cairo got control of Herb's company, he cut Herb out completely. Poor man died destitute and sauced out of his mind."

"Where was Felix in all this?"

"Who knows. I hold Cairo solely responsible."

"Why should Cairo respect any of you, Dad?" Leah says. "You've never respected him."

"Respect is earned, not bought," he says.

"Since when?"

In the biggest insult, Cairo made an offer to Walker's board to buy the company, minus its founder and namesake, not realizing Paxton still controlled the day to day operations. Paxton wasted no time and had taken immense pleasure in letting Cairo know this fact and delivering one of his few defeats. Since the merger with Bickering, Cairo had quieted down considerably, but his venture capital business, which seems to favor minority and female-owned businesses, continues to be a topic of consternation among many in town.

"You just have to do things your way, don't you?"

"Sort of like a certain novice developer in 1969, eh, Dad?"

"Don't change the subject. It's not about me."

"Did you really expect I was going to grovel before your network of old boys?"

"You have known these men your entire life," he says. "You don't even show them the courtesy of listening to their proposals?"

"Funny thing, Dad. Ever since word leaked out about my funding from Cairo, my phone's been ringing off the hook with offers from them."

"Has it?"

"They know a good thing when they see it," Leah says.

"That's neither here nor there," he chuffs.

"If I'd done it your way, I'd have gotten a fraction of the funding but far more condescending advice than I could stand."

"I am never going to live this down."

"That's it, isn't it, Dad? It's not about me charting my own course, but how it all reflects on you. How will you ever face Johnny Portman and Artie Blank on the links, knowing your own daughter had the audacity to go to the wealthiest financier in town?"

"In this town you wait your turn," he says, waving his cigarette at her.

"That's a load of crap and you know it. When have any of your cronies waited their turns? They typically buy their way past any opposition."

"It's bad enough you embarrassed the family by breaking into all those systems. Doug Daft has been giving me the cold shoulder at the club ever since."

"So sorry I broke up your foursome, Dad," Leah says. "The consensus seems to be leaning in my favor. By the time I get Cairo's check, I could have another ten million waiting for me. What's that you always say? Success breeds success."

"Time will tell, I suppose," he says. "Enough about that." He motions for her to sit and she does so she's upwind from his smoking. "This is not why I called you. There's something more important we need to discuss."

"What is it?" she says.

"My estate."

"Estate? Are you trying to tell me something, Dad?"

"Of course not," he says. "But there's no reason not to be ready, just in case."

"Fair enough," Leah says.

"I'm naming you my executor."

"A bit of a surprise, given our discussion up to this point."

"Despite our differences, I have no doubt you'll be a responsible administrator. My alternative is one of the lawyers and I'd rather have someone in the family handle this."

"Uncle Duane used to specialize in financial planning. Why

not tap him?"

"I don't want his wife anywhere near my assets."

"I'm glad you have such confidence in me. What about Alyssa?"

"I don't want her to have to deal with this," he says.

"She's a lot more capable than you think she is," Leah says.

"No matter. I don't want her involved."

"Of course not," Leah says. "Anything in particular I'll need to know about?"

"Not really," he says, "it's pretty straight-forward. I'm evenly dividing my assets between you and Alyssa, including what I got from Peg's estate."

When Paxton's father died, he split his shares of the company equally among his daughter and sons. Margaret gifted her shares to Paxton shortly before her death, giving him a controlling interest in the company — and forcing his brothers to continue to work together to counter his influence, despite the considerable differences in their management styles. In addition, Duane's wife, Jolene, exercises a greater than average influence on his decisions, which rankles his younger brother Boyd. While he had not wanted to run the company himself, Paxton nonetheless uses his influence to attempt to steer things in a direction he feels is best, which often does not meet with the approval of his family.

"I'm not sure I've ever wanted to be a grocer," Leah says.

"You'll still have your uncles to contend with," Paxton says. "In fact, they'll probably be happy I don't have a controlling interest anymore."

"I doubt they'd be much happier with me or Alyssa."

"Individually, you'll each have less control," he says.

"I guess," she says. "Any surprises?"

"I'm not a surprising person. Walker Dev and the grocery business are the major concerns. My personal assets are well-documented."

"I'm sure I'll sort them all out," Leah says.

"Good," he says. "Because I'm not planning to have any further conversations with you on this. After this conversation, we're done."

"You're cutting me off after naming me as your executor?"

"I don't see what other alternative I have, Leah. You've allied yourself with a man I find deplorable. Unless you come to your senses, I don't see what else we have to talk about."

"Great going, Dad," Leah says as she rises. She starts to walk back into the condo.

Behind her, Paxton says, "L. J."

Leah turns. "What was that?"

"You asked how they identified you in the report." He turns. "They called you L. J. Doctor L. J. Walker."

"Did they? Thank you, Tracey. Later, Dad."

Leah is standing at the window in her office suite under renovation. It's late in the day on Monday and she has an important meeting the following day at Bickering Plummet. The outer door opens, and David Cairo enters.

"You know, you should really look into getting a lock on that door," he says. "You never know who might wander in."

"I'm almost on the top floor," she says. "Not a lot of foot traffic. Funny, I always heard you were a hands-off financier."

"Just checking in to see how you're spending all that money I'm giving you. You're certainly wasting no time, nor sparing an expense." He surveys the mostly empty space. "Minimalist. A bold choice indeed." He joins her at the window. "Nice view."

"Isn't it?"

"Tracey turned in her resignation on Friday. I do and do for you, Doctor, and you go and steal my receptionist."

"She'll be happier here," Leah says.

"Undoubtedly," he replies. "She brought her daughter Angelica by to introduce her. I think we'll get along okay."

"She thought you would."

"So, big meeting with Bickering tomorrow. Do say hello to Marty for me."

"Remember, I want to make a positive impression."

"Then wait until you have a signed contract."

"Tracey's coming, that should make Marty happy."

"Nah, she'll just leave again. What did Daddy Leroy have to say about all this?"

"We're no longer speaking."

"Treasure all the time you don't spend together." He reaches into the inner pocket of his jacket. "That reminds me. I need you to verify something."

He removes a packet of photos from Wolf Camera and hands it to her.

"This is a blast from the past," Leah says.

"I've been digitizing some of my photos from the eighties and nineties and ran across a couple you might find interesting. They're on top."

Leah takes it and removes the photos. She's surprised to see they're of her, when she was a teenager. In one, she's mugging for the camera by herself at what looks like Piedmont Park, and in the other, she's with her best friend from high school. "That's me and my friend, Gita."

"I thought so. You don't look that much different."

"When did you take these?"

"Eighty-five, eighty-six," he says. "That's when I got my Minolta. It was stolen from my apartment in Brooklyn in ninety-one."

"I haven't spoken to Gita in years," Leah says. "She and her husband moved to New York. Last time we were in touch, she was working at the World Trade Center. "

"I hope it ended well," he says.

"Yes. Through a series of fortunate mishaps involving her daughter, she was late to work on 9/11 and missed the attacks."

"I was scheduled for a meeting there that morning but overslept," Cairo says. "Fortunate mishaps, indeed."

She replaces the photos and hands him the packet.

He says, "I'll email you copies."

They stare out at the skyline a moment.

"I'm somewhat apprehensive about tomorrow," Leah says.

"You'll do fine," Cairo says. "Atlanta loves winners. I've found you have a better chance here if you go somewhere else and succeed. Then they treat you like royalty."

"You seem to have done okay here."

"I succeeded in spite of this town, not because of it. Before that, nobody cared who I was. Now they claim me as their conquering hero."

"Should have expected that," Leah says. He shrugs. "What's it like? Being where you are, I mean."

"You don't know? You grew up in this world."

"My father's rich, but not like you. His whole family has money, but they've always worked."

He thinks about it. "It's like waking up from a nightmare and realizing you're still asleep and can't wake up again."

"I don't think I've ever heard it described like that."

"I can be as charming and as pleasant as I want, and I never know if people are responding to who I am or what I possess."

"That I can relate to," she says.

"I don't even have to be nice to people. If I disapprove of

something, it's someone else's problem, not mine. Surely you've had your share of that."

"I've had people fawn over me because of my father. People act like he's the second coming, wanting his advice, acting like he can do no wrong."

"My favorite thing in the world to do is walk in someplace cold looking like I do," he says. "Then I get an honest response. Associates running away so they don't have to deal with me."

"If that's what floats your boat."

"Back in the late-90s, a store manager asked me to leave his place of business without bothering to ask what I wanted. Outside, I phoned the CEO of the company and complained. Imagine the manager's surprise when I was escorted back in by the regional director and the head of human resources. The look on his face as the fires of corporate heaven rained down upon him was priceless."

"Frightening. Maybe a little amusing. I've dealt with my share of snooty store managers I'd have liked to have seen brought down a peg."

"A momentary thrill at best," Cairo says. "I felt guilty afterward and ended up giving the poor guy his pick of jobs at a mall I purchased some months later."

"The one thing I've learned growing up with money. It's nice to have, but it's a tool like everything else. It's how you use it that matters."

"That's a lesson I wish someone had taught me sooner," he says. "I'd have saved myself a lot of embarrassment."

"You've had a pretty good ride so far," she says. "At least you knew when to get out of the Internet."

"Timing is everything. Another year and Bickering wouldn't have given us the time of day." He stares out at the skyline. "Remember Templeton Staffing?"

"Templeton?" Leah considers this. "Right. Herb Templeton. Dad brought him up the other night."

"I worked for Templeton just before I started at Bickering. They were a very 'traditional' company. Coat and tie. Whole nine yards. I was fired for not wearing a tie to a job where everyone else wore polo shirts and chinos. When he let me go, Herb told me I wasn't the sort of person he wanted representing his company. He could have told me anything and instead he chose to demean my character. When I took over his company and fired him several years later, I used the exact same words."

"Templeton Staffing was a private company. I find it hard to believe he'd sell it."

"It was, but it was leveraged to the hilt," Cairo says. "Herb went into debt to finance a new home for the trophy wife he married after ditching his first wife while she was undergoing treatment for cancer."

"It's all coming back to me," Leah says. "Mom was friends with Wendy Templeton at one time. Nasty business."

"And you know what they say — if you can't acquire the company."

"Acquire the debt."

"We worked out terms for reorganization, provided they ditched their existing management."

"How'd that go over?"

"Herb sent his young, attractive wife to seduce me so I wouldn't take his company away."

"Were you tempted?"

"Of course, I was tempted. Before being a Falcons cheerleader, she was runner-up for Miss Georgia. Might have won, too, but she did a ventriloquism act for her talent portion."

"Sounds like a real stinker."

"No, I've seen her act. She does it at children's hospitals where she volunteers. She's no Shari Lewis, but she's pretty good. According to her, the judges liked her act, but the winner swayed them with an energetic rendition of My God is an Awesome God."

"I met her once. Delilah. Struck me as an airhead."

"An image she cultivates in public. Behind the scenes, she's sharp as a tack. She dropped the cutesy act when I rejected her advances and told her the timeline for the takeover. I said she needed to get out while she could still take good old Herb for all he was worth, because when I was finished with him, he wouldn't be worth anything. Two weeks later, she filed for divorce. Ended up with the house and half of all he failed to give away to his half-wit son."

Leah nods. "Felix. One of my least favorite people in all the world. Tried to get his father to convince mine to set us up when he was in college. I was like fourteen at the time."

"Sounds like a match made in hell."

"I'm eternally grateful Dad shut that down immediately," she says. "Didn't stop Felix from following me and my friends around when he'd show up at our Christmas parties. Total creep.

Dad told me Herb drank himself to death a few years ago."

"Did he? I'm not shedding any tears over him. You want to know what it's like where I am? I gained everything I thought I wanted. Education, money, power, influence. I came to find out it wasn't what I wanted at all. So, where do I go from here, Doctor?"

"I wish I could tell you. I really do."

He turns to go.

"I believe I'm going to wander off into the night. Give you a chance to get on with your business."

"Thoughtful of you," she says. "Take care of yourself, Cairo."

"I'd wish you luck, but luck is for people like me who don't know what they're doing," he says. "You don't fall into that category."

"I appreciate your confidence."

She watches as he heads toward the door.

"Hey Cairo."

"Yes?"

"Hope you brought your umbrella. Looks like rain."

"Let's hope so."

He exits, leaving Leah staring out at the lights of the city.

Just Kidding

Aileen Delahunt and her husband, Roscoe have never discussed having kids of their own, primarily because neither wants kids and they both know it. There's no medical reason; Aileen has some trouble maintaining her weight, owing to a higher than average metabolism, but the doctors have told her that in every other respect she's perfectly healthy and fully capable of carrying a child to term. Neither of them has a problem with kids; they just don't have much experience with them and never thought they had room in their lives for them.

The subject of children always comes up when Aileen is visiting family. Her older sister Darla is, in Aileen's words, "a baby factory" with five sons, from early teens to a toddler. While she always brags about her boys, she's confided to Aileen that she regrets not having at least one daughter. Darla is deeply religious and always tags Aileen in the Jesus memes she posts on Facebook.

Aileen is the middle of three children, and at the time of her birth, the family was living in a modest brick home near Little Five Points in Southeast Atlanta. Just after the Bicentennial, they moved to Smyrna in Cobb County, where her brother, Kenny, was born. Her father sold insurance, and her mother Barbara worked at a department store in Cumberland Mall.

Aileen's upbringing was modestly conservative, the family being Episcopalians and staunch Republicans at a time when most of Georgia was still led by Southern Democrats. Aileen recalls being the only student in her first-grade class to support Ronald Reagan over Jimmy Carter in 1980. She still finds this fact amusing. Aileen never quite fit in around East Cobb, at least not the way her sister had. Darla was very diligent in her studies and looked forward to worship at their church each Sunday, whereas Aileen did well in school, but had a wider social circle with a lot of extracurricular activities. Aileen enjoyed church more as a social outlet than a spiritual one. She's thankful that her parents weren't very strict, and supported her in her interests, such as chorus and drama club.

She lost her parents when she was a junior in college. They planned a trip to Rome for their twenty-fifth wedding anniversary, and just before they boarded the plane, Barbara called and left a message for Darla, "Hi honey. Sorry we missed you.

We're about to board. Just so you'll have the info, we're on flight 800 with TWA. We have a layover in Paris, so maybe we'll get a chance to explore a little. Hug the boys for us. Love you." Shortly after takeoff, the plane exploded over the ocean, killing all on board.

Darla still has the answering machine tape with her mother's message on it. She also ended up with most of their parents' possessions, now carefully preserved at her home.

Their parents' death had drastically different effects on the siblings. Darla became more committed to her religion, believing God had a plan she didn't need to understand, just accept; whereas Aileen, already exploring alternative beliefs, such as Wicca, became more removed from the religion in which she'd been raised and much less conventional in her clothing, makeup, and hairstyle. Kenny, never much of a believer even as a child, instead focused on the tangible, joining the Army and concentrating on becoming an officer.

Roscoe describes spending time with Aileen's family as "Always an adventure." This was particularly true while Kenny was still living with Darla's family.

Kenny was an energetic child and teen, with a sharp wit and a good sense of humor. He earned a degree during his first tour and completed officer training to become a second lieutenant. His second tour of duty was complicated by the war in Afghanistan, and during an otherwise routine scouting mission, Kenny's company came under what was determined to be "friendly fire" which killed or badly wounded most of the soldiers. Kenny lost his left leg and returned to the States embittered and suffering PTSD. He stayed with Darla's family while he underwent rehabilitation, and by all accounts, it didn't go well.

Darla's husband Shane is affiliated with the local Republican party and Kenny is very contemptuous of politicians and pundits, who he describes as "God-damned Hawks who haven't spent a minute in the damned military."

Around the time Roscoe goes to work for L. J. Walker, Aileen receives separate calls from Darla and Kenny imploring her to find room for him at her house. Darla's bothered by the tensions between Kenny and Shane, who (she says) is afraid Kenny will snap one evening and kill them all in their sleep; and anyway, she doesn't like the influence her moody brother is having on her sons.

"Don't worry," Kenny tells Aileen, "if I do snap, I'll just kill

Shane, I promise."

As it turns out, Aileen and Roscoe's home previously belonged to an artist, who built a large shed in the back to use for a workshop. The "workshop" comes equipped with a kitchenette and a full bathroom. After much discussion, they agree Kenny can come live there, provided he fixes it up and keeps it tidy. He agrees.

One of the alternate religious groups in Little Five Points — referred to by the locals as The Stenographers — is led by an elderly woman named Cecilia Baskin, or as she's known to her followers, The Prophetess. They're well-known for the lavish feasts they prepare each day, welcoming anyone in the neighborhood or elsewhere to join them. Aileen is fond of visiting them at least once a month, where they host poetry readings, karaoke nights, and Bluegrass or Folk jams, and Prophetess Cecilia delivers her latest missive from above.

Hoping to expand Kenny's horizons, Aileen and Roscoe take him to one of the dinners. He goes in very wary of the "weirdo cult" but comes away with a total respect for the group, who he describes as "the most genuine people I've met since being back in the States." He starts spending much of his free time with them. They have a positive influence on him and help with his reintegration into society.

Early in 2009, Aileen gets a call from her cousin Shirley, who she's not seen since they were children. Shirley mentions she's going to be in Atlanta in a few days and asks Aileen if she and Roscoe would mind watching her kids for a few weeks while she looks for work. While it has been years since they were close, Aileen remembers Shirley as a sweet and quiet girl, whose parents' uncompromising religious beliefs made them extremely strict.

"What about Wanda and Larkin?" Aileen asks.

"Who?"

"Your parents. Aunt Wanda and Uncle Larkin. Can't they take the kids?"

"Oh. Them. I haven't talked to them for a while."

"Why not?" Aileen says.

"I wasn't really married to the kids' father and Mama and Daddy didn't like that, so they cut me off."

"I see."

"If it's going to be a problem, I totally understand," Shirley tells her.

"I'll need to check with Scoey," Aileen says. "We don't have a lot of experience with kids."

"Well, we're going to be there the end of the week. Let me give you my number and just let me know."

When Aileen tells Roscoe about the call, he asks, "How old are the kids?"

"I'm not sure exactly. Shirley didn't talk much about them other than saying she had them, but she did mention they're not in school, yet."

"We definitely have room," he says. "I'll need to put some items under lock and key if kids will be running around, but otherwise, we can probably handle them for a week or two."

"Great. I'll tell Shirley to come on then."

The woman who shows up at their home, seems far removed from the girl Aileen recalls. Shirley is wearing short shorts, a floral blouse that's as revealing as it is unstylish, and platform wedge sandals. Like her cousin, she's extremely thin, but Aileen suspects that it's not due to her metabolism. Shirley appears jittery and wired and pushes the two little children into the house as soon as Aileen opens the screen door.

"This is Tyrone — I call him Ty — and Skylar," she tells Aileen.

Both are small, Tyrone appearing to be no older than four or five and Skylar maybe three. Both children are mixed race, but otherwise don't resemble one another. Ty is dark-skinned and Skylar much lighter, with curly, reddish hair like Shirley's.

"I had a falling out with their Daddy, and I'm trying to find a job and get back on my own two feet," Shirley says.

"We're happy to help out," Aileen says.

"Listen, I will pay you back for this as soon as I get my act together."

"Don't even think about it," Aileen says. "You're family."

"Really?" Shirley suddenly hugs Aileen, catching her off guard, but she returns the hug. Aileen detects the strong odor of cigarettes.

"Are you hungry?" Aileen says. "I have some snacks in the kitchen."

"Let me help you," Shirley says, following Aileen.

"That's okay, you just got here." Aileen says.

"No. Really. I don't mind."

While they're in the kitchen, Shirley absent-mindedly takes out a cigarette and a lighter.

"Please don't smoke in the house," Aileen says. "You're welcome to use the deck out back."

"Oh, I'm so sorry," Shirley says. "I sure will."

Once she's outside, Shirley gets on the phone with someone named "Leo" and her conversation becomes very contentious.

"I told you, I don't have it yet," Aileen hears her say. "No. I'm not going to tell you where I'm at. I'll be there when I get there."

While Shirley's outside, Kenny comes in, "Who's the meth addict?"

"Kenny!" Aileen says. "That's our cousin, Shirley."

"That's Shirley?" He leans against the door frame and peers out at her then looks back to Aileen. "What the hell happened to her?"

"We've all had tough times," Aileen says. "You be nice. Her kids are in the living room."

"She has kids?"

Aileen nods. "Two. A boy and a girl."

"Oh, I've got to check them out," he says, moving toward the living room.

"Don't upset them," Aileen says in a lowered voice as he disappears through the door.

"Was that Kenneth?" Shirley says as she comes in. "God, he sure has changed."

"War has that effect on people," Aileen says. "What sort of work are you trying to find?"

"Why do you need to know that?" Shirley says.

"I just thought I could keep my ears open. I know people who are hiring."

"Oh. Of course. I think I'm good. I have some leads, but I'll let you know."

As Aileen gets reacquainted with Shirley, she comes to agree with Kenny that her cousin's frenetic, quirky energy is probably drug induced. She's very excitable, going from sitting nervously on the couch to hopping up and offering frantically to help in the kitchen or clear away dishes or barking at the children to keep quiet. She takes frequent trips out back to smoke and makes lots of calls while she's out there. Kenny's opinion of her does not improve the more he gets to know her.

"She's single-handedly trying to keep the tobacco industry in business," he tells Roscoe and Aileen later that day while Shirley and the kids are resting inside.

"Yeah, I caught her smoking at the kitchen table earlier," Roscoe says.

"I told her not to smoke in the house," Aileen says.

"And I told her again," Roscoe says. "Did she ever tell you where she's planning to look for work?"

Aileen shakes her head. "Nope. She was pretty vague about the whole thing."

"What sort of work does she do?" Roscoe says.

"I think she's been working as a waitress," Aileen says.

"Oh no," Kenny says, "She's dealing drugs. Did you notice she's using a burner phone?"

"A burner?" Aileen says.

"You know, prepaid," Roscoe says, "disposable."

"How do you even know that?" she asks Kenny.

"It was sitting on the kitchen counter the one time it wasn't pasted to her ear."

"I think the quicker she gets on with her job search, the better," Roscoe says. "Probably will be good for the kids to leave them here for a few days."

"No doubt about it," Kenny says. "Those kids are going to have it tough."

In her weekly call to her sister, a few days after Shirley leaves, Aileen mentions the visit.

"So, she roped you into taking care of her kids, did she?" Darla says

"We're looking after them for her, yes," Aileen says.

"She asked me to take them in, but I said, no way, Jose," Darla says. "I have enough of a handful with these five hellions of mine."

"So, you sent her to me, did you?"

"I didn't send her anywhere," Darla says. "She asked for your number and I gave it to her."

"She just said it would be for a few days," Aileen says. "We can handle things."

"Two adults who've never spent a good afternoon with a child and one crazy veteran," Darla says. "Lord help those little ones. Have you even heard from her since?"

"No, but she said she might be hard to reach."

"Right," Darla says. "I'm sure she'll let you know something soon. Maybe after the kids have gone off to college."

When two weeks pass without word from Shirley, Roscoe asks a friend in law enforcement to investigate. This friend summarily discovers Shirley has a record in Alabama for possession, nuisance, and loitering with intent. She's also wanted in Arkansas for leaving the scene of an accident and passing bad checks as well as in Mississippi for solicitation and endangering the welfare of a minor.

"Did she mention anything to you about the father of the kids?" Roscoe asks.

"Not to me," Aileen says. "She got very defensive when I asked her about him. I don't think Ty and Skylar have the same father."

"I tend to agree," Roscoe says.

"Honestly, I doubt Shirley knows who the fathers are," Kenny says. "I'm also pretty sure she's not Ty's mother."

"What makes you say that?" Aileen says.

"Have you not noticed that Ty calls her Mama Shirl?" Kenny says.

"I can hardly get him to talk about anything other than what he wants to watch on television," Aileen says. "How'd you come by that info?"

"Ty helped me with painting my place one afternoon," Kenny says. "And by helped, I mean he stood around pointing out spots I missed. I asked him some questions about Shirley, and he kept saying Mama Shirl. I asked him why and he said that's what he's always called her. She's had him for a while, though. He couldn't remember anyone else taking care of him. Skylar is probably Shirley's, because Ty says he remembers when she was a baby."

"The kids do seem more relaxed since she's been gone," Roscoe says. "Ty was watching me work and seemed interested in computers, so I set him up with a console where he can play games and see educational videos. He seems to pick things up quickly."

"Well, Shirley's voicemail still works," Aileen says, "even if she doesn't return calls. If I lose track of her, I'll call her family."

One afternoon, Aileen is in the kitchen preparing some snacks for the children and hears Skylar singing in the other room. She goes in and as soon as she does, Skylar stops.

"That's pretty," Aileen says. "Why'd you stop?"

"Momma doesn't like me making noise," Skylar says.

Aileen sits on the couch and pats her lap. Skylar hesitates, then joins her.

"You know what?" Aileen says, giving Skylar a hug. "Your mother's not here. I want to hear that beautiful voice of yours."

Skylar smiles and starts singing again. Aileen recognizes the song and sings along with her.

Both the children have come to enjoy spending time with 'Uncle Kenny.' Aileen and Roscoe wonder what they should do about school if Shirley doesn't return soon.

After nearly three weeks of leaving messages for Shirley at three- and four-day intervals, Aileen calls one morning to find Shirley's number is no longer in service. Since she's supplied them with little information on where she would be and when she'd return, Aileen calls Darla to get their aunt Wanda's contact information. Aileen waits another week to contact her. The news isn't good.

"Honey, I'm sorry to tell you but Shirley's dead," Wanda says.

"Dead? When did this happen?"

"About two months ago," Wanda says. "Coroner down in Tallahassee called here to tell us they found her in a drug house. Overdose they concluded."

"That can't be. She was here a month ago."

"At your house?" Wanda sounds surprised. "And you're sure it was her?"

"Who else would it have been?" Aileen says. "Are you sure it was her the coroner was asking about? You identified her, right?"

"Well, we didn't actually go down and look at her," Wanda rebuffs. "They overnighted some photos and it sort of looked like it could have been her. She was pretty messed up. I just told them it was her and washed my hands of the affair."

"After all, she's just your daughter," Aileen says.

"That girl has been a problem since her teens," Wanda says. "We did all we could for her, but once she got mixed up with drugs, there was no helping her."

"She told me you threw her out."

"We sent her off to one of those boot camps for druggies," Wanda says. "She ran off. Didn't hear a word from her for years until the coroner called."

"She had two kids with her," Aileen says.

"First I've heard of it," Wanda says.

"They're here with us now."

"Well don't send them here," Wanda says. "We don't know anything about this person you met. As far as I'm concerned, my Shirley is with the Lord now."

"Don't worry about it," Aileen says.

"Good luck," Wanda says and concludes the call.

That evening after the children are in bed, Aileen tells Roscoe and Kenny, "Pretty much everything Shirley told us was a lie. I'm not even sure it was Shirley who was here. Wanda says she's dead."

"It was her," Kenny says.

"How do you know that?" Aileen asks.

"Shirley has a blemish on the back of her left thigh near her butt," he says. Noting the look this elicits from Aileen, he continues, "I may have noticed it a few times when she was wearing her bathing suit when we were kids. At any rate, whoever was here had the same blemish."

"That's all well and good, but as far as her family and the state of Florida is concerned, Shirley's dead," Roscoe says.

"Where does that leave the kids?" Aileen says.

"Damn good question," Kenny says. "What are you prepared to do for them?"

"Why do we need to be the ones to do anything?" Roscoe says.

"Who else do they have?" Aileen says. "We don't know their fathers, the only mother they've ever known abandoned them. If we let them go, they're going to end up in the system and I wouldn't wish that on anyone, let alone two sweet little kids like these."

"Good point," Roscoe says. "I'll contact our lawyer and start the legal ball rolling tomorrow."

"You know you can always count on Uncle Kenny," he says.

"That makes me feel way better," Aileen says with a hint of sarcasm. "Nevertheless, we're the best chance they have. As Darla said, Lord help them."

Roscoe talks to their lawyer about getting custody of the kids and they file with the court to be appointed legal guardians in the interim. He uses Aileen's family relationship as their justification for seeking guardianship, keeping his suspicion that Ty isn't Shirley's child to himself. Shirley's parents submit an affidavit stating that to the best of their knowledge, Shirley is the parent of both children and forward the death certificate they received from Florida.

"Infirmity prevents us from caring for the children ourselves," their affidavit states, "and we fully support our niece's petition for custody."

Aileen is in the living room one afternoon watching television with Ty and Skylar. During a commercial, Ty comes over and sits beside Aileen.

"Is Mama Shirl coming back?"

"I don't think so," Aileen says.

"Maybe she won't," Ty says. "We can stay here with you."

"Would you like that?" Aileen says.

Ty nods. "You're nice."

She wraps her arms around both of them and gives them a big hug.

"We'll do the best we can, sweetie," Aileen says. "We'll do the best we can."

Woman of God

Mother Avis Collins stands before a packed sanctuary at her church and, as she always does, welcomes the faithful.

"Good morning!" She is greeted by a chorus of replies. "Today is the day the Lord has made. I welcome you all to fellowship with us. I'd like to ask all the home folk to rise and visitors remain seated so we may greet you." Most of the crowd rises. "If you're visiting us today, we hope you'll consider making this your home congregation."

In the decade since starting her church, Avis has seen it grow from a small storefront in downtown Duluth to a majestic cathedral with a sanctuary that can accommodate more than five hundred plus an eighty-person choir and a twenty-piece electrified fellowship band. The twenty-four-hour call center affiliated with the church has a full-time staff of forty individuals, to see to the spiritual needs of people throughout the community; their televised service is seen across the U.S.; and their online ministry reaches every continent. Avis is recognized as an influential figure in her community and beyond, regularly sought out for interviews and spiritual guidance.

Once the choir has finished their number, Avis rises again and opens the Bible in front of her on the podium. "Our scripture today is very familiar to most of you, Matthew 25:14-30." Some in the congregation respond knowingly. "That's right. The parable of the talents. The Lord reminds us that 'For unto every one that has shall be given, and he shall have abundance: but from him that hath not shall be taken away even that which he has.' Friends, the Lord is looking out for his faithful. He's not asking you to hide your good fortune under a rock. He wants you to get it out there and start making it work for you. That's why we ask you to give, so that you may receive."

The crowd responds warmly, and the ushers pass around the offering plates. Since adopting this interpretation of scripture, Avis has seen her own fortunes rise, moving from a modest studio above her storefront church into a palatial McMansion in a gated subdivision in Suwanee. Each morning, a driver arrives to deliver her to the church, where her lunches are catered by the top restaurants in the area. Long a proponent of the belief that God rewards the faithful, she's seen her position as an affirmation of this belief.

Despite the outreach, the influence, and the assurances she gives her parishioners each week, Avis feels unfulfilled in her chosen avocation. She realizes doubts come with the job, but her concerns go beyond simply questioning her calling. Each night, when the workday is done, she heads back to her home alone, without so much as a cat or dog to keep her company. Though she regularly interacts with members of the congregation and counsels them on their spiritual needs, she rarely feels a personal connection to those around her.

Hoping to find answers to her doubts, she's taken to researching the early history of the church. She's intently reviewed the many conflicting systems that claimed to be "the truth" including Orthodox and Gnostic texts. She's also become well-versed with the material contained in the Dead Sea Scrolls, and with portions of the Bible that weren't deemed to be official canon. She's found many divergent viewpoints she finds hard to refute.

In addition to her personal misgivings, Avis finds herself constantly dealing with the church's many detractors. Throughout its growth as a congregation, the Apostolic Awakening Fellowship has fallen under scrutiny from the IRS who questions their religious exemption. The various products sold by the church — everything from essential oils and scented candles, to prayer blankets, Bible translations and concordances, and music videos and recordings of the choir and fellowship band — have led the IRS to believe they are less of a church and more of a religiously oriented business. The church's annual income from these activities regularly exceeds one million dollars, causing many outsiders to question the church's true mission. Given their successes, several high-profile business and political figures have taken positions on the official board, which has guided the direction the church has taken, and often they insist on certain concessions from Avis's ministry.

One group in particular, The Templeton Foundation, has donated much money to the cause and supplies the church with flyers and tracts to distribute. This has earned organization head and founder Felix Templeton an important seat on the board of Apostolic Awakening, where he usually dominates the decision making. Felix is the only son of Herbert Templeton and his first wife, who was gifted a good deal of his father's assets a few months before Cairo Enterprises acquired his company's debt and ousted Herb as president.

Contrary to his father's wishes, Felix refused to return any of the money to Herb in the wake of Cairo's acquisition, placing his father on a very tight allowance. This left Herb with barely enough to sustain himself in the manner to which he'd become accustomed, particularly after his second wife divorced him and took the house and most of his remaining assets. Instead, Felix channeled the money into supporting conservative causes and candidates favorable to the interests of his wealthy business associates. Finding a right-leaning congregation headed by a black woman pastor seemed to Templeton like a gift from the heavens — a gift of which Felix has taken full advantage.

For her part, Avis tries to remain above the fray, allowing subordinates to handle the day to day business of the church. Distancing herself from the nuts and bolts of the operation was a reaction to a notable misstep in 2009, where she commented harshly on what she termed as "sodomites" in a quote for a news report about the Pride Festival in Atlanta, which drew protests from GLAAD and the Anti-Defamation League. Following these challenges, at Templeton's suggestion, the church instituted a public relations fellowship, which clears all requests for statements and carefully monitors any outgoing missives for content while having the added benefit of largely shielding Mother Avis from unscripted press appearances. Over time the fellowship has become the main buffer between Avis and those outside the church.

A new line of inquiry develops in 2011, as the church seems increasingly involved in local politics, with Mother Avis herself stopping just short of endorsing specific candidates. Her close association with Ned Branch, who announces late in 2011 that he's running for a House seat on the Republican ticket, brings another level of concern, which is hardly mitigated when it's revealed that Lonnie Jenkins, a conservative operative connected to the Branch campaign, has signed on as a consultant to the public relations fellowship. Members of the church's staff recognize Jenkins as Templeton's eyes and ears within the hierarchy.

Lately, however, some of Avis's studies into alternate church orthodoxy have been creeping into her sermons, much to the disdain of some of the conservative organizations that fund the church and have seats on the board. In particular, her mentions of an "inner light" and "divine spark" that exists in all have elicited comments from board members who question her divergence from preaching about a stern but loving heavenly father who expects total loyalty from the faithful, and who rewards his followers with riches on Earth and in Heaven. It's been stated in several recent board meetings that she runs the risk of "endangering the spiritual growth of the congregation" if she fails to preach the standard line. This has led to increasing tension between Avis and several board members, in particular, Felix Templeton.

At her last meeting with the Foundation, which she attended with Lonnie Jenkins, Templeton floated a list of right-wing candidates for local office he wanted Avis to endorse from the pulpit.

"I haven't agreed to endorse any candidates other than Ned Branch," Avis said. "And I'm only endorsing him in public statements, as myself, not directly from the pulpit."

"We're going to need your support to help sell our slate of candidates to the faithful," Templeton said.

"Sell? That's an interesting way to state my involvement," Avis said. When they're speaking, Avis can't help noting the owl-like appearance of Templeton, with large, round glasses sitting atop his beak-like nose. She's noticed it before in the past — usually when he turns his hard-sell tactics on someone else.

"A poor choice of words on my part," Templeton said. "We just need you to guide your parishioners toward making the right choice."

"You mean your choice," Avis said. "I know Ned Branch, Mr. Templeton. I don't know these other individuals."

"You only need to know they're working toward a common goal. They reflect the values you've always tried to instill in your followers."

"Like rolling back the Voting Rights Act. How is that a common goal?"

"You've been a good friend to our movement so far, Mother Avis. It would be a shame for that to change at this crucial point."

"That sounds rather ominous," Avis said. "How, exactly, would this change things?"

"You enjoy a lot of support from our organization," Templeton said. "If we suddenly felt our goals were no longer in sync with the messenger, we might need to find another messenger."

"Are you suggesting you would try to remove me from leadership of the church I founded?"

Jenkins leaned forward. "I think we're getting away from the point here, folks. There's no need for any misunderstandings."

He said to Templeton, "Why don't we take a breather on this and I'll meet privately with Mother Avis in a few days to clarify our views."

"That's acceptable," Templeton said. "I'm sure once she sees the larger picture, she'll understand what we hope to accomplish here."

"Perhaps she will," Avis said with her eyes trained on Templeton.

Her meeting with Jenkins is scheduled for Tuesday. Now, facing the congregants, she beams as she says:

"It brings me immense joy to stand before you today to let you know that you are cherished in the eyes of the Lord. His arms encircle you, drawing you into his glory. The riches of the kingdom are spread out before you and this doesn't just mean material wealth, but spiritual. The Lord is preparing his kingdom for all who accept his judgment and follow his commandments. All that's required is for you to believe. If you have but the faith of a grain of mustard seed, you can move mountains. I come to you today to let you know the kingdom awaits us all. We must prepare the way of the Lord."

Many in the crowd show their approval by holding up their hands, or proclaiming, "Amen!" As she looks out upon them, Avis wishes she could still be as assured of the message she's delivering as she tries to sound.

One of the church's harshest critics is a blogger known as "Lady Midnight," who publishes a weekly column where she tackles disability issues, religion, politics, and human rights, often doing so by using Apostolic Awakening as an example of religious excess. In the past few months, she's taken aim at a series of tracts the church has been distributing which she identifies as homophobic, xenophobic and intolerant of Islamic faiths. She's also known to frequently post disparaging comments on the message board at their website. She is notably the only negative poster to whom Avis will personally reply, and their voluminous exchanges often betray not only serious animosity, but also a great deal of familiarity between them.

In one such exchange, Avis states, "You should be grateful the Lord blessed you with the opportunity to be an inspiration to others, rather than the sullen, withdrawn shell of the woman you once were."

Lady Midnight has responded with variations on, "I can't believe this is how your parents raised you. As a Christian, you should know better than this."

Among their outreach ministries, Apostolic Awakening has a weekly radio show, where Mother Avis takes prayer requests and connects with her parishioners, and Lady Midnight sometimes calls in to harass her. The PR fellowship has engineers install voice recognition software to block this, since Lady Midnight is rather adept at disguising her voice. The screening software recognizes both Lady Midnight and several of her followers, including a soft-spoken man with a noticeable Southern accent, who makes little attempt to disguise his voice.

Lady Midnight's followers often listen to the show just to see if she can succeed in getting on the air, and often begin calling in themselves if she fails to get through. The church takes out a cease and desist order against the site that hosts her blog to stop her, but Lady Midnight claims online that she does not encourage others to call. She publicizes her plans to ignore the court order and threatens to sue on First Amendment grounds if the church's "harassment" continues.

At their meeting on Tuesday, Jenkins tells Avis, "You're suffering a crisis of conscience, Mother Avis. I can understand that. But I don't think you've considered all that's important here."

"By all means, enlighten me, Mr. Jenkins."

"The Templeton Foundation is a very influential organization," he says. "They've been instrumental in helping a number of powerful individuals get their start in business and politics."

"I'm well aware of their reach, Mr. Jenkins. But this isn't a business or political establishment. This is a church."

"You and I have a lot in common, Mother Avis. I was raised in a good family who taught me to always do the right thing."

"Indeed. As you know, my father was a minister."

"When I was in college in the 80s. I had a lot of idealism. Reagan had just been elected President and I believed he was going to make a real difference."

"That he did," Avis says. "We'll have to agree to disagree on whether or not that was a positive difference."

"Perhaps," he says. "When I went to work for a congressman after I graduated, I went in there wanting to make a difference myself."

"Did you?"

"I thought I was. Then that first assignment came along where things didn't quite feel right. But I was assured in the legitimacy of our cause. I thought, 'It's just this once.'"

"That's usually how it starts."

"Then once turned into ten times, then a hundred, then more times than I could count. After a while, I realized my job wasn't to change the world. It was about doing what I was told and reaping the benefits."

"That's a rather cynical way to live your life, Mr. Jenkins."

He leans forward and says to her in a confidential tone, "Looking back, there's more than a few times I've wondered if I should have followed my heart instead of my head, but I wouldn't be where I am today if I had."

"Something to consider."

"You preach about all the riches your congregation can receive because of their beliefs. You've been given an opportunity to experience that for yourself. All you need to do is believe in what our associates are promoting and everything else will fall into place."

"I see that, Mr. Jenkins."

"It's not a difficult decision when you get right down to it," he says. "Think of it as a test. You pass and you could enjoy riches of a different sort. Power. Influence. You would become a kingmaker in your own right."

She nods. "I believe we understand one another, Mr. Jenkins."

"Very good." Jenkins leans back and crosses his legs. "On another matter, Lady Midnight is at it again. Twenty posts this morning."

Avis sighs, "What's got her up in arms today?"

"She's off on a tirade about those tracts again."

"What, exactly, are her objections over them? Is there any basis in fact to her claims?"

"They're from a distributor associated with the Templeton Foundation," Lonnie says. "My understanding is that a lot of congregations they're working with are using them."

"I should take a look," Avis says. "Probably more baseless accusations as usual."

"There's really no need for you to trouble yourself with this," Jenkins says. "That's what the public relations fellowship is for. As for Lady Midnight, why don't you just let me and some of our operatives deal with this nuisance? Our associates can be rather persuasive behind the scenes."

"I'm afraid it's not that simple."

"Why not?"

"Lady Midnight is my sister, Annabelle."

"Your sister."

"Yes. We've been estranged for a number of years and she's not happy with the direction I've taken. Believe me, the feeling is mutual."

"Does anyone else know about this?" he says. "We've not had much success in getting the online company to reveal information about her."

"She's fairly shadowy on her blog," Avis says. "It took me a few posts to figure it out from some of her personal references. I'm guessing people in the family know. Maybe some of her acquaintances."

"This presents us with a rather unique challenge, then," Jenkins says.

"I'm open to suggestions."

"Far be it from me to interfere in your personal business," he says. "But in my experience, family matters are best handled face to face."

"I haven't spoken directly to Annabelle in over a decade."

"Maybe it's time for a reunion then."

"Thank you, Mr. Jenkins," she says. "I'll take that under advisement."

Annabelle Collins is on the back porch at her home in Kirkwood, enjoying her morning coffee when she hears the doorbell ring. Paul Searcy is in the kitchen cleaning up after breakfast.

"Can you get that, Paul?" she says.

"Yes ma'am."

Since she went online with The Midnight Hour, the confidence she gained by sharing her voice with her readers led Annabelle to pursue her doctorate in world literature, which, in turn, led to her being offered a position as adjunct faculty at Spelman. She's also started driving again with a specially equipped van, since Paul is still reluctant to get behind the wheel. Given her position at the university and within the community, Annabelle conceals her identity online by not posting personal information or sharing photos and maintaining a private domain registration.

Even with the anonymity she cultivates, Lady Midnight is frequently invited to post on other blogs and is a regular on an Atlanta radio call-in show that covers politics and community issues, as a well-informed voice on human rights and racial justice. A recurring topic of her posts is religious hypocrisy, in particular, churches which profess the teachings of Jesus while ignoring the poor and promoting bigotry against gays, minorities, and immigrants. Online, she's taken issue with a series of tracts distributed by several religious denominations claiming to be Christian. The tracts vilify Muslims, calling them "ragheads" and "jihadists" and call for them to be excluded from the country and treated with suspicion and contempt. Another set of tracts bashes homosexuals and transgendered people with equally inflammatory language.

Her opposition has brought her into conflict with her sister. Avis has taken a stance against homosexuals and mixed marriages in her ministry over the years, but the tracts cross the line into race bating and call for homosexuals to be imprisoned and "converted". Annabelle finds it hard to believe Avis has become that far removed from the respect for divergent viewpoints their parents taught them when they were younger. In their exchanges on the church's various resources, Annabelle has noted that Avis defends her overall message without using language found in the tracts, causing her to wonder how familiar Avis is with them.

Annabelle appreciates the irony inherent in the fact that the only time she ever communicates with her sister is when they're arguing on the website for her sister's church. Annabelle has watched as Avis started and built her congregation and she's noted that often the issues Avis highlights reflect problems she had with one or more of her siblings, in particular, their oldest brother, Alfred. Annabelle suspects that Avis's aversion to homosexuality may have a more personal basis than her other causes, but while they had still been on relatively cordial terms, she hadn't wanted to delve far enough into Avis's personal life to confirm or deny this, out of respect for Avis's privacy.

The family gets together every Thanksgiving at Alfred's home, and each year, he extends an invitation to Avis, which usually receives no response. Lately, he's had to filter his requests through the public relations ministry at the church, which sends a boilerplate response promising that "Mother Avis will give this correspondence the highest priority" and no personal reply. Despite the contentious relationship they had when younger, Annabelle regrets the distance between them.

Paul is gone for a long time and looks surprised when he steps out onto the porch. "Avis is here to see you."

"Tell me you mean the car rental place," Annabelle says.

"No, Mother Avis. It looks like her from television at least."

"She's here?" Annabelle says.

"In the living room," he says. "I just let her in."

"Oh, this should be interesting," Annabelle says as she wheels herself inside.

Avis, dressed in a mid-length grey dress and flats, with a colorful scarf, is in the living room, hands folded in front of her, facing the doorway through which Annabelle enters. Since Avis didn't attend Maxine's funeral, it's the first time they've been in the same room together since the night their mother died eleven years prior.

"Avis," Annabelle manages.

"Annabelle — ah — nice to see you," Avis says. "You look well."

"You appear to be in good health yourself."

An extended silence ensues. Avis surveys the room while Annabelle keeps her eyes trained on her sister.

"I had a brief chat with your man servant when he let me in," Avis finally says.

"He's not my man servant," Annabelle says.

Avis considers this. "He's a man who serves you."

"What do you want, Avis?"

"How are you getting a long?" Avis says. "It's been a while."

"Yes, it has been," Annabelle says. "A lot has happened since we talked face to face. I'm volunteering in the community, teaching at Spelman."

"Spelman? You're taking MARTA?"

"No. I'm driving again."

"You're driving?"

"The van in the driveway is fitted with hand controls," she says. "I ran the Peachtree again."

"Really?"

Annabelle shrugs. "Wheelchair division. Quite a workout."

"That's good to hear," Avis says. "I'm somewhat surprised to find you're employing the man who was responsible for your accident."

"It wasn't easy at first, but we've managed," Annabelle says.

"You've forgiven him?"

"I wouldn't go that far. But I'm open to it someday perhaps."

"It appears he's had a positive influence on you."

"It wasn't him," Annabelle says. "It was me. I figured if I was willing to give him a second chance, I should be willing to give myself one. Finding a voice on my blog helped a lot."

"Yes. Your blog," Avis says. "That's why I'm here."

"Nice to see I can still get your attention."

"You certainly have. I need you to call off your army of followers."

"My army of followers?" Annabelle says. "I don't encourage people to harass you. They do that on their own."

"You don't discourage them."

"They have plenty of provocation, Avis," Annabelle says. "Let's start with the laundry list of those you speak out against from the pulpit."

"I'm not the only pastor who does that. I don't see you protesting them."

"Some of them," Annabelle says. "When it's warranted. I think you need to take a closer look at some of the literature your church is distributing. There's some very incendiary language in the tracts you've been sending out."

"Yes, I've heard that's a target of yours," Avis says. "We don't publish those. They come from a distributor. Other churches use them."

"Yeah. Right-wing race bating churches."

"Race baiting? That's not a message I endorse."

"Oh, you don't? Are you even aware of what's in them?"

Avis looks at the floor. "Not really. The public relations fellowship handles our communications."

Annabelle rolls to her desk and picks up some literature which she takes to Avis. "Take a look." She points as Avis examines them. "Ragheads? Jihadists? Faggots? Don't tell me you approve of this."

"This is not the message I promote at the church," Avis says. "I have always counseled my followers to hate the sin but love the sinner."

"That's not a very inclusive philosophy either, but these are worlds away." Annabelle points to the Apostolic Awakening logo on the brochure. "Whether you endorse it or not, you're condoning everything they say by distributing them."

"One of our board members encourages us to use this publisher. I had no idea this was the message they're promoting. I'll put a stop to it."

"It all started about the same time you became linked to the Branch campaign, if I'm not mistaken."

"This isn't Ned's message either," Avis says. "Obviously, I

need to be more vigilant in overseeing the operations."

"Obviously."

Silence overtakes them again. Avis indicates the door. "I should be on my way." She starts to leave, then turns back. "It's good to talk to you again, Annabelle. Really talk."

"It is. Next time you need something from me, Avis, just ask. Don't send your lawyers after me."

"Noted," Avis says. "Have a blessed day, Annabelle."

"You, too, Avis."

Once she returns to her office, Avis orders that the church cease distributing the incendiary tracts. This prompts another visit from Lonnie Jenkins.

"Are you aware of the content of these?" Avis asks handing him the tracts.

"They're standard religious tracts," Jenkins says. "Mr. Templeton feels they're promoting the proper talking points."

"Have you even read them?" Avis says. "These are a bit beyond a standard conservative message and it's not a message I wish to promote."

Jenkins glances at them without reading. "Perhaps our associates misread your pronouncements about mixing races or the need to bring non-Christians to the light of God. Or has your message changed?"

"I have disagreed with the practice of interracial marriage," she says. "I haven't vilified other races or religions. Yes, I'd be happy to welcome Muslims into the Christian family, but I don't feel the need to call them ragheads or jihadists."

"Not a problem. I'll make Templeton aware of your concerns."

"Very good," Avis says.

"On another matter, it has been suggested that perhaps you should take some time off," Jenkins says.

"Suggested by whom?"

"Members of the board," he says. "They've noted that you haven't taken a proper vacation in many years, if at all."

"I enjoy my work," she says. "Why would I want a vacation from that?"

"You have a very demanding position," Jenkins says. "And you seem to have been under some stress lately. The board just felt you needed some time to yourself."

"The board," she says. "Or, perhaps, a particular member of the board."

"Does it really matter who suggested it?" he says. "The fact is, you give your all to this congregation. It's okay to take some time off for yourself. In fact, the board voted on and approved a brief sabbatical for you."

"Without consulting me?"

"They are the governing authority here," he says. "It's a month. Take the time. Relax. Get back in touch with what you hope to accomplish here."

"It sounds to me like I don't have much choice," she says.

"You can always bring it before the board," Jenkins says.

"That won't be necessary," Avis says. "When does this sabbatical commence?"

"First of next week," he says. "Pastor Horton has already been approached to fill in for you."

"So glad to know the board is looking out for me," Avis says. "Please convey my gratitude."

Once Jenkins leaves, Avis goes into the computer room where Rondul Latimer, the system administrator, is seated at his console. She places her hand on his shoulder and he looks up at her.

"Mother Avis," he says. "What can I do for you?"

"Afternoon, Rondul," she says. "I wonder if you could get me a copy of the church's financial records. I'm going to be taking some time off and I wanted to review some items."

"On vacation?" he says. "Sure, I can get them for you. How far back do you want to go?"

"Complete from the beginning," she says.

"That will probably take me about an hour," he says.

"That would be wonderful," she says. "And, please, don't mention this to anyone. The board is cracking the whip for me to go away and forget about the church for a while. I don't want them getting wind that I'm disobeying their directive."

"Not a problem," he says. "I'll put them on a flash drive."

Avis withdraws a large sum of money from her personal account and drives into the North Georgia Mountains to a bed and breakfast in Clayton. She's become very good at hiding in plain sight when she's in public, downplaying her looks by not wearing makeup, hiding her hair under a headwrap, and using her registered alias, Arielle Flowers. When she arrives in the mountains she pays in cash and explains to the owner of the establishment that she's a poet and novelist looking for some quiet time to rejuvenate and complete a work in progress. Once she's settled in, she mainly holds up in her room with her laptop, only leaving to eat and get some exercise.

She spends several days reviewing the church's finances and notes that the same year the Templeton Foundation came on board, corporate donations increased substantially. Just after the public relations fellowship was established, the church started using Right Think Press, the publisher of the malicious tracts, and the amount billed by the publisher was, in most cases, identical to the amount of money donated by a group called The Ascendancy Collective. She goes online to learn what she can about them and traces the entity back to a post office box in Delaware but cannot learn more about it and can't find a company website. She makes a note of it then looks up Right Think Press, finding their address is also a post office box in Delaware. She can't find a direct link to Templeton for either company.

The afternoon she finishes reviewing the records and making detailed notes, Avis inquires at the desk about vegetarian restaurants in the area and a woman nearby says, "I just asked the same thing and I'm getting ready to head to one, if you'd care to join me."

"What a coincidence," Avis says. "Thanks for the offer. I'd enjoy the company."

She rides to the restaurant with the woman who introduces herself as Jana Roeder, a college professor from Ohio. The whole way over, Jana can't stop glancing at Avis.

"I'm sorry if it seems like I'm checking you out," Jana says once they're seated at the restaurant. "But you seem very familiar to me. Is it possible we've met before?"

Avis chuckles. "Yes. I get that a lot." Whenever someone recognizes her when she's in stealth mode, she's found it's best to address it directly. "Sometimes people mistake me for that preacher in Atlanta. Mama something."

"Yeah. Mother Avis," Jana says. "Sorry if it's a sore subject."

"Not at all," Avis says. "I just wish I knew more about her. I don't own a television."

"Unfortunately, I know too much about her."

"Oh really. What have you heard?"

"I hear she's a closet case for one thing," Jana says leaning toward her and speaking in confidence.

"You're not the first person I've heard that from, believe it or not," Avis says. "She certainly seems to be a lightning rod."

"I wonder how she sleeps at night."

"Alone, I'm certain," Avis says and they both laugh.

"So, what have you written that I might have read?"

"Probably not much," Avis says. "Most of my work up to this point has been very technical. If you buy certain brands of computers, I may have done the documentation. I caught the creative writing bug late in life."

"There's nothing wrong with that," Jana says.

When they're finished eating, they head back to the Inn where they sit on the front porch and talk. They spend a while discussing Jana's life back in Ohio. She details a romantic relationship she's recently ended with a female colleague which she describes as "stormy to say the least."

"What about you, Arielle?" Jana says. "What's your history?"

"Sometimes I feel like I've wasted most of my life trying to be what I thought others wanted me to be," Avis says. "I never bothered to figure out if it's what I wanted."

"We've all been there," Jana says.

"A long time ago, a very good friend tried to tell me it didn't matter what people thought, but I didn't want to listen. I let it ruin our friendship and whatever else we might have had together. I was such an idiot."

"If we're lucky, we get a chance to learn from our mistakes."

"Sometimes we make things worse in the meantime," Avis says.

"Are you still in touch with your friend?"

"We haven't seen or spoken to one another for years," Avis says.

"If she's still around, there's always time," Jana says.

"True," Avis says. "I'm not sure I'd know how to approach her at this point."

As they head inside to go to their rooms, Jana touches Avis's shoulder.

"If you're interested, I have a nice Chardonnay in my room I picked up in Braselton this afternoon," she says. "I've been hoping for the right person to share it with."

Avis smiles and shakes her head. "Your offer is very tempting, but I have a rather complicated relationship waiting for me back home." She gives Jana a long hug. "Perhaps in a different life."

"And so it goes," Jana says. "Take care, Arielle."

Rosalina Cruz has been with the U.S. Attorney since she interned there as a College of Law student at Georgia State University in the early 2000s. She's now a senior attorney working with the division that investigates racketeering in North Georgia. The oldest of four children, Rosalina comes from a family of lawyers, both her parents licensed to practice in Florida and Georgia, her brothers employed by private firms in Atlanta and New York, and her sister, Magdalena, working with the Public Defenders' office in Fulton County.

This morning, she's joined by someone she never thought she'd see in her office, Mother Avis Collins. Rosalina has received complaints in the past from agencies like the IRS to investigate aspects of Avis's church, but has usually passed on taking any action because there's never been any overt evidence of wrongdoing, and their religious observances are protected by the First Amendment. Now, much to Rosalina's surprise, the person asking for an investigation is Avis herself.

She sets a flash drive on Rosalina's desk. "I've found some interesting correlations in our bookkeeping."

"Interesting how?" Rosalina says.

"It seems one of our donors is exclusively covering the tracts our church has been handing out," Avis says. "Tracts which have rightfully drawn the scorn of quite a few outside human rights groups."

"Some of your pronouncements haven't gone over well either."

"True," Avis says. "I'm in a bit of a transitional period now."

"I gathered." She picks up the flash drive. "So, tell me about your concerns."

Avis details what she found about The Ascendancy Collective and Right Think Press. She notes that the association started about the same time she took more of a backseat in running the church.

Rosalina nods, then picks up her phone. "Barbara, please have Rajeev come over. I have some work for him."

A few minutes later, a young Indian man comes in. Rosalina gives him the flash drive and asks him to investigate the contents.

"Let's get down to brass tacks," Rosalina says. "What's in it for you if we find something?"

"A clear conscience," Avis says. "I'll know my work isn't going to help the wrong people."

"Fine and dandy," Rosalina says. "But that might not keep you from behind bars."

"I had nothing to do with this association," Avis says. "I'm the one bringing it to your attention, remember."

"You can bet the people behind this have made sure you're somehow implicated."

"So, what are my options?" Avis asks.

"Cooperate fully and I'll be the best friend you've ever had," Rosalina replies.

"I can use all the friends I can get," Avis says. "Whatever you need, I'm prepared to give it to you."

"Let's start with a deposition. I'll put you with one of our associates and you can tell us your whole story."

On Saturday, not quite two weeks after she left for her sabbatical, Avis enters the computer lab and says, "Rondul. Could you find an assistant and meet me in the storage room?"

"Sure, Mother Avis."

Avis goes into the storage area and finds stacks of boxes labeled Right Think Press. She shakes her head and pulls one down then opens it to find it full of the tracts she's told Jenkins they weren't going to distribute any longer. She takes out a small stack as Rondul enters with another young man and Avis looks at them and points to the boxes. "Please take all these out to the parking lot. I believe you'll see where they need to be."

"Absolutely," Rondul says. "Anything else?"

"Yes," Avis says. "You'll find some cans of gasoline there. Soak these well."

"Are you serious?" he says. "I sort of thought they were over the top but didn't say anything because I thought you were okay with them."

"I was not aware of them and have never been more serious. Be careful not to douse yourselves."

Rondul shrugs to his assistant and they get a cart and begin loading up the cases. Avis takes the tracts and enters Jenkins's office. He's surprised to see her.

"Mother Avis," he says. "I wasn't expecting you back so soon."

"Why are these still here?" she says, tossing the tracts onto his desk. "I said we weren't going to distribute them any longer."

"The board thought you'd have a change of heart once you had time to consider what's in the best interest of the church."

"I see. You're right, Mr. Jenkins. I have thought about nothing other than the best interest of the church." She turns toward the door. "Please come with me. There's something I need to show you."

Jenkins follows her out to the parking lot where the cases are stacked up and dripping. The strong smell of gasoline is in the air. Rondul and his assistant are standing away from the boxes.

"Is this all of them?" Avis says, to which Rondul nods.

"You're not going to do what I think you're going to do are you?" Jenkins says.

"Oh, I am, Mr. Jenkins." She removes a roadside flare from her jacket pocket, lights it, and tosses it onto the pile which bursts into flames. Jenkins watches with a sour expression.

Avis turns to him. "Mr. Jenkins, your services are no longer needed here."

"You are making a huge mistake and you know it," he says.

"This is a house of prayer. It will no longer be a den of intolerance." She waves toward the bonfire. "Tell Templeton this is my answer."

After Jenkins leaves, Avis goes to her office, unplugs the phone, and starts composing her sermon for the following day. Around two-o-clock, Ralph Horton, the assistant pastor, shows up and is surprised to find her there.

"Mother Avis," he says. "I was just coming in to finish my sermon for tomorrow. There appears to have been something burned out in the parking lot."

"Yes, I'm aware of that," Avis tells him. "You don't need to worry about the sermon tomorrow. I'm back and will deliver the word as I normally do."

"Is the board aware of this?"

"They are now," Avis says.

"Welcome back," he says. "I hope your vacation was productive."

"Very much so," she says.

"Would you like me to look over your sermon when you're done?"

"That won't be necessary," she says. "Why don't you take the afternoon off?"

"If you don't think I'll be needed," he replies.

"I have things under control here. Enjoy your afternoon, Ralph."

The following morning, the congregation at Apostolic Awakening is surprised when they arrive and find that the choir and band are not there, nor is Mother Avis in her usual place in the pulpit. About the time the service normally starts, she emerges from the side of the sanctuary and stops in front of the altar.

"We're doing things a little differently today," she says, then leans back against the altar. "I wanted to come to you up close and personal for a change to apologize to you all."

Rumbles go through the crowd as people look back and forth at their seatmates.

"Many years ago, when I started this ministry, I felt I was being called to serve the needs of this community in whatever way I could. In the early days, it was a lot of work over in that tiny little storefront in Duluth. Some of you were there in the beginning and have stayed with me throughout the growth of this church and I have enjoyed making that journey with you." Some in the congregation call out supportive words. "But somewhere along the way, I lost sight of what I was here to accomplish and, in doing so, I have failed you. I have been preaching a false gospel, one rooted in material wealth, while ignoring the spiritual needs of this congregation." A low din goes through the sanctuary. "I have counseled you to seek riches on this earth, rather than serve the needs of your community. I sincerely apologize to you for my failures. I have preached division and intolerance and sown the seeds of suspicion and animosity toward others. In doing so, I have opened up myself and this congregation to manipulation by forces who would seek to divide us further for their own aims."

Ralph Horton rises and moves toward Avis. "Mother Avis, it seems you're under some stress. Perhaps it's best if I take over the service."

"No, Ralph," Avis says. "I'm perfectly fine. In fact, for the first time in a long while, I'm seeing things clearly." Ralph returns to his seat. "All these years, I've been quoting the parable of the talents, but I never really understood it. Why would the Lord take from those who have nothing? Now I see it's not about earthly riches. It's about goodness. Those who have it will be rewarded with more, but those who don't have nowhere to turn. That's the lesson I should have been teaching you, but one who does not possess wisdom cannot impart it on others. I now see there's so much I've been wrong about. I've led you all astray, but no more."

Avis pushes away from the altar and continues. "We've been waiting for the Lord to establish his Kingdom on Earth when it's been here all along. It's not a goal to which we should aspire but a reality for us in the here and now. It lives inside us all. Every one of us is a manifestation of that goodness and light. It's up to us to nurture it and let that light shine in the darkness of this world. Don't question what God can do for you but ask yourself what does God require of me? What can I do to make my fellow human beings more comfortable and welcome? How can I best serve the needs of my community and the people in it?"

She raises her hands. "I strongly suspect that this will be the last time I appear before you in this sanctuary." Some in the crowd react with shock. "So, let me say what an absolute honor it has been for me to serve you throughout this ministry. Please forgive me for losing sight of my purpose but know that the Lord is all about second chances. If you find this isn't a journey you'd like to pursue, I won't hold that against you. You must determine your path and let that guide your actions. Whatever your decision, I wish you all the best."

With that, Avis walks out of the sanctuary and returns to her office. A short while later, Rondul Latimer looks in on her.

"Mother Avis, are you okay?"

"I'm fine, Rondul. You stayed?"

"Yes ma'am," he says. "A lot of people left, and Pastor Horton went with them, but there's still a good crowd here. They're in the fellowship hall, hoping you'll join us. We'd like to hear more."

Avis rises. "Thank you, Rondul. I'll do just that."

On Monday morning, citing gross mismanagement of the church's affairs, the board at Apostolic Awakening announces that they have removed Avis as pastor and order her and her followers to vacate the grounds where they've remained since Sunday. She responds by chaining the gates to the driveway closed and refusing access to her replacement, Ralph Horton, and any member of the board. After Felix Templeton and others are turned away, a contingent of county police arrive and take up non-confrontational positions across from the church. The police chief goes onto the grounds to try to mediate with Avis but exits a short while later stating she's adamant about staying.

Once a day, for about an hour, the congregants appear on the front lawn to sing hymns and receive a message from Mother Avis, using a bullhorn.

"Jesus tells us that it's easier for a camel to pass through the eye of a needle than a rich man to get into heaven," she says during one sermon. "And we know that's true. Oh, yes. Jesus died on the cross for our sins and you can't spare some comfort for those in need? You will be judged."

People in the surrounding community and the local media gather for these messages and the national press appears late in the week. Avis announces to the congregants that she's reversed her position on gay rights and interracial marriages and if anyone wishes to marry, she'll perform the ceremony. Several take her up on this.

"James asks us if faith alone can save us," Avis says during another of her sermons on the lawn. "And he lets us know that faith without deeds is dead. Jesus counseled us to care for our fellow individuals and that's regardless of what the politicians or the business community or the leading citizens in our community say. Jesus said if anyone would come to me, deny yourself, pick up your cross and follow me. To those who say we're wrong, we're violating the law, we're the criminals, your cross is waiting."

As the standoff wears on, Felix Templeton calls on police to storm the compound and subdue Avis.

"This isn't Jonestown, Mr. Templeton," the chief says. "We don't need another Waco."

Ned Branch approaches the chief and volunteers to go in and speak to Avis in the hope of resolving the situation without further escalation. Despite objections from the board, the chief agrees to Ned's request and mid-morning on Friday before the start of the daily ceremony, he goes to the church and heads inside. He finds Avis in her office on the phone.

"Looks like my escort has arrived," Avis says to whoever's on the other end of the line when she sees Ned. "Thank you, Ms. Cruz. I look forward to coming to you when this is over."

Avis hangs up and addresses Ned. "So, they sent you to reason with me, did they?"

"I volunteered," he says.

"It certainly won't hurt your standing with the voters, will it?"

"That's not why I'm here. We're friends. I'm just here to talk."

"I'm sorry, Ned," she says and indicates a set of chairs across from her desk. Ned sits in one and Avis comes from behind her desk to join him. "As you might imagine, I'm a little suspicious of people dropping by for a visit these days."

"Understandable," he says. "So, what's this all about?"

"It's about living up to who I am rather than who everyone

expects me to be."

"What brought this on?"

"Every week, I stand before hundreds of people, telling them what God expects of them, how they should live. People listen to me; they say they love me, respect me. And when it's all over, I go home to an empty house. Recently, I've been wondering if that's really what God expects from me."

"You're a very important leader to many. Your followers are led by your example."

"My words, not my deeds."

"Until now, of course," he says. "A lot of your followers are out there now, waiting to see what you'll do next."

"I don't know what I'm going to do next," she says. "I never thought I'd go this far."

"Just so we're clear," Ned says, "the men you're opposing don't like hearing no."

"Are you aware of some of the debates that took place in the early centuries when the Christian church was forming, Ned?"

"No. I'm not much of a scholar."

"One of the important questions was whether we are redeemed by faith alone or faith and good deeds. The Apostle Paul concluded that faith alone was sufficient, but Jesus stressed the importance of taking action in one's faith. 'Do unto others as you would have them do unto you' would seem to contradict Paul's belief."

"A lot of people believe that faith is the key."

"My sister is an atheist, Ned. She was never firm in her faith when she was younger, but she was injured by a drunk driver and can no longer walk. That only confirmed her lack of belief."

"Sorry to hear that."

"I recently found out that the man who caused the accident has been working for her, taking care of her house, tending the garden. She says she hasn't forgiven him, but she gave him another chance. An atheist. Christians are supposed to be in the business of tolerance, and I can't even remember the last time I gave anyone the benefit of the doubt. I've pushed everyone out of my life that I ever cared about."

"This situation doesn't have to escalate further. We can end it here, before you lose everything you've worked so hard to build."

"I've already lost everything that really matters. My family. My friends. There's nothing anyone can say or do to me that's worse than what I've done to myself."

"Maybe not, but your followers don't have to pay for that."

"You're absolutely right, Ned." She leans forward. "Please speak to the police and let them know these are my terms."

A short while later, Ned exits the grounds and goes to the police chief. "She says she'll surrender if you'll allow everyone else to leave unharmed."

"That sounds reasonable," the chief says. "I'll make sure everyone gets the message so there's no misunderstandings."

Ned returns inside and finds Avis waiting for him outside her office.

"It's ironic, isn't it?" Avis says. "Looks like I'm going to get you elected after all."

"Our friendship has never been contingent on you endorsing me for public office," Ned says.

"I know and I appreciate that, Ned," she says. "Lead on."

As they leave her office and head toward the exit, Ned says, "I have the name of an attorney who's willing to represent you."

"Thank you, Ned," Avis says. "I have a feeling that won't be necessary. But I appreciate the gesture."

"If you ever need anything, my door is always open."

They step out into the early afternoon sunshine to the sight of everyone who's been there in support of Avis lined up to either side of the drive, watching the door. As Avis emerges, they burst into cheers.

She stops, looks around at all the parishioners and says, "Thank you all. The police have assured me that if you leave now, there will be no charges filed against you. It's time to end this."

"What about you, Mother Avis?" one of them calls out.

"Don't worry about me," she says. "I'm going to be fine. Just remember what I've tried to tell you the past few days. Go out and be a blessing to someone."

Many of those lined up go to Avis and hug her, then head to the gates where they remove the chains and exit unhindered. Once they're all gone, Avis says to Ned, "Let's make this official, shall we?" She taps her right cheek. "Kiss me."

Ned shakes his head, then gives her a peck on the cheek. He walks Avis down the drive and through the gates, where she's promptly arrested.

The morning after Avis's arrest, Annabelle is at home when she gets a call from Alfred.

"What the hell's going on with Avis?"

"It would seem she's gone crazy. I kind of like it."

"It's definitely a departure. Do you know if anyone is representing her?"

"I haven't heard. Paul called police headquarters last night and they had her in lockup."

"I guess we should go bail her out."

"Make the arrangements and I'll pick you up tomorrow morning," she says.

Sunday morning, Annabelle drives over and picks up Alfred and they travel to Gwinnett County to get Avis. When they arrive, they're informed that she's no longer there.

"Someone from the U.S. Attorney's office showed up with a court order and spirited her away," the officer says. "They say she's a material witness in a federal case."

"Where have they taken her?" Alfred asks.

"No idea," the officer says.

"I guess she'll reveal herself when she's ready," Annabelle says.

The board of the church releases a statement accusing Avis of mismanagement and embezzlement. It's the top story on local news for a week or so, and at least one national outlet picks it up. When no one is able to find Mother Avis for comment, the story dies and the news cycle moves on.

Several months later and with much less fanfare, representatives from The Ascendancy Collective and Right Think Press are indicted in Delaware on charges of money laundering and racketeering and several representatives from the Templeton Foundation in Georgia are implicated. Founder Felix Templeton states in a press release that he was "shocked and disappointed" to learn that employees would engage in such behavior and pledges full cooperation in the investigation. That same month, the board of Apostolic Awakening announces that the church, which lost most of its following and has stood empty since a month or so after Avis's removal as pastor, has been dissolved and the buildings and grounds, including the parsonage where Mother Avis resided, will be sold to a real estate developer.

With the publicity surrounding his mediation of the standoff at the church, Ned Branch surges in the polls and easily wins the party's nomination. The evening of the primary, he receives a text from a number he doesn't recognize. The caller ID states it's from the West Coast. It reads, simply, "She says: You're welcome."

When she graduated from Carver High School in 1983, Myesha Kittredge left Atlanta and hasn't looked back. She headed to San Francisco, where she spent two years living and working to establish residency, before enrolling in City College to study social work. Halfway through, she transferred her credits to UC Berkeley where she earned her Bachelor's, Master's, and Ph.D. A brief relationship with a classmate during graduate school produced her daughter Lacey, and after earning her Ph.D., Myesha settled into a long-term romance with a woman she met while serving on a community board. She's now the head of a foundation that counsels gay, lesbian, and transgendered teens.

Her coworkers and the individuals who receive services from the foundation know Myesha as a loving, supportive, and encouraging presence, never too busy to stop and talk to someone who needs an ear. She's full of energy, with a loud, easily distinguishable laugh, who's fond of giving hugs, but also conscientious of the other person's space and level of comfort with physical contact. She's usually the first one in the office in the morning and the last one out in the evening and has a reputation for being a tireless advocate on behalf of the community and the people she serves.

One of their activities is a weekly support group where people can share their stories, talk about their lives since coming out, or discuss topics of mutual concern. Tonight, the group has a new face, an older woman seated in the back, who Myesha recognizes though they haven't seen one another in person for nearly thirty years. Myesha is surprised to see her. "Avis?"

"It's good to see you again, Myesha," Avis says.

Someone in the audience says, "I recognize her. That's Mother Avis, the homophobic preacher from television. Why's she here?"

"Our doors are open to everyone," Myesha replies. "You all know that. We welcome anyone to tell their story here." To Avis, she says, "Is there anything you'd like to share with us?"

"I'm not here to talk," Avis says. "I'm here to listen. I didn't listen to you before and look where that got me."

Myesha indicates the seat beside her. "You have a room full of people willing to tell you their stories, if you care to listen to them."

Avis goes up and sits and for the next several hours, members of the audience stand and talk about their lives, the struggles they've endured and the challenges they face.

"My partner died, and the courts wouldn't give me custody of the child she and I were raising," one woman says. "We were the only parents she'd known and instead, the courts gave her to an aunt she barely knew after considerable lobbying on the part of her church."

A trans woman in the midst of her transition rises. "When I came out in my teens, my parents forced me to go to a boot camp where they basically tortured us into being straight. I ran away. Haven't seen my family in years."

One man in the back holds up some of the brochures Avis's church had been distributing. "This is a perfect example of how organizations like yours contribute to the violence we all experience."

"I was unaware of the message in those tracts," Avis says. "But that's not an excuse. I accept responsibility for them none the less because I should have known and put a stop to it."

Others relate stories of having to conceal their sexuality to keep their jobs, having to introduce their partners as "tenants" or "roommates" and not being able to have photos or other mementos at their desks. A woman tells Avis she has to lie and say her emergency contact is a cousin instead of her partner because the company insists only family members can be contacted. Many speak of the rights afforded to spouses that are denied to them. Through it all, Avis listens intently.

Finally, one young man in the front row stands up. "I don't have a story. Just a question. Why do you hate us?"

Avis looks down and clears her throat. "It's taken me most of my life to realize, I don't hate you. I hate myself. Once you start there, you don't have anything left in your heart for anyone else. Maybe I'm finally ready for that to change."

Myesha stands and holds out her arms. "You came to the right place for that."

Avis rises and they hug. Others come and join them.

Following the meeting, as they're having coffee and socializing, Myesha tells Avis, "You know, an awful lot of people are looking for you back in Atlanta."

"I'm not surprised," she says. "As far as they know, I vanished into thin air."

"I've been following your career the past few years," Myesha says. "You've turned up in my prayers many nights."

"Well, I appreciate that," Avis says. "You look like you've been taking care of yourself."

"I work all the time," she says. "It's tough but very fulfilling. How long are you in town?"

"As long as it takes," Avis says.

"Don't you even think about staying in a hotel," Myesha says. "We have plenty of room and you and I are long overdue for one of our all-night talks. You'll probably get an earful from my partner, Delia, but she's usually forgiving once she gets to know you."

"I welcome your hospitality."

Once she feels sufficient time has passed for her to move about freely, Avis returns to Atlanta and heads over to West End to a non-descript, two-story warehouse, that houses the Cairo Foundation. She enters the lower floor and walks toward what looks like a reception desk that's unattended. Behind it is a large sign with a Biblical reference on it, "Matthew 16:26-27". A man with long, brown hair and a full beard enters and approaches her.

"I'm guessing you recognize the verse."

"I do," she says. "For what does it profit a man to gain the whole world yet lose his life; and what would a man give in exchange for his life? For the son of man will come in the glory of his father with all his angels and he will repay each man for what he has done."

"Indeed," the man says.

Avis presents herself to him. "Mr. Cairo, I'm Avis Collins."

"I thought that was you, Mother Avis."

She shakes her head. "Different life. I'm just Avis now."

"What can we do for you," Cairo asks.

"I hear you're planning another relief effort in the Congo. I wanted to see if you could use a few more hands. Jesus tells us we need to lose ourselves to find ourselves. I can think of no better place to do that than Mother Africa."

"We can use all the help we can get," he says. "But we don't have much need for preachers over there."

"No. I didn't think so." She looks down. "I once thought I could use my faith to punish those who I felt had hurt me. In the end, the only person I punished was myself."

Cairo nods and says. "I can sympathize. I shall forever be

haunted by the souls of fifty-eight people I never even met, who were in the right place at the wrong time because I wanted to show what a big shot I was."

"Sounds like we both have our crosses to bear."

"A reasonable observation."

"I'm not here to preach, Mr. Cairo. I'm here to serve — in whatever capacity I'm needed."

"Then welcome aboard, Ms. Collins." He extends his hand.

They shake hands. "Please, call me Avis."

"Only if you call me David."

A petite woman with curly, dark hair and an olive complexion, wearing dark coveralls enters and approaches Cairo.

"Here you are. Everyone's looking for you upstairs."

"That's why I'm down here," he says.

The woman stops and notices Avis. "Is that Mother Avis?"

"She's just Avis now," Cairo says. "She's not a Mother anymore."

"Oh. Sorry for your loss," the woman says.

"That's quite all right," Avis says with a laugh.

"This is Angelica McIntosh," Cairo says. "She's the real authority here. I'm just a strawman for people to pelt with dung. Avis would like to join us in Africa."

"Doing what?" Angelica says.

"Whatever you need me to do," she says.

"If you could get the paperwork going," Cairo says.

"Sure," she says. "Have you been to Africa before?"

"A time or two," Avis says. "Not to the Congo, though."

"Not to worry," Cairo says. "Angie runs a tight ship. She takes after her mother."

"When are you planning on leaving?" Avis asks.

"First of the year. Probably after the holidays," Angelica says

"That will work out well," Avis says. "I have some people I need to see in the meantime."

Thanksgiving morning, the Collins family assembles at Alfred and Chizuko's home for their annual gathering. Annabelle is there with Paul, who's treated like part of the family. Avery has some free time and flies in with his fiancé Eloise, a model from England. Ishmael Branch and other members of his family circulate in and out from their own get together across the street. Ishmael brings some of his teammates over to meet Midori's uncle.

"What's it like working with Arnold?" one of the guys asks Avery.

"Couldn't tell you," Avery says. "I ran lines with a stand-in. I thought I'd have the chance to meet him at the Golden Globes this past year, but no such luck."

The doorbell rings, and Midori goes to answer it. She's gone a moment, then calls out, "Dad?"

Alfred goes into the living room to find Avis there.

"Avis? We were wondering when you'd reappear."

"Hello, Alfred. I finally decided to accept your invitation — if you'll still have me."

"Of course. Come on in."

Chizuko enters, and, seeing Avis, hurries to her and gives her a hug. "Avis! Welcome. So good to have you back with us."

Avis tells her, "Chizuko. I am so sorry for everything I have ever said that was hurtful to you."

Chizuko shrugs. "You lost your way. That happens sometimes. You're home now. We'll work it out."

She takes Avis's arm and leads her into the family room where the others are. When he sees her, Avery greets Avis with a hug. Annabelle, who's been speaking to Paul and some others turns her chair around to face her sister.

"Let us eat and make merry," Annabelle proclaims. "She who was lost is found!"

Avis goes to Annabelle, takes her hands and says, "Annabelle. Thank you so much for helping to open my eyes."

"My pleasure," Annabelle says. "Good to have you back."

"It's nice to feel welcomed again," she says.

"You've always been welcome," Alfred says to Avis. "Hey, at least, I won't be calling you Mother Avis anymore."

"Then my plan worked," Avis says with a wink.

Avis retreats to the couch and spends time getting reacquainted with her niece and nephews.

Later, at dinner, Alfred taps a wine glass with a spoon. The others in the room give him their attention.

"It is our custom every year to relate that which we're most thankful for. I can say for certain that I'm thankful that for the first time in a long while, our family is reunited." He puts his arm around Avis and gives her a squeeze. "We've missed you, Avis."

"Thank you, Alfred," Avis says. "It's been a very long and strange journey so far, but I'm thankful I was able to find my way back to my family. It may not have seemed like it, but I missed you all and I'm happy to be with you again."

"You can't get rid of us that easily," Annabelle says. "You're stuck with us."

They enjoy a festive dinner together. Afterward, Charlotte Murdoch drops in to invite them to the festivities across the street. They all head over for an evening of singing and music.